THE THIRTEENTH

ALSO BY L. A. BANKS

VAMPIRE HUNTRESS LEGENDS

Minion

The Awakening

The Hunted

The Bitten

The Forbidden

The Damned

The Forsaken

The Wicked

The Cursed

The Darkness

The Shadows

CRIMSON MOON NOVELS

Bad Blood

Bite the Bullet

ANTHOLOGIES

Love at First Bite

Stroke of Midnight

THE THIRTEENTH

L. A. BANKS

ST. MARTIN'S GRIFFIN ❧ NEW YORK

THE THIRTEENTH. Copyright © 2009 by Leslie Esdaile Banks. All rights reserved. Printed in the United States of America. For information, address St. Martin's Press, 175 Fifth Avenue, New York, N.Y. 10010.

www.stmartins.com

Library of Congress Cataloging-in-Publication Data
Banks, L. A.
The thirteenth : a vampire huntress legend / L. A. Banks.—1st ed.
    p. cm
  ISBN-13: 978-0-312-36876-0
  ISBN-10: 0-312-36876-3
  1. Richards, Damali (Fictitious character)—Fiction. 2. African American women—Fiction. 3. Vampires—Fiction. 4. Armageddon—Fiction. I. Title.
  PS3602.A64T47 2009
  813'.6—dc22

                    2008037581

First Edition: February 2009

10 9 8 7 6 5 4 3 2 1

ACKNOWLEDGMENTS

I want to first thank the Most High Creator for allowing me to begin and complete this twelve-book epic. When I started it, I had no idea where it was going or how long it would be. That just goes to show you that sometimes there is something bigger than you out there orchestrating things in a way you could not conceive of . . . therefore, with that said, this last book is in honor of the fantastic, cosmic beauty, love, and intelligence that is the alpha and the omega . . . referred to by many names, but the one source of all Divine. Thank you, Tua.

I also thank the ancestors for guiding me with the whispers of angels, for the abundant blessings poured down on me . . . pressed down and overflowing. I thank the readers who all hung with me till the very end: Three Feathers Light, for her guidance on Atlantis; Bill Harvey, for his deep consciousness and readings he shared with me about all things metaphysical; and as always, the Street Team, whom I affectionately call "my Guardians," bless you all for the love! Through this process, we literally became family. What a truly wonderful, extraordinary gift.

★　★　★

Special acknowledgment: As always, Manie Barron, coconspirator, creator, collaborator—*big smile* . . . I love you, man! Monique Patterson . . . lady . . . wow . . . we did it, huh? *LOL! Thank you* and all the fine folks at St. Martin's Press. Plus I must give kudos to Denise Dorman and team at Write Brain Media for their creative PR fire, as well as to Walt Stone at Dream Forge Media for keeping the communication channels up on all Web sites. And most important, I want to thank my daughter who stood witness and gave me her love and support through it all! Much love.

THE THIRTEENTH

PROLOGUE

Bermuda—Seventy-two hours after the battle in Washington, D.C., BBC World News has just learned that the USS Ronald Reagan, one of the United States' nine most significant supercarriers, is en route to the Atlantic Coast to take a position that will enable strategic air strikes on U.S. soil for the first time in military history.

The USS Ronald Reagan is a ninety-seven-thousand-ton, twenty-story supercarrier, with state-of-the-art hospital facilities on board. Normally stationed by Korea, and boasting a six-thousand-member crew, it will now moor in the deep Atlantic waters just beyond the Chesapeake Bay.

Following the collapse of the Washington Monument, the still incalculable loss of human lives, the destruction of countless Washington, D.C., city streets, and a major section of the Metro subway network, the United States of America is under martial law. The decision was based on the inexplicable attack that left unfathomable structural damage to the White House as a result of the catastrophic blast that toppled the Washington Monument and sent it spiraling like a pike to pierce the iconic building from a source that has still yet to be determined.

The world is watching to understand what vast implications all of this will have on the global economic front, and non-ally countries around the world are bracing for a potential military backlash from the threatened United States. America's closest neighbors, Mexico and Canada, are also reeling from the tragic events.

Both Mexico's and Canada's national leaders had entered into what was then coined the "North American Union" during a closed-door pact with the president of the United States on March 23, 2005, in Waco, Texas. Without needing to go through Congress, the Security and Prosperity Partnership of North America was announced, inextricably linking the three nations through a proposed new currency, the amero, which will effectively blend the struggling U.S. dollar with the peso and the Canadian dollar in the near future.

Likened to the African Union, Asian Union, and European Union, the newly formed North American Union, which seeks to evolve to one currency and to have several laws transparent to its trilateral agreement, will now also feel the violent shock waves of the recent terror attack throughout the three linked nations. World economic and military experts suggest grave consequences ahead for this pivotal collaboration.

American, Mexican, and Canadian borders have been shut down, all civilian planes grounded, and a massive military offensive is under way to sweep the area for potentially deadly biohazards that could have been released in the blasts. White House spokespersons have issued a short written comment: "The nation is doing everything possible to analyze and contain the pale cloud that eyewitnesses saw rising from the site—which may have merely been debris, dust, and vapor from the multiple explosions. It is too early to tell whether the United States has also been the victim of bioterrorism."

Rider got up from the bamboo-framed sofa not even looking at the team, and simply turned off the television set in the large villa living-room suite they occupied.

"Thanks," Carlos said, his tone flat and hollow. "I was sick of hearing that shit anyway."

Rider glanced around at the exhausted team and then at Carlos, who was sitting on the floor with his elbows resting on his knees, head hung low with fatigue, clearly heartsick. "Don't mention it," Rider muttered. "Face it. We ain't getting out of this bull called life alive anyway."

Yonnie pounded Rider's fist as he passed. "It's a damned shame to say it, but I know more people dead than alive—so hey."

"Please don't be so cheerful on my account, gentlemen," Marjorie snapped, losing patience. "I'd hate to have something crazy like hope ruin our morning."

"Sorry, fresh out of hope this early in the day. Will pick some up along with a carton of fairy tales when I make a supply run," Yonnie said, staring out of the wide sliding glass doors that led to the deck. He spat the toothpick out that he'd been gnawing on, watching it disappear before it hit the floor, and walked to the doors to stare out at the ocean. "Ya think they let out the old-fashioned bubonic plague or smallpox with the pale horse or some zombie-making bullshit, C?"

"Five bucks says all three," Big Mike said, shaking his head.

"I'm waiting for the locusts, myself," Rider said sarcastically while rubbing the stubble on his jaw. "I'm so disappointed in the darkside's lack of creativity this time out. Anybody got a cigarette? Rhetorical question."

"Your attitudes are pissing me off," Marj snapped, her gaze deadly before seeking Marlene's for support.

"It definitely is the end of days," Rider said, his voice hardening with additional sarcasm as he flopped down in a chair. "Finally pissed Marj off . . . so you know if Miss Mary Sunshine is losing it, then what chance do the rest of us poor bastards have?"

"Oh, just—" Marlene stopped midsentence and stared at the door with the rest of the team seers.

The sound of a golf cart pulling up, the engine being shut off, followed by slow footsteps drew everyone's attention. They quickly concealed the weapons they had been holding.

Damali and Carlos gave each other a look as Dan nervously approached the door. Seers nodded and he finally turned the locks and swung open the door.

"May I help you, Mr. Fontaine?"

"Uh, yes. Good morning, Mr. Weinstein. I'm so sorry to trouble you so early in the morning. May I have a word, er, in private?" The hotel manager's cultured voice wafted through the hostile vibes in the room and his dark walnut-hued face seemed to flush as his gaze briefly slid away from Dan's. His crisply starched, white, short-sleeved shirt and khaki Bermuda shorts seemed to wilt under a fresh rush of perspiration. "It is regarding a delicate matter best saved for a more discreet conversation."

"We don't do 'private' on group expeditions," Rider said, folding his arms.

The hotel manager peered around, seeming more nervous than Dan as his wide brown eyes assessed the team. Every seer in the room tracked his thoughts, feeling the immaculately dressed, highly cultured man make a decision about whom to approach with the embarrassing news he held.

Mr. Fontaine glanced around the room and a dull ache began to throb in his temples as hard-set eyes stared back at him.

Clearly something tragic had happened to these people and he felt awful having to bring them bad news this morning. Maybe they'd lost loved ones or colleagues in the Washington disaster?

But perhaps the most disturbing of the group was the young dreadlock-wearing woman who sat yogi-style on the coffee table, her gaze so distant that she seemed to be somewhere else. Yet her eerie serenity drew him, as did her peaceful brand of beauty. He knew her face from somewhere, the recollection probing at his mind, but he continued to draw a blank. Then she looked up at him and he felt positively spellbound. The most serene, gorgeous face held his breath within his lungs as a pair of large brown eyes held him entranced. He took in her cinnamon skin that seemed to radiate from an inner light and watched it cascade over her pretty locks.

"He's cool," Damali said calmly. "Don't kill the messenger."

Immediately the man's hand went to the door frame to steady himself as unbeknownst to him each seer released his mind. Gasping and suddenly afraid, he thrust a thin black leather portfolio at Dan.

"It didn't work. Your credit card didn't accept the charges. Oddly, it did when you initially checked in, but when we began adding incidental charges, everything simply reversed. All charges, including your initial fees, canceled out. We're not sure what happened, but I'm sure your tour group has the resources . . . for such accommodations; however, you understand that our establishment must have some guarantees." The manager dabbed his forehead with the back of his wrist and looked around. "We ran the card several times, sir. You understand our predicament."

"We do," Dan said coolly. "It was my error. We were rushed and hadn't had time to transfer monies from our London account to cover balances from our last travel junket. We'll make arrangements. Just give me a few hours to do a wire transfer from Great Britain."

"Thank you, thank you, sir. Again, my apologies for bringing you such inconvenient news this morning." Mr. Fontaine nodded, seeming relieved that there was a reasonable explanation and peaceful conclusion, and hurried away from the door.

Dan shut the door and waited until he heard the golf cart roll down the gravel driveway. "Fuck *me*." Dan closed his eyes.

"Couldn't have said it better, Danny boy," Berkfield muttered, and stood. "The darkside screwed our accounts or what, Carlos?"

"That is *so* cold, yo. Half a billion dollars that I'd been moving lovely on the market up in fuckin' smoke," Yonnie said, shaking his head. "I *cannot* believe it. But, then again, yeah I do."

"Whatchu talkin' about, man?" Juanita yelled, jumping up and beginning to pace. "All of our money is gone? Don't play."

"It was *their* money, girl. Easy come, easy go. I ain't with them no more, so . . . my vamp three-card monte got busted. Ask Tara," Yonnie said coolly, watching the group blanch.

Tara nodded and looked at Berkfield. "Back when I found Yonnie and we hooked up to locate Carlos, we found out the feds only gave Carlos a pittance for his work with Berkfield. Yonnie sent him a hundred million to match whatever Damali had, like a safety net."

"That was a far sight better than what I could wrestle out of the authorities for the man," Berkfield said, shaking his head. "Damn."

"You know I was taking care of your shit, right, C? Had everything offshore in Swiss accounts, Cayman Islands, you name it. But it was still vamp illusion. Guess they took issue with how we've been on their asses and finally siphoned their cash back, huh? It was good while it was good, but damn."

"I know, I know, man," Carlos said, closing his eyes. "It's just the timing is so fucked-up. But then how else is it supposed to be, coming from them?"

"Maaan, you ain't said a mumblin' word," Mike muttered, releasing a hard breath of frustration.

"I don't know why I was even surprised," Marlene said flatly. "We've been skating on grace a long time with those resources."

"But what the hell about whatever *I* was working on Wall Street from the Warriors of Light?" Dan's eyes held Marlene's. "Those earnings weren't illusion and didn't belong to the darkside!"

"It doesn't matter," Damali said in a weary tone. "Whatever wasn't vamp illusion that was ours, the Warriors of Light, has probably been seized by Homeland Security now. Every credit card, bank account, asset of any kind is on lock in the system. I'm sure the darkside saw to that in order to make up for the hundred-million-dollar loan from them that Yonnie and Carlos took out for the last coupla years, then grew to a half billion on the market. So now they've led the feds to everything we had in order to freeze our accounts worldwide."

"Ain't no getting around that shit, either," Shabazz said, standing and raking his dreadlocks. "First thing they've gotta do is starve out what they think are potential terrorists, which unfortunately, in this case, seems like it's us. We got played by the darkside, once again. They do the dirt, we take the weight."

"At least when the Light delivered us here, they made humans unaware of who we are," Tara said in a far-off tone, looking toward the door where the hotel manager had been. "You could see him struggling to remember, trying to put the pieces together."

"But how long's that gonna last?" Rider shook his head. "Like all we need is for some human with darkside leanings to be able to see through that veil or to get accidentally tracked somehow and it's over people." He looked at Marj. "Now you see why I woke up on the wrong side of the bed this morning? I had my reasons."

"Rider's got a point," Shabazz said, his gaze raking the group. "Check it out. Radio frequency chips are now in the new passports, new money, and after this last disaster, you can bet U.S. citizens are gonna have to carry a real ID card, or get stopped and hassled. The same GPS chip they want everybody to embed in their bodies, just in case there's another catastrophe."

"The mark of the beast, bro," Jose said, nodding. "We gotta go off the grid."

"I've gotta get to my baby girl and my momma," Inez said in a quiet, urgent tone.

"We will," Heather said, taking up one of Inez's hands.

Jasmine nodded. "Remember what the teams that met us in D.C. said? They were sent to protect the unborn. Dragon Rider said, 'I'm your new nanny.' Remember?"

"Yeah, but we've gotta get back to the States to recon with the teams there and pray our contacts didn't get blown away," Bobby said, panic lacing his voice. "They took a goddamned fallback position in Atlanta to get away from the plagues about to hit and all the military roundups, and a twister . . . a freaking *twister,* hit downtown Atlanta for the first time in history? Be serious. How in the hell can we expect Carlos and Damali to do an energy pull through the fucking Bermuda Triangle with everybody's wife pregnant, huh? Or even risk trying to pull little Ayana and Mom Delores through that? The only reason we got here was because the Light shot us here—which I still haven't reconciled in my head. And we're talking about going off the grid, which back home and with stupid resources was possible . . . but how far off the fucking grid can you go on an island when you owe people two grand a day in hotel fees you can't pay? How long will it be before they round us up, fingerprint us, then it's ball game!"

"The young blood is panicking, C. Got any remedies for that? I don't, 'cause as crazy as his ass sounds, he's speaking truth." Yonnie sighed and continued staring at the ocean through the door. "We have just officially become America's most wanted, like it or not. Maybe the world's most wanted, who knows."

"Maybe the angels will continue to conceal our identities long enough for us to find our hidden warriors? Uriel said to wait for word . . . we must abide the archangel's command to the letter," Val said, her worried gaze traveling around the group. "We cannot be outlaws. But for now, no matter the truth, we are blamed for the tragedy."

"That is so not right!" Krissy said, excited. "We didn't kill all those innocent people that got hurt during the battle—we tried to avoid that! The darkside did it, not us. Didn't the people see the angels; didn't they see how we were blowing away demons? How come none of that hit the news? What's wrong with people!"

"They didn't see it, baby," J.L. said quietly. "Council Group Entertainment is spinning what's on the networks and what eyewitnesses took into their minds that day. So, people saw fear, pain, blood, explosions. Everything was masked by dark illusion. They saw cops getting shot and choppers getting blown out of the sky by shoulder-launched rockets coming off our man, Big Mike—not him blowing away clouds of demon bats and Harpies, trying to give the choppers aerial assists. They saw what the darkside wanted them to see. They saw *us*."

"But that's just not fair. . . ." Krissy's voice trailed off in a horrified whisper.

Carlos just looked at Krissy in disbelief for a moment, ignoring the way Damali shook her head. "We were on the scene when the freakin' White House got skewered by the Washington Monument . . . y'all didn't figure there'd be consequences? Being broke is the least of our worries. Fair ain't nowhere near a rule in this game."

CHAPTER ONE

Damali rolled up the legs of her jeans, stood up, and absently ran her fingers over the stones in her silver divining necklace as she gripped it tightly in her left hand. Then she opened the deck doors and walked barefoot out toward the deserted beach. Even with a lightweight, white tank top on, the early morning sun beat down hot rays on her scalp, face, and shoulders. She squinted toward the beach and lifted her dreadlocks up higher in a ponytail scrunchie, searching for Carlos, then let out a hard breath of frustration when she didn't immediately spot him.

Why did everything on the team always have to be done by committee? Okay, sure, every man in the house whose wife was pregnant was freaking out, and the Berkfields were having a fit because their daughter, Krissy, and daughter-in-law, Jasmine, were carrying their first grandchildren, but she and Carlos couldn't just do an energy fold-away this close to the Bermuda Triangle! Basic quantum physics made that impossible. The Triangle was magnetically unstable. J.L. knew that. Every tactical Guardian on the team should have been able to grasp the implications. Why they had to argue that fact with the team was beyond her.

It was simple, at least in her mind. Deviations in the magnetic field around the phenomenon were caused by micro-wormholes, otherwise known as transit tunnels—the same tunnel system that the team seemed to have forgotten that Cain had used to lead a full aqua-demon army out of Nod before.

Damali blew a stray strand of damp hair up off her forehead, exasperated. The damned Bermuda Triangle, just like all the other vortexes on the planet, was filled with rips in the cosmic fabric, some only a gigafraction of an inch—a tear so small that it could be represented by a decimal point and the number one preceded by something crazy like thirty-three zeros, where unstable mini–black holes of virtual matter and mini–white holes of virtual antimatter fluxed on a dime in and out of the geometry of space.

Only Cain was insane enough, and driven enough, to risk bringing his armies through a temporary black hole flux . . . just like the angels must have jettisoned the team through a quick flicker of white hole opening to get them here. But neither she nor Carlos was down for chancing that. Hell, no—that'd be like trying to jump into a millisecond-turning double-Dutch rope that was changing from black to white and white to black and hoping they could snatch the entire team through on white. *Not.*

Pulling a team through that, where one burp in the interdimensional vortex could land them God only knew where, was not an option. No wonder Carlos was freaking-out.

After a moment of walking to calm down, Damali steadied herself. The team was panicked, and her gut told her that was why unity was so hard to achieve right now. Everybody had to chill. Marj and Berkfield had their parental worries about Krissy and Bobby, as well as their kids' spouses and unborn grands . . . just like Marlene and Shabazz were no doubt scared to death for her and Carlos. Maybe Yonnie and Val, along with Rider and

Tara, would be the balancers of sanity this time out, she prayed. Inez and Mike were too freaked-out about the whereabouts of little Ayana and Mom Delores, rightfully so, to be of much help. But Bobby, J.L., Jose, and Dan would probably have a cow once they finally learned she was pregnant, too . . . which was why she knew Carlos needed to go take a long walk before he'd said something about her state that had been forbidden by the joint Neteru Kings' and Queens' Councils. Why was everything always so hard?

She'd left the team to its collective squabbling about the potential next steps to take without looking back. They'd still be at it by the time she got back, she was sure. This was the part of communal living that Carlos couldn't stand; she knew her husband well. After the team meeting, that Scorpio was going to need a private, quiet place to get his head together. Fury waves had been coming off his body so intensely that they were threatening to either fuse the Turkish rug to the hardwood floors around him or start a blaze. That's when he simply got up and left the villa.

Yeah, Carlos had to get up, get out, and walk it off. It was easy to understand. The darkside had jacked with Carlos Rivera's cash flow, which represented *major* disrespect where he came from, and she knew his old street ways were wrestling within him. That part of him would never fully die. It would always resonate in his being, no matter what. Once from the streets always from the streets. Mess with a brother's money? Oh, hell to the no. Damali just shook her head as she searched the beach for him. Some things were simply embedded in the man's DNA.

Armageddon notwithstanding, with a wife and a baby on the way, the darkside was playing to all of her husband's deepest fears—all of which centered on basic survival. For Carlos, she knew cash meant flexibility, maneuverability, strength, a backdoor escape. If he was liquid, he could flow like the water sign he was and get out of whatever. But they'd taken that option away and Señor Rivera wasn't having it.

By the time she found him, his aura was radiating so much heat it had turned the sand around him to glass. Actual grains of sand had fused together right under him without burning him and then had quickly cooled from the trade winds and surf. It was eerie to see him sitting all alone, yogi-style, wearing jeans and a red T-shirt, hovering several inches above the beach in heavy meditation, aura glowing white-hot silver and him taking in long, deep breaths, practically shaking with rage. A deep crimson V of sweat marked his shirt as his broad shoulders and back slowly expanded and contracted beneath it.

Stopping for a moment, she wrestled with how best to approach him. He needed to know that she was on his side, even if she didn't agree with the waste of energy being expended on rage. They had shit to do and had to do it quickly before Mr. Fontaine at the resort began to inquire further.

Caribbean sun beat down on Carlos's bronze skin, making the silver aura around him shimmer until she had to partially shield her eyes with her hand. Small beads of silver perspiration cast a glow to his damp hair, and his normally ripped, athletic frame had bulked ever so slightly, adding bricks to his abdominal six-pack, chest, and thickly muscled biceps. He was two seconds from a full vamp battle bulk, she could tell, and the only things missing were the sabertooth-length battle fangs.

Damali sighed quietly and tested the brittle surface of the beach before she stepped onto the smooth, shiny coating, wondering as much about how to restore what had once been pale pink sand to its previous pristine beauty as she was worried about how to restore Carlos's peace. He was creating an ecological disaster while in angry-meditation repose. What the hell was he gonna do when he finally came out of the trance?

"You're levitating," she said calmly, walking toward him as she murmured a prayer that their conversation be Light-sealed.

Carlos opened his eyes, pure silver staring back at her as he unfolded from the yogi position and stood. "You ain't seen nothing yet," he said in a low, furious tone.

"Okay, so they messed up our money—"

"No," he said evenly, cutting her off. "What the darkside did was box us in, bleed us out, and make us have to come out of hiding to eat . . . a daylight exposure move. Sudden death. Old-school vamp. Starve 'em out."

She nodded, having to give credit where credit was due. "Yep. Okay, but we're still unrecognizable, courtesy of the Light. Last I checked, that side was providing for us, any ole way. We got here safely, which is more than you can say for a lot of people. We ate well. Got cleaned up, rested, and got new clothes—anywhere there's a church mission we can pull in resources so we're not raiding stores and gift shops like thieves. So what makes you think we're gonna be without for long? Might not be as fly as we're used to, but we won't be completely ass out, and you know it. This just pisses you off because it's definitely gonna cramp our style—*a lot*."

Carlos looked away from her and folded his arms over his bulked chest.

"Do *not* let ego get a chokehold on you, brother. I know you and Yonnie loved having deep pockets . . . but if the entire planet blows up, how much does that matter?"

When he whirled on her, she knew she'd accidentally pushed the wrong button.

"It's not about that, D!" he shouted. "It's about being able to move, roll smooth without a trace, buy supplies and ammo, and have the basic cover we need when we need it. Don't make this about some old bullshit, Damali. Not this morning. Don't go there."

"All right, all right, my bad," she said, holding her hands up in front of her. "But you have to admit—"

"I don't have to do jack shit but get this family out of here in one piece. How am I supposed to do that when they have all my closest land options in a direct route through the Bermuda Triangle?"

"Uriel said to wait for word."

Carlos briefly hung his head back and closed his eyes. "I know. And I was ready to do that. But where are we gonna wait, D?" He opened his eyes as he opened his arms and simply stared at her. "They dropped us at a hotel where we can't pay the bill. Even if I could successfully jettison us out of here, the humans at the hotel will by rights call U.S. authorities, which will alert the darkside to our last location—here—which will put pure Hell hot on our trail."

"Uriel said to wait for word," Damali repeated calmly, not blinking as she stared at him.

Carlos let his breath out hard. "Yeah, I know."

"You try the Kings?"

He stared at her for a moment. "You try the Queens?"

She nodded. "Seems all of Heaven pretty much emptied out searching for the pupa."

"And in the meantime, we're ass out."

Damali fought a smile. "Yeah, I guess our credit card problems aren't a top priority, given what the Light is hunting . . . or as much of a priority as trying to contain the pale horse of the Apocalypse, huh?"

"I don't even see how you can crack a smile at a time like

this." Incredulous, Carlos raked his fingers through his hair and shook his head. "We've got a serious problem, boo."

"Yeah, I know," Damali said, finally going to him. "Listen . . . I wasn't making fun of you; I was just trying to put things into perspective. So, we leave Mr. Fontaine a Rolex—which should cover the nights we stayed, along with a note saying that due to the Wall Street crash, everything liquid we had got jacked. This way, we're not breaking cosmic law by stealing, which means the darkside can't track us . . . then we—"

"We what, D?" Carlos pulled away from her to begin pacing. "What the fuck are we supposed to do!"

"Go to the hills, and—"

"That's just it, Damali. They're *hills,* not mountains! The whole island is only twenty-one freakin' square miles big. You can get from one end to the other in an hour. Hide? Hide where, boo? You wanna go to the place called Shadow Mountain here, which is really a big hill—or maybe wall-up underground in their crystal caves that look like you've entered Level Seven of Hell? No, no, better yet, we can hide in Hungry Bay or Mangrove Swamp with you being pregnant! Or maybe we'll just hang out at the golf course green of the Duns Resort until we bump into Tiger Woods and then I'll ask him if he has a coupla C notes he can drop on—"

"Or maybe we could just go to a church, and call the Covenant?" She stared at Carlos. He was starting to get on her last nerve. "The oldest church on the island, Marlene said, is the Cathedral of the Most Holy. To me it's as good a place as any to wait for word from an archangel, don't you think?"

Carlos gave her his back to consider as he put his hands on top of his head and walked off a ways. She'd wait. She knew the drill—he had to blow off enough steam to let good, old-fashioned logic kick in. The fact that Father Pat was no longer around had simply closed off the Covenant as an option for support in her husband's mind. She could feel it, knew it as much as she knew her name. There were so many things eating the man up from the inside out that it was obvious he couldn't think straight.

"Listen," she said quietly after a moment. "The Light always works in code and yet always provides. We're in *Bermuda,* man. No one knows who we are, courtesy of the Light. Truth be told, we could eat off the trees and live off the fish in this weather for a long time, if we had to, and we've avoided the pale horse plagues for now. We could still be scraping in the streets of D.C. trying to get past military checkpoints. So, there's gotta be something about why we got dropped here, of all places."

When he didn't immediately respond, she pressed her point, trying to give him something positive to hang on to. "Did you ever consider that maybe the Light put us here because during this all-out war, even the darkside would be afraid to send their troops through the Triangle to risk their resources right now? That network of interdimensional tunnels fluxes both black and white, right? So, this could be the safest place at the moment . . . I'd bank on that, since an archangel set us down here and not in a hot zone. Make sense?"

To her relief, she watched the intricate tumblers in Carlos's mind begin to turn with that new awareness, as though her words were the necessary lubricant to get the heavy mental gears that had been paralyzed by rage to move.

Damali motioned to her necklace. It was important to give the man who she knew wanted to rip out an entity's heart something more productive than vengeance to focus on.

"Twenty-one square miles—do the math." Damali looked at her husband in an unblinking gaze. "Two plus one is three, a trinity. Even after the Light sent old man Cordell back to rejoin his

D.C. team, there are still twenty-one members of core Guardians and clerics combined on our team—eighteen Neteru Guardians here with three remaining members of the Covenant back in the States. This place is made up of seven main islands within the cluster of tiny coral islands and islets—*seven,* Carlos. A lucky number; a power number. C'mon, I thought you were a betting man."

Carlos looked out to sea, his eyes glazing over with a seer's mild trance. "Yeah. Blackjack. Twenty-one, a trinity. All right, I hear you. Spanish mariners got here in 1503, which when you do the math comes to nine . . . an end number. But if Bermuda is being represented by an end number, and they left us off outside the Bermuda Triangle—why would they drop us near what is also known as the Devil's Triangle, baby? Cain got his troops through this way before, and you know his granddaddy, old Lu, is crazier than him." Carlos turned to look at her, the trance suddenly gone.

Damali shrugged and looked down at the necklace in her fist. "Let's ask Pearl."

"He released the pale horse," Fallon Nuit murmured to Lilith discreetly. "Does this mean Sebastian was correct in his theory that the Neteru heir has been conceived? We've scoured the eastern seaboard for three days and three nights, have sent out search-and-destroy teams everywhere, and it's as though the entire Neteru Guardian team simply vanished without a trace. This can only be the work of angels . . . perhaps there is information that we should be apprised of by our master? Why aren't the Neterus here at the epicenter of the disaster fending off our demon attacks and helping the innocent as they are so led to do? Something's wrong, Lilith."

Lilith shot Fallon a glare. "Do you want to be the one to question my husband about his war strategy at a time like this?"

She waited a beat as they stood in the shadowed ruins of the White House. "I didn't think so."

Undaunted, Nuit lifted his chin, wanting to make use of the rare opportunity of having Lilith's ear in a private conference. "Then what of your heir? Surely this contagion that has been unleashed could harm his development."

"Have you seen the angelic dispatches?" she hissed with a smile. "They are of more harm to him than mere pestilence—which, by now, he thrives on like the rest of us. He has been safely moved, rest assured. But the heavens will pour out to attempt to protect their precious humans. A beautiful diversion, don't you think?"

Nuit didn't immediately reply as he watched demons scampering between the rubble with bits of dead human flesh in their clutches. It would be weeks before all the bodies were recovered and the damaged structures were repaired. Chaos reigned . . . but there was a part of him that was actually sad. He allowed the odd sensation to invade him for a moment, letting it coat his insides and flow over his evil palate like a new wine that he'd never tasted.

"I shall miss the old days," Nuit admitted quietly, waxing sentimental in a rare display of truth. He lifted his chin to stand taller, brushing flecks of dust from the rubble off his black designer suit and then tugging on his cuffs a bit. The glimpse of vulnerability he'd given his Council Chairwoman could have been a mistake, but it was so close to his surface that she would have sensed it regardless.

Resigned to whatever she would do with the information, he turned his black-glowing gaze on the carnage and ran his fingers through his thicket of onyx curls. New Orleans was calling him, as were the good old days of plantation ownership in his Creole bayou.

Clearly horrified, Lilith didn't immediately answer. Instead she pressed a graceful hand to her voluptuous chest and allowed a slight scowl to overtake her eerily gorgeous face. She studied Nuit with soulless dark eyes.

"I have not grown soft, dear Lilith, calm yourself." Nuit let out a deep sigh and then motioned before him. "There was once a certain order of things. A balance. There was exquisite beauty in that balance. The greatest honor to become daywalkers, and no longer haunted by the searing sun, will unfortunately allow us to witness a loss of what we'd been."

"Fallon," Lilith murmured, coming closer to him, "what have you learned? What haven't you told me at this critical hour of battle?"

"We were bound by the blood and the night . . . now we will all become flesh-eaters before long. The human populations will soon be thoroughly diseased. Pristine blood in the goblets of old shall be no more, shall pass away as have all the old-world ways that once held a level of dignified charm. The erotic thrill of turning an innocent will be a thing of the past as well . . . once the humans all become the walking dead." He shook his head. "Such a pity."

Lilith stroked his jaw, seeming relieved as her black irises considered his for a moment. "I will never admit this in open council . . . but I understand you, *mon ami*. It is quite a pity and I will miss the days of pure vampires, too. Pure bloodlust. The beauty of deadly seduction versus brute force." Lilith sighed. "We were majestic creatures, yes?"

"*Oui*. It was *très bon*." Nuit allowed her silky, raven-hued hair to fall through his fingers as he slid it off her bare shoulder with strange affection. "Vlad will also weep . . . how could the count, for all his insanity, not miss the old empire?"

Lilith nodded and looked out to the smoldering battlefield

that had previously been intact city streets. "He will weep, as will all the ones from the era of the night, but yet we shall become used to the new order of things. This chaos is temporary . . . the heir brings the promise of perpetual night and with it a level of evil that the world has never known. Humans will shudder in fear, the fumes of it rising with their every breath, and we will feed off that as much as their blood and flesh."

"I will still miss the game. The enchantment of the hunt. This is pure slaughter. Not very sporting, after it has all been said and done."

Lilith clucked her tongue and petted the side of Nuit's face until he closed his eyes. "There, there, yes, I know," she whispered seductively. "I think this is why he's left us the Neterus and some Guardians to still hunt, don't you?"

Their eyes met and an evil smile found its way between them to silently savor, but neither would openly say what was on his or her mind. To even breathe that the Dark Lord had left the Neteru team alive because he'd been bested by the Light was a death sentence.

"I suppose I should rejoin the battle," Nuit said, sensing that his private moment had come to an end as Lilith's hand fell away from his cheek.

"You are aware that our Dark Lord only knows brute force as an extreme measure. For centuries he toyed with the chess games between him and the dreaded Light. And now it has come to this. He is tired, stressed, and has grown impatient for unequivocal victory. My suggestion is that each of you show yourself to be of constant value to the new empire he's creating . . . or I don't know how long I will be able to protect any of you. He's on a mission."

"No country for old men?" Nuit said with a sad smile.

The sly half-smile Lilith had been wearing disappeared from her face. "No. Not at all, Fallon."

The moment Damali dipped her necklace into the balmy Bermuda waters, the six precious stones in it lit and the oracle pearl blushed rosy pink and cooed. Small waves lapped Damali's calves and she had to admit the water felt great against her skin.

"Oh . . . Damali . . . that feels so good after all the drama." Pearl giggled.

Damali and Carlos stared at each other.

"She's been hanging around the team too long," he muttered. "Since when does an ancient oracle start talking about 'drama'?"

"Hi, Carlos," Pearl said in a sexy voice. "I'm so glad you're all right."

"Hey, Pearl, glad you made it, too," Damali said, slightly peeved.

"Oh, yeah, hi, Damali." Pearl laughed in a good-natured tone, totally oblivious to the slight. "Glad to see you, too."

Damali just shook her head as she held the oracle under the water in the shallows. "So, I hate to rush you, or anything, but we're in—"

"Bermuda," Pearl gushed. "Just off the coast of Atlantis. There's so much white-light power beyond the vortexes."

Carlos shot Damali a look. "Okay, you can say I told you so."

"Told her what?" Pearl asked, her voice curious and playful.

"Uriel said to wait here for word, and our credit cards just got slammed by Homeland Security and the darkside," Damali said, not answering the pearl's question as she launched into the problem at hand. "So, we're trying to figure out a next move. At least what the Divine motivation was for dropping us off here."

"With no money," Carlos interjected, walking onto the damp sand to stand closer to Damali, and not caring that his jeans and Tims got wet.

"Right," Damali said, looking up at Carlos from where she squatted.

Carlos bent down to get a closer look at the small bubbles rising from the submerged necklace.

"Hmmm . . . I'm not sure," Pearl said, giddy from the rush of water that flooded over her.

"The oracle is not sure," Carlos said flatly. He gave Damali a look and then stood up and stretched his back with annoyance. "Perfect."

"Give her a minute, baby," Damali warned, when Pearl's glow dimmed. "You'll hurt her feelings."

"I'm not a machine, you know," Pearl snapped, her tone hurt and defensive. "I need to acclimate myself to the environment, Carlos, and it's not as though anyone had the courtesy to immediately revive me in these crystal-blue Caribbean waters . . . oh, nooo . . . you just left me on a dresser until you wanted something. No one thought that maybe Pearl might need a little sea surf after all the horrible things I saw in those battles with you. Humph!"

"Apologize," Damali whispered. *Or we won't get anywhere,* she added in a telepathic barb.

Carlos let his breath out hard and then looked at the necklace. "I'm sorry, boo . . . I'm just a little tight. Didn't mean to take it out on you."

"But you have money, Carlos," Pearl said, sounding much improved. "Didn't Father Pat come to you, yet? You've been so angry that maybe his spirit couldn't get through?"

Carlos came closer and squatted down. He motioned to Damali to allow him to hold her necklace. "Talk to me, baby."

Pearl giggled and released a bubbly, underwater sigh as the necklace slid from Damali's hands to Carlos's.

"Oh, brother," Damali muttered under her breath. "You might as well put her in a ring or a damned—"

"Hey, hey, hey," Carlos said, laughing softly. "You'll hurt her feelings and will have to apologize."

The glare Damali gave him made him swallow a smile and return his attention to the oracle.

"Pearl, baby, you know she doesn't mean any harm . . . but I really need to know what you're talking about."

"The Templar treasures. Those are human-gathered, but the whereabouts are not known of by common man—only other Templars—so the riches of the vaults cannot be confiscated by the human authorities. They were consecrated by Templar priests and hidden on hallowed ground to be used in the mission of protecting the innocent and for the service of the Most High, so the darkside has no access and cannot make it disappear, either. I'm also sure that they would have collected a considerable stash of weaponry to be used against the darkside throughout the ages, as they were warrior-priests."

"Yes!" Carlos leapt up and kissed the necklace, making it laugh out loud before returning it to the water. "I love you, Pearl!"

Damali stood, hands on hips, thoroughly annoyed. "I told you the Light provides. How many times have we had this conversation, Carlos?"

"Okay," Carlos admitted with a wide smile, briefly looking up at Damali before studying the necklace again. "You're right, I'm wrong, Mrs. Rivera. But, Pearl, how do I find the Templar vaults?"

"The Templars were once the strongest banking network in the world and only those sworn by their oath know where their vaults are," Pearl added proudly. "But I hear their resources are far vaster than the little bit of money, comparatively, that you and Yonnie had. Don't worry, Carlos. It's going to be all right."

"But that's the problem—we've gotta drop some cash on the hotel pronto . . . so, c'mon, Pearl. If you have the smallest clue . . ."

"You have to wait for Father Pat to show you," Pearl murmured. "I'm sorry, Carlos, even I can't see that. Their vaults are Light-shielded so that only those given direct permission can access them. They did that after that evil French king burned so many of them at the stake and took their treasury the last time. Now that they've reclaimed it and rebuilt it to hefty reserves over the years, not even oracles can see their hidden resources. All I know is that Father Pat will come to you to reveal resources to you. I wish I knew more."

"It's cool," Carlos said, trying to remain calm.

"If they're not showing us resources right away, there's a reason," Damali interjected.

"That is true, Damali," Pearl said brightly.

Damali stooped down staring into the warm, clear blue water. "You said something about Atlantis . . . and before when we were in Washington, D.C., you said something about something being brought out of Ethiopia. What's up with all that?"

"You will soon be told about what came out of Ethiopia. Right now it's important for you to remember that they found a pyramid off the coast of Bermuda that was twelve hundred feet down below the surface of the sea."

Damali glanced at Carlos. "That reduces to three, in numerology."

"Yes," Pearl murmured in contentment. "It is also three hundred feet higher than the Cheops Pyramid in Egypt. The Bermuda Triangle stretches from here to Florida to Puerto

Rico, three . . . also a pyramid—but it also encases the Bimini Islands. *Bimini* is Taino for 'mother of many waters.' Your team is that now. Many mothers, many waters . . . water is your safe haven, water can be blessed as you travel across it, and in northern Bimini there is a saltwater mangrove forest that has a healing cove. Go there for a while and await word."

"That's our way back into the States," Carlos said, now looking at Damali. "From here to Puerto Rico by small charter boat, skirting the Triangle so the darkside can't detect us, through the Bimini Islands, and back in through the Florida Keys. From there, sheeit. If me and Yonnie get back on Miami soil, we *definitely* know how to navigate that terrain. We go from there, recon with our Atlanta team, and go get Ayana and Mom Delores, as well as get Dan's parents, out of harm's way . . . but we've gotta circumnavigate the Triangle as our cloak against the darkside while on the open seas . . . also probably the huge destroyer that's stalking the Atlantic, you feel me? We could get blown out of the water by a nervous U.S. military move, too. This shit ain't no joke."

"Stay as close to the edge of the vortex as you can," Pearl murmured in delight. "That's what Uriel wants."

"With the pyramid they found underwater here as our touchstone?" Damali said, glancing from the oracle to Carlos and back. "I still don't understand the whole Atlantean energy thing, but when you said pyramid, I'm on it."

"The energy will be good for the babies." Pearl giggled. "Atlantis is where Tehuti hid the knowledge of the Kemetian empire before it sank . . . your Kings' and Queens' ancestors all hail from there, just as the Kemetian, Mayan, Aztec, and Incan empires were vast, then disappeared without a trace or reason, so went Atlantis before them . . . where positive soul spirits came forward to dry land to rebuild what had sunk, bringing advanced knowledge forward through the seven rays of consciousness."

Damali and Carlos stared at each other and then down at the oracle as it prattled on in a cheerful voice.

"Every continent that owns pyramids or mounds, superstructures, and standing stones has an Atlantis vortex off its coasts—that's why no one can find it . . . Atlantis isn't in just one place or associated with just one race, it was a vast, advanced network of diverse races all called Atlanteans, just as before them were Lemurians and the Mu. Therefore, you must have your female seers lock into that to guide you past the dangerous fluxes in the Triangle. All seven pregnant female Guardians need to hold the energy. Each new child being formed must gain strength in one of the seven rays, in addition to the extrasensory gifts genetically passed by their parents."

Only four of our Guardians are pregnant, Damali shot to Carlos in a private, telepathic barb. *She said seven!*

I know, I know, but be cool, Carlos shot back, wiping his brow.

Be cool? Be cool! Damali's eyes were wild. *The only other possibilities are Tara and Val . . . or Inez . . . which means half of the team is down, literally!*

"Are you two listening to me anymore?" Pearl said in a sweetly sarcastic voice.

"Yeah," Carlos said, giving Damali a look to table the telepathic conversation. "We hear you. If the area has crazy energy, maybe our stoneworkers and seers can lock onto the pyramid to help whomever we charter a boat from hold his course—that part we got. But, damn, that gets right back to the problem of resources. Me and Yonnie are gonna have to—"

"No, Carlos." Damali gave him a hard look.

"What do you mean no, D? It is what it is—we need cash to function. That's just being real. What are we supposed to do until the Templar treasures and any other mystical shit is revealed?"

Damali stood, stretching her back, her gaze boring into Carlos's. She hesitated, wanting to say so much more about the additional pregnancies that Pearl just casually mentioned, but let it go for the sake of time and priorities. What did that matter anyway, really, when they were already in deep doo-doo?

"If we pull in money from some dirty source or so-call borrow it from an unsuspecting, innocent source, then we open ourselves up to the darkside," Damali said evenly, slowly folding her arms over her chest. "That's why we've gotta pay our bill at the villa, even if we do that using one of the team members' Rolex watch or something. We can't go back to the old ways. I don't care, draw lots and give up the wrist candy. As it is, the angels made poor Mr. Fontaine think we'd booked months in advance and hooked up the resort's computers to reflect that—stealing might unravel who knows what, Carlos. Be serious."

"You can't charter a yacht without money, D."

He folded his arms over his chest. She stared at the sea, and then glanced up at him with a half-smile as the pearl in her necklace blushed again. Damali immediately squatted down and submerged the necklace under the surf.

"Didn't seer Marlene mention the Cathedral of the Most High?" Tiny bubbles broke the surface of the water as a small wave lapped against Damali's legs. Pearl's voice cooed with contentment before she practically sang out her next statement. "I'd bet they have a parishioner there who might help you for free . . . if you ask him nicely and don't scare the poor man half to death, Carlos. After all, this is a mariner land with members of the British Navy heavily populated here, too."

Damali stood with a triumphant sigh. "I keep telling you we need to go to church more often, Carlos. But what do I know?"

CHAPTER TWO

"Oh, that's just lovely!" Rider shouted, throwing up his hands as he walked to the other side of the living room. He looked at Damali and Carlos in disbelief. "On the advice of a flaky, several-thousand-year-old pearl oracle, who has had her bouts with personal issues, we're supposed to leave a twenty-thousand-dollar watch on the coffee table as though this exclusive resort were a pawn shop, and then mist into a freaking cathedral in broad daylight—one that probably has tourists—and then hope to charter a yacht from some guy we have yet to meet with the goal to circumnavigate the goddamned Bermuda Triangle with a boatload of pregnant Guardians, and then try to work our way into Miami during U.S. martial law, praying we don't get blown out of the water by a naval destroyer or the coast guard at the very least—in *Miami,* a port *known* to shoot smuggler ships on sight—so who can guess what'll be waiting for us *if* we make it to shore with the Devil literally on our asses on the open seas. . . All this during the end of days, when lady luck ain't exactly been in our hip pocket. Maybe it's me."

Rider looked around at the team getting confirmation glances, and then settled his hard gaze on Carlos and Damali.

"What did I miss? Did you two go out on the beach and smoke a joint to relieve the tension or something? Are you *high*?"

Big Mike didn't say a word, just crossed the room and slapped Rider five after Yonnie pounded his fist.

"Look," Carlos said, his voice tight and urgent as he glanced around the team. "This ain't up for negotiation. We don't have a lotta options, given where we landed. You wanna take a short-cut through the Triangle on a wing and a prayer, hoping we don't get sucked into a black hellhole? You wanna risk the lives of four pregnant Guardian sisters?"

"Five," Tara said quietly.

Stunned speechless, Rider simply looked at her.

All eyes went to Tara, but Damali looked down at her sand-crusted bare feet. Carlos dragged his fingers across his scalp in agitation. The Neterus glimpsed each other. Their secret was finally out. Just as Damali was about to offer an explanation, Val pushed off the edge of the sofa she'd been leaning against.

"Six," Val whispered.

Carlos and Damali shared another look.

"Whoa, whoa, whoa," Yonnie said, slowly pushing off the wall, his line of vision fixed on Valkyrie. "Talk to me. My ass is dead—I'm just a vamp with an undefined reprieve. Whatchu talkin' about *six,* ma?"

"Five?" Rider said so quietly that the group left Val to ricochet and focus on him. He stared at Tara. "Baby, you were dead for forty years . . . I mean . . . something's wrong with the math here . . . I'm damned near—"

"Angels don't lie!" Tara shrieked, and then hugged herself and turned away.

Rider immediately crossed the room, trying to gather her in his arms. "Hey, hey, easy . . . I was just—"

"Is that all you had to say to me, Jack Rider—that I was

dead for forty years?" Bitter tears streamed down Tara's face as she hauled off and slapped him hard enough to make his lip bleed.

Two tense seconds passed; not one Guardian moved. Then all of a sudden Rider burst out laughing and hugged Tara up off her feet until she started laughing with him.

"Our asses are in a world of shit now," Rider said, laughing, finally putting her down. "Okay, I'm in for a penny, in for a pound." He staggered around in a circle, intermittently chuckling and becoming morose.

"You okay, man?" Shabazz asked, going up to Rider to land a hand on his shoulder and to get him to stop walking in a circle.

Rider just shook his head. "No. Actually, I'm having a nervous fucking breakdown, if you don't mind. How are we supposed to defend all of humanity against the forces of the Ultimate Evil and not be scared shitless that something could happen to the most precious thing on the planet?"

"Wow . . . oh, wow," Yonnie repeatedly muttered, rubbing his jaw. "This is deep . . . I'm dead, yo. Maybe it's, you know, psychosomatic, baby . . . not that I'm not down with it, if that's what's up, but I just never thought, I mean . . . we be getting it in, but I'm not able to . . . like . . . yo, C, you know what I'm saying, here, bro—you've got a heartbeat, I don't . . . like how is this possible? You sure we ain't got double-crossed?" Yonnie went to Val as huge tears of disappointment welled in her eyes. "Baby, listen, for real, now . . . I am a dead man walking. If you're pregnant, this could be the darkside seeding you, somehow, you know." He looked at Carlos and then Damali as worried glances passed around the group. "They do foul shit like that from where I'm from."

"I can scan her," Damali offered, but Carlos blocked her path.

"Uh-uh . . . that's a job for the Queens. If something's

inhabited her," Carlos said carefully, "we need to just be sure it's not contagious."

Yonnie closed his eyes and wrapped his arms around Val, kissing the top of her head. "We'll get it out of you if it ain't right, okay, boo. Carlos is right . . . but I'ma be with you no matter what."

"It's not evil," Val shot back, trying to wrest herself out of Yonnie's hold.

"Baby, how do you know?" he murmured, cupping her cheek with his hand. "I can't make life; I can only take life like I am now."

"Uriel told me," Val said in a quavering voice, her eyes filling with tears as she wrapped her arms around herself and lifted her chin. "The Neteru born must have seven Guardians for protection—ours plus Ayana, the new mother-seer, makes seven, Yolando. It's part of the prophecy."

Marlene rushed forward and gently grabbed Val by the arms as the team suddenly looked at Damali. "What's the full prophecy the angel told you, honey? Talk to us."

Val nodded. "What Damali is carrying has the power, when fully matured, to stop the one-third destruction of humankind foretold in Revelation. If this progeny is born and can reach maturity, then the one-third population wipeout can possibly be averted. This will help tip the scales toward the balance of the Light. Every one of these children must be a part of the new team."

A tiny squeal rang out in the room as the pearl in Damali's grasp fought to speak without water.

"Dip the oracle under tap water or something," Marlene commanded, eyes frantic.

J.L. rushed forward with the ice bucket, sloshing melted ice water, and offering it to Damali, who just stared at him. Carlos reached back, feeling for the wall to lean against with a thud.

"Dunk the pearl," Carlos said in a raspy voice. "I thought we weren't supposed to tell anybody yet . . . just dunk the pearl."

A high-pitched squeal wafted up from the bucket as soon as the necklace hit the water. "I was just bursting to tell. The Queens said I couldn't—not until Uriel made other announce-ments! So, now it's official. Congratulations, everybody!"

Damali yanked the necklace out of the water and simply stared at the rivulets cascading down her forearm.

"Oh . . . shit. . . ." Jose bent over, hands on knees, and began to hyperventilate.

"Like, what does this mean?" Berkfield asked quickly, his gaze furtive and haunted. "Like what are we gonna do, all this at risk and down a Neteru? Anybody hearing me?"

"It has to be all right," Marjorie said, wringing her hands as she spoke. "There must be a plan."

"Don't freak, people," Shabazz warned, taking temporary com-mand of the team. His dark, intense gaze swept the room, his regal African features set hard in his dark ebony face as a blue static charge ran down his dreadlocks and then connected to the charge running down Marlene's long, silver dreadlocks. "You saw how crazy strong C got in Detroit when Drac came after Damali and the team, right?" He waited until shoulders began to relax. "I don't know what the plan is yet, but I know I've lived through enough bullshit to know there is a plan."

Marlene swept her arm around the group. "We've got, for all intents and purposes, two sets of grandparents here—me and Shabazz, Marjorie and Berkfield. Between the four of us, we've got the skills of two seers, a strong veteran tactical, sharpshooter, aikido master, healer, and stoneworker . . . practically an entire squad, just from us. We represent the four cardinal points now. Plus, every man on this squad that's a father-to-be is still a viable warrior—and is probably more insane now than ever before. Every female who's carrying is still a force to be reckoned with, Ashe. So let's not get our heads all twisted, like Shabazz said— not yet. We've got months before we have to worry about all that."

"Ashe," Inez said. "But I have to get to my momma and my baby."

"First order of business, as soon as we can get to the States, suga," Big Mike assured her. "But we can't be bringing Mom and boo through no crazy energy distortions."

Inez nodded and leaned against his huge, six-foot-eight, tree-trunk frame, which made her seem even shorter.

"I just wanna know how all this happened at the same time?" Berkfield said, wiping the perspiration away from his bald scalp.

Shabazz smiled. "C'mon, man. It ain't been that long since you got some—you know how the birds and the bees work."

"That's not what I mean!" Berkfield yelled, growing peevish. "I mean the timing."

"Communal living," Marlene said in a cheerful voice, un-fazed by Berkfield's tone. "Fertile women who live in the same home, same tribe, all cycle around the same time . . . all the children born within a community like that are normally con-ceived and born around the same time. Lots of cousins. This is life still happening, even in the darkest moments in history. The human spirit will prevail, no matter what. These children will all need one another." Her tone sobered as she looked around the room. "And in a family like this, if one or both parents don't make it—which is a reality we have to be at the ready to always deal with—that child will not go parentless. We will raise all of them like the village we are. Ashe."

Murmurs of Ashe filled the room as each Guardian couple fell quiet to contemplate Marlene's and Shabazz's words.

Rider went to the mini-bar, opened the door, and just stared at the selections. Yonnie followed him, and then materialized a pack of red Marlboros in his hand, pulled out a cigarette for himself, and offered one to Rider without lighting either one. Both men simply stood shoulder to shoulder dragging on their unlit butts, smelling the tobacco while lost in their own thoughts.

"Uriel told me, too," Tara murmured thickly, finally breaking the silence in the room as she drew in deep breaths looking out the glass doors toward the unending blue sea.

She pushed a strand of her dark brown hair behind her ear and turned her face toward a shaft of sunlight that bathed her beautiful Native American features in tones of gold.

"My womb was dead for four decades, but was needed . . . I am needed and what grows within me is needed. I'm not dead anymore. I'm alive." Tara looked at Yonnie. "You might be alive, too . . . when's the last time you cut yourself to see if you bled red blood? The Light works quietly, subtly, and when we least expect it."

"I ain't been cut since D.C. . . . everything healed the moment we came through the Light and we got dropped here."

Yonnie stared at Tara for what felt like a long time and then opened his palm. Guardians gathered around him, craning to see the results of his test. With a shaking forefinger he willed forward a razor-sharp vampire fingernail and sliced into his palm. Thick, red blood oozed to the surface, painting his palm crimson. Yonnie clutched his chest like a man having a heart attack and staggered backward until he crashed into the dining-room table. Val caught him under an arm before he fell, and then pressed her fingers against his jugular.

"You're warm," Val murmured in awe. "For the last couple of

days and nights you've been burning up . . . and I just thought it was your body trying to regenerate from internal injuries." Then suddenly she snatched her hand back and pressed it to her heart, beginning to sob. "You have a pulse."

"Oh, shit. . . ." Yonnie wheezed, tightly closing his eyes. "When? I didn't even feel it."

"You had a better transition from the darkside to the Light than I did, bro," Carlos said, going up to Yonnie to pull him into a warrior's embrace. "Welcome to the Light, man. And congrats on the kid."

Yonnie opened his eyes and then burst out laughing, hugging Carlos back hard. "Damn, man! Like . . . we did it! We gonna be dads? Oh, shit! Me, too?"

"So, what in God's name do we do now?" Rider said quietly, still staring at the bar.

Tara wrenched her gaze away from the ocean and stared at Rider. "We take the path the Neterus have set."

"It's always the little things. The devil is in the details." A deep thunderous voice rang out followed by an evil laugh, unsettling transporter bats and dislodging rubble from the vaulted ceiling above.

The massive, black double doors leading into the Vampire Council Chambers eerily creaked open. Both of the large, golden-fanged door knockers that normally struck for blood authenticity cowered with their slit eyes shut tightly. The sound of hooves in the distance kept all eyes trained on the gaping maw of total darkness just beyond the doors. Wall torches began to flare in agitation to the new screams and moans renting the air from the Sea of Perpetual Agony just outside the grand chamber.

Every vampire went still as they sat in nervous repose awaiting the next set of orders to be given by their Dark Lord. Tiny gargoyle-bodied Harpies scampered to hide in the crags behind each of the huge, onyx-hued marble thrones, avoiding their normal sanctuary beneath Lilith's hemline like the plague—just in case she'd somehow lost favor with the master. They seemed to sense his foul mood before he arrived, as did the fanged crest in the center of the pentagram-shaped black bargaining table that had stopped spewing black blood. Even the veins within the black marble floor had stopped pulsing with the elixir of life, as though every inanimate object was also trying to avoid being the object of Lucifer's wrath.

Lilith sat deadly still on her throne. As Chairwoman, she knew that if a mistake had been made by one of her council members, she would be instantly targeted to take the weight . . . unless she could skillfully deflect whatever charge was being levied. Self-preservation, at all costs, was necessary.

Her three-hundred-and-sixty-degree peripheral bat vision studied each council member with care. If Lu needed a blood sacrifice to abate his fury about some yet unknown offense, who would she offer? Which member of her council was most expendable? The pale, devious Elizabeth, with the porcelain skin—wife of Count Dracula?

The fact that Elizabeth Bathory was a ruthless, sadistic bitch was reason enough to give her up; those character traits weren't unique in Hell. What did Liz really bring to the table, other than the very crafty reanimation of Dracula at Sebastian's expense . . . which was priceless. But the question was, however, would she be enough to sate Lu? The aquiline brunette with smoky, dark, exotic eyes was reed-thin, tall, and handsome, but no stunner. Lilith released a very slow exhalation, considering. No.

But then, what about Liz's husband, Dracula—Vlad the Impaler himself, perhaps? She glimpsed his strong, warrior jawline that held massive fangs when provoked and studied his athletic carriage, watching torchlight make strands of gold and red glisten in his dark brown hair. No, he was too valuable to the empire. Like Nuit, he was a master strategist, but had the added asset of owning the prowess and loyalty of a full demon army.

Maybe the sallow-skinned spell-caster and regular pain in her ass, Sebastian . . . but an expert necromancer during these times was also an asset. Lucrezia, then? Lilith studied Lucrezia Borgia's delicate features, startling green eyes, and beautiful thicket of auburn curls, and then discreetly dragged her gaze down the councilwoman's shapely body. But Lucrezia's expertise in poisons had served her well, not to mention, she had an evil pope in her line that was a strategic chess piece in the game that could be used later. Besides, to sacrifice Nuit's wife would cause an indelible rift between her and Fallon, and he was truly the closest reminder of Machiavelli that she had left. Decisions, decisions . . .

Glimpsing Fallon from a sidelong glance, she wistfully considered the tall handsome rogue from New Orleans, knowing that she'd throw the whole lot of them at her husband, if necessary, to buy herself more time.

Sulfuric ash spewed into the entranceway, making Lilith wrinkle her nose and halt her endless musing. Messengers had been killed . . . lovely. She made a tent with her fingers in front of her mouth and waited. She'd clearly heard hooves, but to her surprise, upon his arrival, her husband entered chambers in his human form—handsome as always and well coiffed, wearing one of his best black business suits.

His dark hair was well barbered. He'd put away his horns and bat wings, with no evidence of fangs gracing his seductively lush mouth. The spaded tail was gone and he wore a pair of expensive Italian slip-on leather shoes. He'd even come wearing his fanged crest ring, the one she so adored with the pentagram and black diamond in the center of it. Very nice. What game had he come to play today? She almost smiled.

The entire council prostrated themselves as the Dark Lord approached the bargaining table and took up a golden goblet, waiting impatiently for the fanged crest to belch black blood into it.

"The pale horse is running amok, how shall we make use of this fine hour?" The Unnamed One lifted his goblet with a droll smile and waited until Lilith slowly gazed up at him. "You have no idea how dismayed I was to have my hand forced like that. But all is fair in love and war, they say."

"We tried to contain the battle with the Neterus to Detroit and end it there," Vlad said in a defeated tone, "but—"

"My dear count, do stand." The Dark Lord swirled the blood in his goblet and then took a healthy swig from it as Vlad pushed up and stood. "You were the only one man enough to attempt to offer an explanation, and out of respect for all you've done for the empire, I'll allow you to cast the first suggestion for a strategy."

Seeming unsure as the Devil's smile broadened, Vlad hesitated.

"Oh, come now . . . you don't trust me?" The Dark Lord set down his goblet very carefully on the edge of the table and clasped his hands behind his back, beginning to circle Vlad. "You gave me much," he said in *Dananu,* beginning the negotiation by employing the centuries-old bargaining language. "Here is your chance to make a fair exchange. Sebastian is too weak to call me on what I really owe him; therefore, I will give it to you—if you can guess what it is."

A loud swallow made the Devil turn toward Sebastian, and then he laughed as Sebastian lowered his gaze. "Don't even attempt a late entry into this game, you pussy . . . you had your chance."

"You have released the pale horse of the Apocalypse to divert attention away from your heir," Vlad said quickly in *Dananu*. "It was a wise move necessary so that the warriors of the unnamed place above shall be too busy saving human lives to send a substantial retinue of warriors after the dark prince."

Clapping slowly, Lucifer narrowed his gaze on Vlad, the echo from his strong palms slapping one against the other deafening the vampire until blood began to leak from Vlad's nose and ears, staining his black council robe. Then in a sudden fit of rage Lucifer grasped Vlad by the jaw and stared deeply into his eyes. "Only half the story, old friend. Your obliviousness disappoints me. Perhaps I allowed you to suffer in the Sea of Perpetual Agony too long and your sensory awareness is dulled. Pity."

Gently removing his grasp from the count's jaw, the Dark Lord spoke in a quiet, lethal tone. "Please tell me what happened in Detroit?"

"The moment I surfaced with my army," Vlad said, gasping in *Dananu,* but still standing tall and proud, "I attacked with all my might. We impaled innocent humans and Guardians alike. We ravaged the area—"

"You attacked," Lucifer said calmly, refilling his goblet. "And not once did your dick get hard for the Neteru . . . a centuries-old vampire that still has the look of a young, virile, handsome warrior from the knights of old?"

"No," Vlad said proudly. "I was focused on victory."

Lucifer shook his head. "Fallon . . . stand and tell me what's wrong with that picture?"

Fallon pushed up from the floor and stood, head held high, shoulders back. "Dracula lusted for the Neteru in the Sea of Perpetual Agony until he nearly went mad when she ripened," Fallon murmured in *Dananu,* staring at Vlad first and then the Dark Lord with dawning awareness. He ignored Elizabeth's hiss of jealousy and a sly half-smile tugged at his mouth as he finally settled his gaze on Vlad. "*Mon ami* . . . you didn't even try to take her as a hostage for a lair prize later—you tried to kill her outright . . . the female Neteru."

"Of course I did, you backstabbing harlot!" Vlad shouted, about to lunge at Nuit. But Fallon Nuit's eerily calm countenance gave Vlad pause as Lilith covered her mouth.

"That could only mean one thing," Fallon said, his *Dananu* now ringing out with confidence as his line of vision shifted to become steady on the Dark Lord. "She no longer lures . . . the female Neteru's once-irresistible scent has been tainted by the Light that now inhabits her womb. Damali Richards Rivera has conceived! Always efficient in your evil, you released the pale horse to kill two birds with one stone . . . to lure the angels away from your heir and to infect the Neteru prophecy child."

"The *devil* is in the details—did I not say that when I first came in here? Give the man a seat at the head of the table, Lilith. He was the only one who stuck to his guns, figured it out based on a known variable—Dracula's behavior—and had the balls to present the theory. I like that," the Dark Lord said, laughing as he offered Nuit his goblet. "The game just got very interesting, and I have much work to do."

Time was pressing down on Damali like an invisible anvil. While the team absorbed the shock of what they'd just learned, something very instinctive kicked in and made her stop all conversation. She couldn't worry about how people were processing any of the news. They had to get out of there. *Now.*

Damali rushed forward to the middle of the room, her second-sight sending a hot poker of pain through her temples until it bloomed behind her eyes. "Everybody chill!" she shouted. "I can see the inside of the church. We've gotta move, come out of the energy fold in the long corridor just before you get to the sanctuary. Then we'll blend in with the tourists. There's a man there now, seeking his life's purpose . . . he's going into a confessional booth. If we wait, we'll miss him—he's our contact."

"Baby, you all right?" Concern laced Carlos's expression as Damali doubled over, beginning to pant.

"No," she whispered, standing up slowly. "I'm really not."

CHAPTER THREE

"It's been three days, and no word." Rabbi Zeitloff turned his heft away from the television in the Brooklyn safe house and closed his eyes against the violence being broadcasted from around the world.

"They have finally arrested the Dalai Lama," Monk Lin said in a quiet, angry tone. Lines of worry had begun to mark time on his otherwise ageless, bronze face. "A spiritual man of peace, Chinese government officials have dredged up false charges against a man of impeccable character, simply because of his words of truth and enlightenment . . . our Neteru Guardians are nowhere near as iconic, and thus would never stand a chance against an organized campaign of propaganda. We must go and protect those children. They must not fall into the hands of misdirected human authorities."

"How do we get to them, get into Washington, D.C., where they were last seen?" Imam Asula's calm gaze raked his fellow clerics as he unfolded his towering height from the small, white, vinyl-covered chair. He walked to the window and stared out at the city that never slept, his large, dark presence swathed in white linen almost blotting out the sunlight within a full pane.

"Perhaps our goal should be to secure their loved ones? We do not know where the Neteru Guardian team has hidden themselves, but we must ensure that baby Ayana, her grandmother, and Dan's parents do not perish at the hands of evil."

"Yes," Monk Lin said quietly, moving a worry bead through his graceful fingers as a rare breeze from the window caught the hem of his Tibetan robes. "But with the chaos, do we even know for certain where they are? We can try to get through the barricades to drive to Philadelphia to seek the child and her grandmother . . . perhaps Dan's parents will remain safe in the synagogue refuge here?"

"But Dan's mother and father must be confused and frightened by what they are hearing," Imam Asula said in a sudden boom of rage. He pointed at the television. "What mother or father could withstand such an onslaught of lies about their child? Even if they are physically safe, we must go to them and for once and for all reveal to them the truth of their son's sacrifice . . . they must be able to have peace in their souls, if not in their minds."

Rabbi Zeitloff stared at the television for a moment and then out of the window. "Don't you find it odd that the communications channels—radio, television, and such—are still functioning as though nothing unusual is going on, when the entire monetary system has temporarily shut down? They said the money is dirty and could pass the virus from human hand to human hand—so who would still be on the air at a time like this? Who would still be trying to document events while *everyone* is at risk, even newsanchors?"

The elderly rabbi turned to his fellow clerics. "While all of this is happening, and the people on television are still looking freshly showered and clean, stray dogs and cats are fleeing down the streets. Pit bulls are savaging homeless people for food. Vermin is pouring out of the sewers, rats are just ambling down the street with cockroaches, and no trucks are coming in to bring food back into the city. Is it me, or is this strange? How long do you think it'll be before the military and cops abandon their city checkpoint posts? Those young men and women have families . . . they will soon be as afraid of the contagion that's got pigeons falling off the wires and ledges as well."

Imam Asula closed his eyes and dropped his head. "Then there's no other way. We cannot wait this out—this tide will not pass quickly. We must get to the Weinsteins and to Inez's loved ones . . . in the final days there will be floods and famine and fire to complement the plagues. We must get off the island and cannot stay on hallowed ground paralyzed by fear. We must act. May Allah the Beneficent be with us. "

"Then we must also pray that the Weinsteins will hear us and still be where we left them," Monk Lin said in a serene tone. "We will then anoint them and pray the contagion that follows will not touch them. I will try to get word to the Philadelphia team to move baby Ayana and her grandmother. We must at all costs protect the new young seer, the child of Inez."

"That is the only way. Monk Lin is right, and so are you, Imam. We must pray for their Passover . . . that the contagion that will come will pass them by. Then we must act." Rabbi Zeitloff motioned to the window with his chin. "The air is sti-fling, the weather uncertain. All the signs are here."

"Our departed warrior brother spoke of this day, when the pale horse would ride and, according to his faith, the fourth seal would be broken," Imam Asula said, leaving the window to walk deeper into the living room. "One-fourth of the world would perish by the sword, and hunger, and death by the beasts of the earth."

Monk Lin nodded. "In Nepal, the monkeys have gone

wild . . . have become rabid, and are attacking pedestrians on the street. The banks of the Ganges are overflowing with bodies. There are indeed wars and rumors of wars. The current pope is ill; cyclones are sweeping the Asian plateau." He pushed another worry bead along the leather cord. "Here, it is the stray dogs and the rats that carry the fleas of bubonic plague. Look outside. As hot as it is, only military patrols . . . where are the people? In New York City, if the rats completely flee the subway and sewer systems when the floodwaters come, there will be pure chaos. We must find the remaining family members of our Neteru team or die trying."

"The Old Testament, Book of Daniel—all of it." Rabbi Zeitloff took off his thick glasses and wiped a handkerchief across his eyes. His brows knit like furry white caterpillars in the center of his forehead as he stared at his Covenant brothers. "I feel things in my gut. Monk Lin gains impressions from meditations. Imam, you have been our tactical strength . . . but we are missing our eyes. We are missing our dear, dear friend, Father Patrick—our seer." He clenched his fist to his chest and swallowed hard. "Without his eyes, it is hard to see in the dark."

"Nana?" Ayana whimpered, pulling her small body from beneath the rubble.

Pitch-blackness surrounded her. Sharp, hard objects made her afraid to move. Dust filled her lungs, making her cough, and she could still hear the howling wind outside. That's what Nana had told her it was—just the wind. But spooky noises of things creaking and groaning made her shut her eyes tightly and try not to breathe. The grown-ups Nana said were there to help had fallen down, just like Nana, when the big wall fell on everybody.

She kept telling Nana that they shouldn't leave where Mommy and Uncle Mike had left them. They shouldn't have gone back to Atlanta because the wind was mixing around with trees and cars in it and windows would break. She'd heard the windows crashing in her dream, everything crashing. People got cut and had blood on them. But the grown-ups said things like that never happened in Atlanta, not downtown where they would be safe in the big, pretty hotel on Peachtree Street. The name sounded pretty then, but she still didn't like the idea. The grown-ups were using a word she didn't know . . . *tornado.* When she asked them more about it, they just said it was a little storm, but their eyes seemed scared.

It wasn't a little storm.

It was a big, big storm.

They had to hide in the basement. But there were so many people running into the hotel and down the steps that Grandma fell and lost hold of her hand. People who'd come to help Nana fought to get to her . . . but she was so teeny and the people running were so many. She was three and a half, almost four, a big girl, Nana said . . . but right now she felt really teeny and re-ally scared. Then the lights went out and a big explosion hap-pened. That's all she remembered for a long time. She had to remember everything to tell Mommy and Uncle Mike . . . and Aunt Damali.

Two big tears rolled down Ayana's nose and she sniffed hard, too frightened to cry out loud. There was something scary in the dark that other people couldn't see. She knew it. She could feel it.

Ayana closed her eyes tighter, remembering what Aunt Damali and her mommy said to do. Pray hard in her mind. Don't move her mouth. Ask the angels for help. See inside her eyelids.

She ducked her head down lower, laying her cheek against broken concrete, and curled up into a little ball. Something cold crawled over her and she kept her hand clamped tightly on her mouth, shivering . . . saying the prayer to be invisible to monsters. Then she saw it.

Huge red eyes looked through the dark. Big, dripping, yellow teeth. Big, sharp claws. Stinky, stinky body that was skinny like a big spider's. It was looking for her, she knew it. She could tell. But if it found Nana first, it would eat her!

Ayana's eyes rolled back and forth behind her tightly shut lids. Then she saw a shoe. Her nana's shoe! Ayana's head jerked in the direction of it at the same time the demon's gleaming eyes spotted it. The creature pounced on the fallen column that had Delores wedged beneath it and began to savage her limp body, becoming frustrated as it tried to extricate her from the debris.

Seconds put Ayana on her feet. She knew the monster would tear off one of her grandma's arms or legs, and would make her bleed. If it did that, Nana would stop breathing and die. A high-pitched scream exited Ayana's body and rent the air.

"No, no! Leave my nana alone!"

The creature whirled and held its head for a moment with several of its hooked-claw appendages, and then lunged at the three-year-old child. Ayana's scream brought heavy footfalls. Men and women were frantically calling out her name. Something huge was hurtling toward her. The pitch of her scream intensified. Gun barrels lowered. An explosion wet her face with green slime.

"Over here!" a Guardian yelled.

Coughing, sputtering, Ayana went to the first adult that opened her arms to her.

"Nana, Nana—it was gonna get Nana!"

Someone wiped her face. She heard somebody hock and spit.

"Yo, Quick . . . the kid went up against an arachnid demon . . . Level Four—you see that?"

A tall lady that she couldn't see too well held her. The gunk on her face stung her eyes, and all she wanted to do was keep her face pressed against the soldier lady's neck, in case some more monsters came out.

"I'm Shaun, baby. We got you. It's gone. We're gonna get your grandmom out, okay?"

Ayana just nodded. Her stomach felt jumpy. "I want my mommy," she whimpered. "I want my nana. I didn't wanna come here. I don't wanna stay here. We have to go where it's high, high up in the mountains."

"I know, I know," Shaun soothed. "But we had to bring you all here . . . because there's some bad germs where you were. The sickness hasn't spread here yet, you understand, pumpkin? Your mommy and Uncle Mike don't want you and Nana to get sick."

"Dragon Rider, you see that?" Craig's voice made everyone look as he stood over demon remains. "She's a reverse audio . . . whoa. Kid uses her voice like a weapon, you see that?"

"Yeah," Quick said, stepping over rubble, her gun barrel at the ready to blow away anything demonic that might slither out. "That's why we listen to the kid and head toward the Appalachian Mountains as planned to rendezvous with the Philly team. They took all the Guardian kids from the safe house school and headed west out of the madness toward Pittsburgh, to higher ground in the mountains."

Ayana peeked up from Shaun's neck. A big man picked up a hairy monster leg and threw it away from the pile of rocks, trying to get stuff off her grandmom.

"If she's got that kinda skill to see demons coming and to explode 'em from a scream at three or four years old," Dragon Rider said, checking her weapon magazine, "imagine what she'll do at twenty-three."

"Yeah, well, we've gotta make sure we get her to twenty-three," Michelle said, glancing at her teammate and stashing a 9 mm in the back of her fatigue pants waistband. She tossed a couple of grenades to Dragon Rider to hang on to as she bent and grasped the edge of the cement slab that trapped the unconscious woman. "C'mon, Rayne . . . this is your detail. Healing. Remy, you and I lift with Craig, then Rayne, you pull the grandmother out with Leone while Quick and Dragon Rider cover us. Might be more of these suckers down here crawling around in the dark looking for a Neteru team hostage—so look alive, folks."

Craig spat and pounded Quick's fist, hoisting his Uzi up out of the way as he tightened his grip on the edge of the concrete slab. "Atlanta ever had a tornado before?"

Quick gave him a look. "Hell, no. New York City ain't had one, either, till this past year."

He nodded. "Just what I thought."

He could feel himself being followed as he left the safe house and headed toward the Masjid. He didn't care; he had been ready to die all his life in the service of Allah. When the unmarked car skidded to a halt and bounced onto the sidewalk, followed by another screeching to a halt, Imam Asula stood very, very still.

Men in dark suits and white shirts drew weapons on him without identifying themselves. Within moments he was forced to the ground by what felt like twenty men. He could have resisted, but that would have given them license to shoot him in broad daylight. People leaned out of windows with camera phones, screaming, yelling, trying to make the police hear that he was a man of faith, a cleric. But they had pictures of him with the most wanted. His obvious religion and garb also didn't work in his favor.

With hands shackled and his dignity in shreds, he was roughly forced into a black van. A dark hood got yanked over his head. The burlap dug into the fresh cuts and bruises on his cheek. Angry words pelted him, as kicks and jabs from boots and elbows thrashed his body. Then suddenly all motion stopped and he was yanked forward, falling, banging his shins and knees, and then yanked upright. He heard a door open, could smell the cool dankness of a basement.

He could have fought them, could have used his years of martial arts training. Could have concealed a weapon under his robes. But his mission was to divert them from Rabbi Zeitloff and Monk Lin . . . who had to make it to Dan's parents, had to get word to the Neterus, had to complete what they had all given their lives to the Almighty One for. Allah was with him.

Suddenly pushed back, he hit the ground with a thud. Dazed, he could barely catch his breath. Then came the water. Drowning—he was drowning! He fought, shackled, struggling to breathe. The sack over his head sucked up into his nose and mouth as he gagged trying to get air, but he accidentally sucked in water that scorched his lungs. Blood rushed to his head as they inverted him even more, causing him to gag, causing him to vomit and choke on his own refuse.

"What the fuck did they put in the dirty bomb?"

Voices thundered around him in muddy waves.

"People are dying! What's making people go insane and begin eating each other, asshole? What is it, an airborne drug?"

"Or is it some kind of airborne toxin that eats into the brain stem? What is it, motherfucker!"

"Did you and your terrorist cronies release the bubonic plague with the Ebola virus, too? You poison the water—shoot up a bunch of animals with rabies and let them go in cities all over the world?"

"Who do you work for?"

"Where are the Weinsteins? What are their real names? Did all you Middle Eastern bastards brew up some nasty shit in a lab together, or what? They're not Israelis, are they?"

"Is that why the dogs and cats are turning on their owners? What. Did. You. Do?"

"Let him up, Frank. See if he's got something to say."

Voices had become so distant. His dear friend smiled and held out a hand. He had made it to more than threescore and ten years of age. They laughed together. His face suddenly felt clean and fresh. His chest no longer felt like it was about to explode. The taste of vomit was gone from his throat. He watched dispassionately as frustrated men yanked back his hood to stare into his glassy eyes. He walked away with Patrick, who slung an arm over his shoulder.

"Goddamn!" the lead interrogator yelled, and flung down the hood. "You held him under for too long. That was our closest Middle Eastern lead!"

"His body was still moving," another man nervously argued.

"He was fucking convulsing, you moron. Look at him. He suffocated under the hood in his own vomit!"

"Quickly, quickly," Rabbi Zeitloff urged, holding Mrs. Weinstein's hand.

"But my Daniel, he couldn't have done those things they claimed." Stella Weinstein's tear-glazed eyes sought the rabbi's and then her husband's. "He is honorable, has a good job working to help the president—so does his superior officer . . . that General Rivera. His wife is a good girl. They have a baby on the way. Tell me my world is not coming to an end!"

"Stella, we must go. Now. There is no time," her husband said, shaking her. "We must trust the rabbi and the monk. Do you see they are rounding people up? Have we not seen this in history before? Open your eyes!"

"Please, I beg you," Rabbi Zeitloff said in a rush. "Follow us out through the safe tunnels that were built under this place when we bought it, then we'll go up to the streets. We'll get you onto a ferry, from there—"

"Where is *my son*?" Stella cried out as they hurried her down the long corridor into the basement.

No one answered her as the rabbi opened a door with shaking hands and then gave Monk Lin the key. "Lock us in and may Yahveh be with you."

Running, running, his breath came out in waves of pain as he fled the building and headed uptown. Monk Lin's frantic gaze took in the chaos around him. Dogs snarled in the street, fighting over the dead bodies of the homeless—the first to fall. Those with weak immune systems. Those without shelter and with a limited stash of food or water. They now lay dead in alleyways, food for the rats that battled the dogs, a job too voluminous for a public health system in shambles. Alleys were disease pits. Garbage cans a death sentence. Men and women had rightfully abandoned their jobs hauling refuse. It meant certain death now that the Black Death had settled like a toxic cloud over the eastern seaboard.

Knowing wounded his soul. He'd felt his dear friend Imam leave this plane not a half hour ago. He would not weep; he and Father Patrick, even the young Padre Lopez and the others, were fortunate. This was no way to live. The Buddha was weeping.

Monk Lin jumped back as pigeons began dropping from the sky like small gray bombs of jellied feathered flesh. Dead squirrels littered the streets, even the cockroaches ran about as though disoriented. Sewer openings belched rats. Screams of humanity chilled his bones as he ran through the sweltering streets, dodging the occasional wildly veering car.

Only those who were sick, or without resources, or hiding from the law were still trapped within the city. Basic services had finally shut down, collapsing under the weight of human panic. There were no more civilian trains. No buses. No trucks renewing supplies. Monk Lin looked around. Just military checkpoints. Just military occupation of all civilian carrier systems—trains, ferries, buses, trucks—everything had been commandeered to transport the sick and dying, or to remove bodies. Stores had been looted for food and water and were now just shells. Money was worthless . . . was outlawed as a cause of passing the contagion.

How would Rabbi Zeitloff ever hope to get the Weinsteins off the island and past checkpoints at the harbor?

Tunnels unused since the fifties shimmered with moisture as the rabbi led Dan's parents to what they all prayed would be salvation. They were healthy—had no signs of the contagion. Phony ID had been drawn up. Hair colors had been changed, size augmented by theatrical prosthetics. Makeup added, enough to get them past harried checkpoint guards. At least they'd be out of hell's kitchen. The safe house network stretched to the harbor. Monk Lin would hold the line and continue to signal for the Neteru team and local Guardians, continue to try to interpret word from the spiritual realm, while he couriered the innocent to a haven beyond the walls of insanity.

Disease was imploding in the major cities, but where the population densities were lower, there was still some fragment of civilization left that had not begun to unravel. Getting to the mountains was the only hope.

Rabbi Zeitloff kept that goal in front of him as he hustled

down the dark corridor with a lantern flashlight, blotting out Stella Weinstein's whimpers. His heart ached with hers, but he couldn't focus on that now. He had to deliver her and her husband to higher ground. That's where he needed to get these good people.

They could be safe on hallowed ground of a mission in New England until he could break through to Carlos or Damali to whoosh them into an energy fold and make them vanish without a trace. Worse case, they could trek to Hartford, then head west from there and go toward the Appalachian Mountains. Higher ground. Once in the mountains they could maneuver.

He would focus on that and couldn't think about how his bones ached, his age and weight made his breathing labored, or how his heart now beat in arrhythmia from the heat, exertion, and fright. If it was the last thing he did, he had to keep pushing the Weinsteins forward to reunite them with the core of safety—the Neteru team.

The narrow passage only allowed one body to get through at a time. The air was stifling, the lantern becoming so heavy . . . the gap widening between him and the Weinsteins ahead. Just as well. Tears filled his eyes as the sound that he heard in his head and in his soul slowly filled his ears. The door behind him was a mile away and locked. He leaned his forehead against the wall, his black clerical hat toppling off his head.

"Rabbi!" Dan's father turned around.

Rabbi Zeitloff waved him off. "Push forward and live to see your grandchildren."

A woman's bloodcurdling scream drowned out the high-pitched squeals that echoed in the narrow tunnel behind him.

The rabbi braced himself against both walls, using his body as a shield. They would run for him, the closer meal . . . would scramble over his blood and flesh first, and once sated would continue forward. The rats would eat well on his leathery, fat meat. He laughed, insanity and fear colliding with courage. They had killed his friend Patrick. He could feel Imam was no more. "Run!" He would be a human body plug, a flesh and blood dam to keep the disease-carrying rodents from tearing into Dan's heart by tearing into his parents.

And they came as a biting, clawing, searing wave of filth and pain with red glowing eyes and razor-sharp fangs. They covered his legs and back, a writhing swarm of gnashing teeth, tearing at the soft flesh of his neck and eating away his ears, until the tide of them swept him off his feet.

But one seize of his elderly heart brought two familiar faces toward him. A large dark hand with the strength of a giant clasped his within a familiar palm. Asula brushed off his suit and Patrick lifted him under his arms, a sad smile gracing his face.

"Dead but not broken, the Covenant is still empowered and could be more dangerous to us than alive, Elizabeth. I applaud your work but remain skeptical about its effectiveness." Lilith hissed as she looked into the depths of the illusion beneath her fanged crest. She circled the black pentagram-shaped table in her chambers and glanced up at the Vampire Council. "Once the pale horse rides, never forget that the fifth biblical seal can be broken. That will allow the Light to bring back martyred souls to aid in their cause from the spiritual realm . . . hence why our Dark Lord was so furious that the Neterus' actions prematurely forced his hand." She waved toward the huge chamber doors. "The next time he comes back, unless we have phenomenal progress to report, I guarantee he will not be in such a good mood. Instead of bargains, there will be bodies—do I make myself clear?"

Lucrezia stroked the armrest of Fallon's throne. "But Madame

Chairwoman, the moment the fifth seal is broken, does not the match point revert to us? My poisons and plagues are making it impossible for the team to hide as it spreads across the land. No agricultural stock animal will be fit to eat. Nor fish. The adverse weather will blot out crops. Once the human stockpile dimin- ishes, there will be war in the street for food."

"I have already risen the undead," Sebastian said with a sal- low grin. "Those who succumb to Lucrezia's plagues reanimate and wake up with a hunger for human flesh . . . there will be more than war in the street. So let the Light open the fifth seal and call their martyrs. As soon as they do so, all we have to do is open the sixth seal, and it will be our turn."

Nuit's eyes met Lilith's as Vlad made a tent before his mouth with his hands, waiting.

Lilith nodded. "But it is not that simplistic. The sixth seal was hidden eons ago because it is our nuclear alternative, if we elect to employ it. It seems some angels playing dirty allowed it to be removed from the astral plane and after such treachery, we have been hunting it for millennia."

"You almost had it," Vlad murmured in *Dananu,* cutting a glare at Fallon Nuit. "Residue of that time whispers in my throne. I'll share my impressions for a reinstatement of my po- sition as head of the table, beneath you, of course, milady."

"Still green with envy from Fallon's subtle coup, eh, Count?" Lilith chuckled. "Make it interesting; time is not on our side."

Vlad ignored the curious gazes from his competitors. "There were four masters who Carlos Rivera bested in the Outback, yes? This, of course, after he'd already bested Fallon." Vlad leaned forward as Lilith held a goblet of blood in midair. He gave a triumphant glance in Fallon Nuit's direction before returning his gaze to Lilith. "I believe all that occurred during the time Fallon was in repose in the Sea of Perpetual Agony . . . after having been fang-neutered by the inimitable Mr. Rivera." Vlad chuckled as Nuit issued a low, warning snarl. "You see, I, too, am a student of history, especially epic battles. Being so close to claiming the sixth seal is what nearly drove our former Chairman, Dante, insane. He was *so close.*"

With a snap of her fingers Lilith created a dark globe in front of her throne and then blew on it to make it spin. A long graceful fingernail soon became a talon as it scored the crust of the earth, causing it to bleed where Rivera had been during his vampire incarnation. "Carlos was primarily in Sydney—not the Outback, to be exact—with that Neteru bitch of his. He spent a brief time at the late Master McGuire's castle, just off the sandstone cliffs overlooking the Great Barrier Reef. But where the real travesty occurred was on the high seas on McGuire's yacht and at the docks in Sydney—which is presumably why Sydney is already under Lucrezia's plagues and Elizabeth's chaos. What more do you suggest?"

Vlad stood and swept away from his throne to meet Lilith by the globe. "Rivera bested Nuit, and then subsequently all four master vampires that confronted him and—"

"Yes, yes, I know! Dante revoked Rivera's freedom, bat-snatched him in a swirl of Harpies off the yacht, killed his first conceived child, and brought him here to these very chambers, where he ripped out Rivera's innards, then sent him into the sun. What more was there to do to the man? He was as good as exterminated, had the Light not cheated and called in the soul determination clause. Whatever."

"Your husband taught me something earlier—taught me not to overlook the details—and I respect his wise counsel." Vlad offered Lilith a charming bow and then took up her hand. "Follow Rivera's blood trail from the night he won the Master's Cup . . . from the castle, through the desert . . . to the border of sunrise."

Lilith pulled away from Vlad's hold and waved her hand dismissively. "He was with the Neteru female—many a male vampire would have braved ash for a ripened—"

"No," Vlad said, cutting her off and catching her arm by the wrist. "He was to bring Dante the sixth seal *and* the woman. Love blotted out the female's whereabouts, and the Light blinded us to the seal's location . . . but the fact that Rivera saw it out there in that desert and left it out there for the love of a woman, for the love of humanity, registered as treason in his throne! Feel it! *That* is what drove Dante wild. It was a multiple offense against the empire."

Lilith yanked away from Vlad and quickly swept to his throne, caressing the armrests before she sat down. Her glowing black irises slowly widened as dark energy entered her body.

"Throne of darkness that nearly took residence in Rivera's spirit, speak to me," she murmured. Slowly she closed her eyes with a satisfied sigh and then opened them.

"We do not need an exact location," Elizabeth cooed in *Dananu.* "Just a general area."

Vlad nodded and held out a hand to his wife, who floated over to him to receive it. "Let the full wrath of the fourth broken seal drive the beasts of the earth to ravage the ancient Aborigine population . . . then send the plagues. In death, they cannot keep up their dreamtime Light chants that blind us from the exact location. As the plagues take their toll, sooner or later we will find their hiding dens and will rout them out. All we needed to know was a general location of who had it, and from there we can apply pressure to the area until the humans in it cave and give up the seal."

"As with all things," Lilith said, standing slowly, choosing her words in *Dananu* with care. "You and your wife only win an elevation in power if your theory proves correct and you can defend it to Lu." She cast a withering gaze toward Sebastian, who simply hissed. "Isn't that correct, Sebastian? Being right isn't the full monte—you must have the balls to execute."

Walking slowly, she gave Vlad a long, contemplative look and tapped her forefinger to her mouth. "That area is extremely dangerous. It is crisscrossed by twenty-thousand-year-old prayer lines and sacred didgeridoo sound lines, hence why we haven't returned. An educated guess is that once the keepers of the seal had been discovered, they would have moved it . . . . I just don't know. We have already expended a lot of resources, but you may have a point. Time will tell."

"Rather than playing long shots, why not allow a real artist to go to work?" Sebastian snarled in *Dananu*. "I can raise the Berserkers from all of the Nordic lands, as well as from the old Slavic empires and Germanic tribes, to search and destroy the planet for the seal." He turned to Vlad with an evil challenge in his smoldering eyes. "If my reanimated demons find the sixth seal first, I will claim lead councilman—and your fucking wife will lap dance me!"

Nuit came between both snarling combatants, blocking Vlad's and Elizabeth's lunge at Sebastian with a cool smile. "You take the high road, Sebastian, by raising the Berserkers. Allow Vlad and Elizabeth to take the low road, namely ravaging the Aussies," Nuit offered in *Dananu*. "But until such time as either of you bring in the goods, you will do things my way. Right now, I say we concentrate on locating the Neteru female who is carrying the Neteru child."

☙ CHAPTER FOUR

No matter what I tell you, do not let the team see it on your face.

Then tell me what's wrong. Carlos's gaze was hard with worry as it raked her body, searching for anything that could have made her sick.

Everyone was looking at them, waiting for word that it was safe to move out. Damali stared at Carlos, her eyes imploring him not to tip the team off to the multiple tragedies she'd sensed. She waited till he nodded and then glanced around the desolate hallway inside the Cathedral of the Most Holy.

"It's safe here," she said quietly, glancing around. "Tourists haven't started arriving. Priests are probably in the sanctuary. Go two by two and slide into the pews, spread out like we didn't just jettison in here together. Keep your head low like you're praying until we can figure out how to approach our contact."

"Whaduya mean *like* we're praying?" Jose said, running his fingers through his hair. "At this point, D, that's all we're doing."

"You ain't said a word," Mike muttered, moving out first with Inez.

Carlos gave the group a nod and he and Damali watched as

each couple slowly fanned out, moving into the sanctuary quietly and then hiding their identities behind clasped hands.

"Talk to me," he said in a low, private murmur as soon as they were alone.

Damali closed her eyes and then reached out to hold his face with both hands. "Oh, Carlos . . . Imam, Rabbi . . ." She shook her head and allowed the horrific images to flow from her mind into his.

"Jesus . . ." Carlos tore his gaze from Damali to look at the team that had spread out in the pews.

"Yeah," she said, opening her eyes. "They went after Ayana. Mom Delores almost didn't make it. The Weinsteins are trapped in the safe house tunnel system . . . Rabbi went down with the key to open the other end around his neck . . . in the panic he wasn't thinking about all that. There's no time left to get them out. What are we gonna tell Dan?"

Sweating, nauseous, he pulled his wife behind him with one hand and held the heavy flashlight with the other, running. The sound of flesh being torn away from bone was far behind them, but the pants of their breaths and the smell of their humanity in the tight confines made him know it wouldn't be long before the ravenous hordes sought them out.

The door in sight was their only salvation and he kept his blurred vision trained on that. Frank Weinstein turned and caught his wife as she stumbled, grabbing her by her arm and her shirt to urge her forward. He couldn't expend energy on words. They had to move. He could hear the squeaking mass starting to move. Survival depended on staying ahead of the rats.

He reached the panic bar on the door, thrusting his body against it with all his might. But the heavy steel door didn't budge. His wife covered her head with her arms and released a wail of despair as she sank to the damp ground. He tried again, throwing his body against metal and concrete until he heard a rib crack. Then his fists bore out his frustration as he banged and yelled into the nothingness, the flashlight dropping to his feet to reveal what was headed toward them—a crawling river of plague-carrying death.

His wife's screams made him sob. If she had at least made it. If she weren't there. If he weren't impotent to protect her or his son! Why was God punishing his family?

As Frank gathered his wife into his arms, the couple huddled against the locked door. He put his body between her and the on-slaught, hoping to buy her a few moments more while also pray-ing that she'd have a heart attack before they ate out her eyes.

"Yo! Yo! Anybody down there?" a strong male voice bel-lowed into the abyss.

"Help us—the rats are coming!" A collective wail greeted the question as the Weinsteins began banging on the door with open palms.

"Get back from the door—we gotta blow it!"

The couple scampered backward, falling against the rocky sur-face as they monitored the oncoming, writhing threat.

A sudden blast deafened them as they covered their heads and bright lights and dust stung their eyes.

"Get those people outta there!" a loud voice yelled.

"Yo, Phat G—flamethrowers, man!" another voice hollered.

Strong arms pulled the dazed couple from the tunnel.

"Go, go, go!"

Chaos surrounded the Weinsteins. People in military fatigues and weapons. Flamethrowers. Their ears rang, their vision was blurred. Their bodies were being pulled and shoved to safety. Sewer water sloshed in their shoes and the stench filled their noses and mouths. Gunfire report and the heat from flamethrowers gave them the strength to climb up an iron ladder. A strong soldier flipped open a street manhole and brandished a weapon. They watched as he quickly drew himself out and then turned around to pull them into the fresh air.

Using a machine-gun barrel, the soldier motioned toward a covered military truck. "Get in and get your head down."

There was no time for questions. If they'd been abducted by the government, it was still survival. The couple looked at each other and then complied, running toward the vehicle. Women in fatigues with hard eyes and toting weapons pulled them into the truck and gathered a tarp.

"Listen," a tall African-American woman with braids in her hair said. "We're the New York squad, all right. We got Monk Lin's SOS. We're friends of your son, and gonna get you somewhere safe."

"I'm Carmen, that's Adrienne with the braids, and Roshida—ex-cop and sure shot—and Chantay—from up south . . . South Carolina, who's gonna get us through the mountains," another shorter woman replied, handing the Weinsteins a bottle of water.

"Glad we got to you in time, was *literally* a monster getting up here from Harlem," the soldier pointed out, as Roshida said.

Carmen nodded. "No lie. But we want you to know that we're not some terrorists kidnapping you—that's why we're giving you names. We don't want you afraid of us, all right? We lost a lotta good men trying to get to you to help you."

The couple looked up from where they sat on the truck floor, uncertain, eyes wide with terror, but nodded in agreement nonetheless.

Adrienne gave the other female Guardians a look. "They're gonna be all right. Just need time."

"Yeah," Carmen said quickly, and then looked at the Weinsteins, trying to get through to them. "Lisa was the little chick on the flamethrower that got the rats. Nyya was on your six keeping back demons in the sewer till we could get topside. Phat G blew the door, and my boys the Professor and Rene will be driving. If you haven't noticed, the world has gone crazy. Me, Phat G, and the rest of the squad got your backs. We've gotta go through a coupla military checkpoints and pass through like we're military—hiding in plain sight. That's why you've gotta go under the tarp. Don't panic, Mr. and Mrs. Weinstein . . . we're not gonna hurt you. We're trying to save your lives, cool?"

As the back flap of the truck opened, and more soldiers piled in, the diesel engine engaged, lurching the truck forward.

"All clear. Move out!" a bulky soldier with dreadlocks shouted.

Carmen pounded on the truck frame and repeated the command. "Yo, Professor—Phat G said to move out!" She looked at the couple on the floor and handed them the tarp. "You all cool? You know what to do?"

The Weinsteins looked around, dazed, and simply nodded, still shaken as they guzzled the offered water and then hid.

Cordell left the safe house in Georgetown, not caring what his fellow Guardians had to say. The darkside had killed his Dougie, his protégé . . . a young Guardian that was more like a son to him than anything in the world. What else could they do to him? Death would be an honorable conclusion. D.C. had gone insane.

Troops in jeeps, Humvees, and armored vehicles crisscrossed the city grid, sweeping the terrain with flamethrowers to exterminate rats, stray rabid dogs, anything that didn't seem normal. Tanks rolled down Sixteenth Street and guarded bridges. Black

Hawk helicopters nearly blotted out the sun. The occasional F-16 fighter jets soared in formation overhead.

He knew what the remaining team feared, that the authorities would see him walking down the street, dazed, and assume he was one of the walkers—and then torch him on sight. Maybe. Maybe not. Or he would take a single shot to the head by a military sniper, just for being considered a threat. Every soldier was on high alert. He was an old, out of shape black man ambling down the street as though the world hadn't changed. His teammates said he was crazy for insisting he go alone. He'd be gunned down, detained, or possibly attacked by the walkers, feral stray animals, or worse.

But that wouldn't stop him. He had work to do. A priest had come to him in a daydream, more like a vision. An older man with a shock of silver-gray hair and a Templar crest had shown him a series of carvings on a wall that moved when pressed hard.

The hieroglyphs opened a façade that hid a secret room that had standing knights in armor with medallions on their chests. Each of the four medallions linked together to create a key that fit into a specific east wall brick. Turning the key gave way to what was behind the door—a long corridor that opened out to a wider room. There was a single bench table at the center of it. The walls were bare, just highly polished stone. Wall torches sputtered.

Then he'd seen the stone floor that had prone statues of dead Templars in the four corners of the room. The one guarding the western cardinal point held a scroll in his hand. This was the map he was to find. He saw the engraved medallion on the stone statue and then looked at the key in his hand, fumbling to separate out the four medallions he held.

Setting the right one from the western armored knight into

the carved stone replica of it and turning it made the wide slate floor tiles around the prone statue drop four inches. He looked closer and in the dusty space was a parchment roll.

Cordell looked up, suddenly coming out of his medium's daze to find himself standing in front of the Scottish Rites Temple. How he'd gotten there he wasn't quite sure. That much didn't matter. The fact that he'd made it alive did.

Maybe the reason the soldiers hadn't shot him, even though he was walking down Sixteenth Street, was because they viewed him as just an old man heading in the direction of Columbia Road and Harvard Street, an intersection that held All Souls Church, National Baptist Memorial Church, and the former Church of the Latter-day Saints that was now a Unitarian church. Perhaps there was some mercy in their hearts, no matter what their training dictated, and they'd let old folks that reminded them of their parents and grandparents go into a house of worship to lie down and die. He didn't know. Didn't care. He just scratched his balding head, wondering how the time had escaped him.

Not lingering, Cordell rushed up the steps and entered the abandoned grand hall. Nothing was locked; people had fled, the power was out. He didn't need lights.

The vision guided him, pulling him around corners, taking him down stairwells, making his breaths labor as he wielded his heft at a frantic pace. But as soon as he entered the chamber that held the four armored knights, an immovable force gripped him and held him firm. Terrified, he struggled against the supernatural hold, his heart pounding in his ears. It had been a trap! He wasn't armed; had to be that way in case he got stopped by military street patrols. The younger Guardians had been right. Now the darkside had him!

To his horror, a sword unsheathed from the scabbard of the

western standing knight just as the force thrust him onto his knees. The weapon flew at him, but didn't cut, hovered only an inch away from his neck, then gently lowered to his right shoulder and then his left, before clattering to the floor.

When he looked up, the warrior-priest of his vision stood before him with a sad smile. He had on the same medallion with a heart on a cross pierced by a dagger and crowned by a ring of thorns.

"Only a Templar knight can know our secrets," the priest said. "I am Patrick. Memorize the maps. Use them to feed the remaining teams. You may pass. *Ex Orient Lux . . . ex Occidente lex*. From the East comes Light, from the West comes law. Follow the Light for knowledge as you head west toward the mountains to establish new laws."

Within the span of a blink, the apparition of the priest was gone.

Carlos rubbed the perspiration from his face with his forearm and waited in the shadowed hallway with Damali. The cool sanctuary, while beautiful and still, put him en garde. There were columns and shadows everywhere. Corners he couldn't see around, obstructions of view, and a hundred places something could slither out from. The fact that he was standing on hallowed ground brought little comfort. He'd seen Father Patrick attacked by the Ultimate Darkness with his own eyes while standing in a cathedral. Who knew if this particular church's history or the behavior of the presiding clerics would be enough of a barrier? He didn't have that information. And that was the overall problem—the lack of information.

But he was sure that his side seemed to be losing.

Father Patrick had been attacked by the Devil and sacrificed by the Light.

Imam Asula had been murdered at the hands of ignorant men.

Rabbi Zeitloff had been assassinated by possessed creatures.

Monk Lin was on the run.

The Covenant was no more.

A three-year-old baby and her grandmother had almost been killed.

A warrior's parents were in flight with the remnants of a Guardian squad.

There was a wanted dead or alive bounty on his team's heads.

And he was stuck just outside the Bermuda Triangle during U.S. martial law with Hellfire bearing down on him, his wife, and his squad. This was bullshit. His heart broke for the elderly clerics. The loss was so visceral that he was beyond pain, simply numb. Those guys went all the way back to his beginning, his first steps toward redemption when Father Pat first found him. Their deaths tore open a fresh wound just remembering that. Now they were gone, their lives lost in the foulest way possible.

Carlos allowed his head to drop back for a moment and he took in a deep breath before opening his eyes. It disturbed him no end that, at a critical time like this, his gut instinct was way off by a long shot. He should have gotten those horrible images, not her. He should have been the one to intercept them and filter the transmission of information to her verbally, not have such gore taking root in his pregnant wife's mind.

But right now, for whatever reason, Damali's second-sight was ridiculously strong, just like it seemed as though the other female seers on the squad had increased in their ability to pick up the subtlest changes in the environment. But he and his boys were missing everything. That was not good. Not at a time when they should have been on point protecting precious cargo.

He looked at his wife, a deep sense of reverence overtaking

him as he watched prisms of sunlight wash over her beautiful, cinnamon-brown skin. Her eyes were closed, her thick natural lashes dusting her cheeks. She bit her plump bottom lip, an endearing nervous habit that just made her expression prettier in his eyes. Shards of stained-glass color dappled her face and played over her shoulders and throat, splashing against her white tank top.

The delicate cleft in her throat fluttered with each long inhalation and exhalation that she drew in while trying to sense who and where their contact for a charter would be. Her breasts were full and her face was beginning to round ever so slightly, although she wasn't showing yet. Even her aura was different . . . more serene, stronger. He could envision her nude with her broad, white wings out, belly full and slowly moving with life, her graceful hands covering her breasts . . . his angel . . . his reason for existence.

And they'd taken her stage away from her, making her a fugitive so that she couldn't sing for the world. Could never perform live in concert . . . couldn't jam with the team band to the thunderous applause she so rightly deserved. That was a high crime, if ever he witnessed one. It just wasn't right that he and the baby would probably be her only audience from now on. He only hoped that would be enough, and he'd try his best to make up for the darkside's robbery.

Though he did not want to disturb her mild meditation, it took everything within him not to reach out and allow his fingers to trace her butter-soft cheek or to gather her into his arms. Yes, they were both warriors and he respected her as such. But damn he wished he could take any- and everything this cold hard world had to throw at her for her. If he could just spare her some of it, to hell with destiny and fate. *She was his wife.*

Her thick ropes of velvet-soft brown hair were swept up in a ponytail that he wished he could set loose just to see it cascade to her shoulders. That was what he could never seem to make her understand. To him, she was more important than the Armageddon. What she carried within her was even secondary to her. He loved their child with all his might, all his heart . . . but she owned his soul. There wasn't even a definition for that. Maybe that's why he couldn't ever fully describe for her how he really felt. Women sometimes didn't understand that words were inadequate. There simply were none.

If anything ever happened to her, air would cease to fill his lungs. If anything evil broke her heart and took their child again, his hands would be useless in picking up the shattered pieces of her. But he would try. He would bloody himself to make it right, even knowing that it wouldn't help. What did a man do who had the entire world trying to destroy his heart?

Didn't she understand that after all they'd witnessed, and for all his strength and all his power, he was helpless when it came to her . . . and perhaps more than anything, having that Achilles' heel mirrored and magnified times six Guardian brothers . . . watching them also struggle with their new weaknesses, with their eyes looking to him as a squad leader, made any vulnerability within him all the more intolerable.

People had died on his watch. Clerics had succumbed— hadn't made it to the end. Men of faith; men of valor. Guardians had been ground to dust. Innocent humans had been collateral damage in Detroit and D.C. There were families in mourning, people's lives irrevocably changed by monstrous injuries. Hellish diseases now swept the land. Fear permeated every living thing. And he and his squad had been helpless to avert this catastrophe when the Unnamed One came to call. What would he do when the Unnamed One came for his wife?

Heaven help him; Carlos looked out at the pews where his

fellow team brothers waited for word of the next move with their heads bowed. It was no act. He knew each man, no matter what his faith, was deep in prayer—each praying the same thing, *God, don't let anything happen to my pregnant wife. God, what do you want from me? God, how can I protect my family and do your will at the same time, be a warrior, when the world is coming to an end?*

Carlos lent his own prayers to the collective, adding one more, *God, please don't let me have to choose between saving my wife and child and that of another man . . . I am not that strong.*

Montrose Sinclair simply stared at the screen in the empty confessional. There would be no tours, most likely no clerics. Everyone was holed up in their homes, hoping the Black Death never reached Bermuda's shores. This was nothing like what he'd planned for his life, nothing like what he'd thought his golden years would be.

He closed his eyes. First cancer had taken Eleanor, his beloved wife of thirty-five years. In hindsight, he would have gladly traded more time with her for the wealth he accumulated working like a fiend, only to have that wealth totally eviscerated on the London Exchange. It all seemed so pointless. All such a wickedly evil game. Then, again, what did it matter? The money was naught. There was no one to leave an inheritance to in order to give his life any semblance of meaning. If he died today, who would bury his remains? Like the old days of London, would the dead wagons come to fling his corpse in a mass rotting grave?

His son had lost his life in Iraq. His beautiful daughter gone at the hands of a panicked driver when the plagues began to hit.

A single tear slid down his weathered, brown face. God help

him, grant him peace. Monty folded his hands tightly and bit his lip to hold back a sob. What was his purpose? Just show him a sign that his life had had some meaning.

An ex-patriot of Britain, what did he have left but a small house he'd saved and saved for but never had a chance to enjoy, and a boat that was way too big for a man without a family or surviving friends to enjoy it with. Everyone on the mainland was gone. The things being broadcasted on the news made his blood run cold. If an angel of mercy would just set his direction, he would never question God again.

"Mr. Sinclair," a soft female voice murmured through the screen.

He jerked his attention toward the sound and pressed his hand against the carved wood. He'd thought he'd heard a slight rustling, but had been so absorbed in his own thoughts. "Yes," he said in a garbled voice, embarrassed that it hitched with raw emotion.

"You don't know me, sir . . . but I heard your prayer."

He pressed his fist to his mouth and dragged in a deep breath.

"We need your help . . . and your life has meaning. I asked if you were the one who would help us, and if I had the right to approach you like this, and I received word that I could. All is in divine order, sir. I'm not here to mock your pain, just to give you some comfort and possibly a new start. Please hear me out."

"Who are you?" he whispered, shaking.

"I am a Neteru."

Lilith waited at the entrance of her husband's war room, watching him sit on his dark throne in quiet contemplation, staring at the globe. As it turned slowly on its axis before him, a blue marble hovering in midair, he made a tent before his mouth with his fingers. The look on his face was one of calm confidence.

But still she hesitated, never sure of what a summons by her Dark Lord could bring.

"You sent for me," she said as evenly as possible, waiting for him to invite her over the threshold.

"I did," he said quietly, not looking up. "We have made progress. I want your opinion."

Lilith didn't move. He looked up with a smile.

"My apologies. I should have said that to you in *Dananu*." He allowed his seductive gaze to rake her and then chuckled as she gasped from the pleasure jolt he gave her.

"My opinion?" She stepped forward, her eyes never leaving his.

"Yes," he said in *Dananu,* issuing her a slightly fanged smile. "You have been in touch with the female Neteru's weaknesses from the beginning . . . which led to the creation of our heir. You knew she'd attempt to save the host in Nod and have earned my respect. Therefore, now that we are in the final, delicate stages of the game, I would be remiss to overlook your input." He rubbed his handsome jaw and stood, allowing his raven-black wings to unfold to their full thirteen-foot span as he walked.

"I am at your service, as always," Lilith replied in *Dananu* with a slight bow, but still on guard for entrapment. To ask her opinion in the language of barter meant that he was unsure of his next move. If she chose wrong, his full wrath would fall on her—but if she chose correctly, her power would increase exponentially.

He chuckled, having read her conflict within her dark eyes. "There are always consequences, darling," he said in a mellow tone. "Care to wager on a strategy?"

"What's your dilemma?" she replied with a sly smile, pressing a forefinger to her lips, waiting.

He let out a long sigh. "After seventeen hundred years, the humans found the Coptic version of the Gospel of Judas. Of course I did everything I could to play a shell game once raiders lifted it from an Egyptian tomb in the seventies . . . it went to Switzerland, then the United States in the early eighties—greed is a marvelous thing. It sat in a bank vault until the late eighties, and finally got sold in ninety-nine," he added, walking around the globe as he mused. "But I broke up that sale—checks bounced," he said, chuckling. "The books were broken up, and finally given to a credible source, but I tampered with the translation, completely reversing the meaning."

Lilith cocked her head to the side and frowned. "I fail to see your dilemma then. You were successful in making the humans think there was a possibility that Judas was a hero. And?"

"Those who see through it will know the true name of my most cherished and powerful demon. The Thirteenth. He is the one that the original Coptic text says held sway over Judas Iscariot. In the bad translation, they call him by his origin, a daimon—but think it means spirit—albeit you and I are the wiser. It means what it means—demon—and he is the one who made Judas trade the one I refuse to name for a few pieces of silver."

"Yes," Lilith said flatly. "I do recall the incident—which is when silver gained power as a weapon to be forever used against us as a result."

Her husband waved his hand to dismiss the loss and kept talking. "This text that came out of Coptic Ethiopia was hidden in the Valley of the Kings and protected by the Kemetians until the grave was robbed. My goal then was to have the graves disturbed by mortal men, knowing we were coming upon the end of days . . . and then have the manuscript with the secret name burned. I had to get it out of the hands of the Neteru

Council—because as you and I well know, if anyone with a soul knows a demon's true name, they can rebuke it. At a time like this I can ill-afford to have the two Neterus come into such knowledge. Their Neteru Council in spirit cannot say the name of the Thirteenth, cannot tell them, as no being of Light can outright call a demon's name. That was the beauty of my plan to have the manuscript stolen."

He let out another hard breath. "I thought I had procured the manuscript, but as you know, human will and human greed is a very fickle thing—a double-edged sword that cuts both ways. Greed led those humans to try to profit from me and then attempt to sell it for three million dollars, rather than listen to my whispering and bring it to me. Damn free will! Although I punished the troublesome fools, that information is still out there in general circulation."

"But it is out there in a mistranslation . . . and with all that is going on, and with almost all of the Covenant clerics gone, who shall interpret obscure texts for the Neterus, hmm?" Lilith soothed.

"When I release Ialdabaoth upon the earth, his job is singular—to dry up the Euphrates and cause havoc in the region so that I may release my four dark avengers, which he will then lead . . . the ones who have been prepared for an hour, a day, a month, and a year to slay a third part of men. The Thirteenth will ready my troops during the yearlong drought and then release my four dark angels, those most loyal to me when I fell from grace."

He turned to Lilith, excitement shimmering in his bottomless black eyes. "His horsemen will number two hundred thousand thousand. They will wear brimstone breastplates and fire and brimstone will issue from their mouths . . . it will be beautiful."

"It will come to pass . . . I do not understand your concern."

Lilith said, walking to stand before the globe. She stared at the Euphrates basin that encompassed Turkey, Syria, Iraq, and Iran.

"Look at all the hell that's breaking loose over there as we speak. Why would you doubt that one of the four rivers that flow from the original location of the Garden of Eden would not dry up in the end of days as prophesized? It is in the Old Testament, even in some of the hadiths of the Prophet Muhammad that this will happen . . . that when the riverbed dries, men will fight over the riches they find there, and ninety-nine out of a hundred will die."

Concern knit her brow as she studied her unresponsive husband. "After the sixth seal is broken, the Light gets to do the Rapture—fine, fine, so they get to take all their goody-two-shoes people up to wherever . . . and then the world is *ours*. We get to break the seventh seal and just become ridiculous . . . six great plagues come after that. You know we'll have something particularly dreadful planned by then . . . like a coming-out party for our son. He'll bring order to the chaos, once we're finished having a little fun with the left-behind humans, and he'll seem like the dark prince he is. He'll have them eating out of the palm of his hand, just to have their old creature comforts back— principles and moral compasses be damned. Humans are so gullible. Don't worry. They're weak. Easy to guide and tempt."

She opened her arms, going to her husband when he still didn't answer her, his eyes fixed on the globe. "You are winning, darling," she murmured, hugging him. "The mark of the beast is only a matter of time—humans are afraid of the virus carried on currency worldwide. Survivors will have to embed a chip in their bodies to buy or sell, to eat, to survive. What brings this unusual bout of melancholy to you at a time like this?"

He wrapped her in his arms and then covered them both with his dark wings. "What concerns me is that Sebastian was right and I didn't catch it early on . . . the female Neteru was pregnant. I didn't give him his due because he pissed me off. That little bitch should have stood his ground and made me hear the truth—if he hadn't caved we would have known sooner. Still, I shouldn't have missed that!"

"That's all right, because we know now," she said quietly, laying her head on his shoulder.

"What also concerns me, Lilith, is that as much as I hate to admit it, Nuit and Vlad are right. All this is bullshit, if I can't find my sixth seal and that Neteru child lives."

CHAPTER FIVE

The moment Damali stepped out of the confessional and the man who'd been in a booth next to her came out crying, he knew this had been a bad idea. The older man was no soldier, was just an innocent—a potential victim. Carlos pushed off the stone wall and walked toward the twosome and shook his head as Damali hugged the man.

"Mr. Sinclair, this is my husband, Carlos."

"Monty," the man sniffed, clearly overcome as he continued to wipe his eyes and nose with a very used handkerchief. "It's short for Montrose and what my friends and family call me . . . used to call me when they were alive." The short, stout man wiped his eyes again and then dabbed perspiration from the bald horseshoe in the center of his head.

"Your wife is an angel," Monty pressed on between stifled sobs. "She knew things about my life that not even some of my closest friends knew. She told me things about my Eleanor . . . and told me she could communicate with my wife on my behalf to tell her things I never got to say to her. I am indebted to your wife for the rest of my life. I will pilot you wherever you

want to go—free of charge. I've been waiting all my life for my
life to have meaning."

"Yeah, she has that effect on people," Carlos said flatly, gently
tugging on Damali's arm. "Can I have a word with you, D? Before we go upsetting Mr. Sinclair any further?"

Damali arched an eyebrow. "Sir, if you just give me a moment to talk to my husband?"

Monty nodded and staggered to a pew. "Take as long as you
need."

The moment Mr. Sinclair was out of earshot, Carlos dropped
his voice and spoke through his teeth.

"D, are you crazy? What's the matter with you? I thought we
were supposed to be getting the boat without a civilian passen-
ger? You know how dangerous this shit is!"

"Shush!" she hissed back, and glanced around. "First, stop
cussing in church."

"Aw'ight, my bad," he said, holding up his hands in front of
his chest. "But you feel me, D? That old guy just lost his wife
and kids, is in mourning, and probably never shot a gun in his
life, let alone seen any of the craziness we have. Now you want
to put him on the high seas with a boat of targeted Guardians,
during the last days, and—"

"I know it sounds bad, Carlos," she said, talking low and fast.
"But—"

"Sounds bad? Sounds bad? It *is* bad, Damali. It's *insane*—
socially irresponsible, is what it is!"

"Keep your voice down. He's doing this of his own free will.
I told him—"

"No, no, no, no, no. That's the same game the darkside plays,
and I ain't having it—so-and-so knew of their own free will.
Gimme a break. If that old man dies on our watch, you think
the Light is gonna say, 'Oh, she told him, so it's his bad'? It don't

work like that, woman, and you know it. Plus, that mess will haunt you for the rest of your life."

Damali's hands went to her hips as shock overtook her face. "Do you think for a million years I'd use some tragically unhappy old man like that, Carlos? Just for a boat? I can't even believe you'd think something like that about me!"

"Keep your voice down," he muttered, pulling her more deeply into the vacant hallway. "Listen, I know how focused you get. I also know how badly you want off this island so we can go get Ayana, Mrs. Filgueiras, and the Weinsteins, okay. That's all I'm saying that sometimes . . . when you get like this, and while looking at the big picture, the details get fuzzy. That's all I'm saying."

"The details aren't *fuzzy,* Carlos," she said, pointing at him, biting off every word as she spat it out. "I might be focused, which last I checked wasn't a crime . . . but I have never, ever, *ever* put an innocent in harm's way—not even for the cause."

"All right, all right, I'm sorry," he said, dragging his fingers through his hair and beginning to walk in a circle. "But . . . why?" Carlos stopped pacing and stared at Damali. "Why *this* guy? Why *this* civilian?"

Damali folded her arms over her chest and looked away. "I don't know. Just got a feeling I could trust him."

"Okay," Carlos said, letting his breath out hard. "Look at me, D." He waited until she turned around and faced him, but when she only glimpsed him and then sent her line of vision to the floor, he put a finger under her chin and lifted it. "I want you to replay this conversation in your own mind again. What about this doesn't sound right?"

"All of it," she finally said, letting out a deep sigh. Her shoulders sagged as Carlos's finger dropped away.

"All right . . . progress," he said, glancing over his shoulder toward Monty Sinclair. "But I respect your gut, D. Something drew you to that guy."

Damali looked at him and perked up. "It did, and it was weird, Carlos. It wasn't like my normal second-sight. I didn't see—I felt. The connection to him was hand in glove . . . then all these things about his life poured into my head. So I said a little prayer before I said a word to him. I asked if he was the one I should trust and if I should tell him what I knew . . . and this really bizarre, strange sense of peace flowed over me. That's when I told him what we were up against and what we were—"

"Wait," Carlos said, placing both hands on top of his head and squeezing his eyes shut. "You told him what sounded like mythology . . . about us being Neterus and whatever?"

"Yeah, because it felt right . . . and he started crying and saying that just knowing he had something to do during all of this chaos made him feel like his life hadn't been in vain. He said that evil had been making a mockery out of all he thought was important and this was his way of fighting back, however small a measure that was."

Carlos opened his eyes and stared at Damali. "Did you tell the man he could die?"

"I told him it was extremely dangerous and that we were wrongly being sought by authorities and—"

"Did. You. Tell. Him. He. Could. Die?"

"Not in so many words; you know I like to stay positive about these things."

"D . . ."

"Oh, all right!" She began walking in a tight circle. "Why do you have to be so negative all the time?"

Carlos folded his arms again. "Where I'm from it's called *being real*."

"Yeah, yeah, yeah——"

"No, D, I'm serious," Carlos argued, pointing toward Monty Sinclair without looking at him. "Before we even get on that man's boat and risk him having a heart attack at sea, we are going to tell him the realio dealio. We're gonna show him fangs, wings, shape-shifts, the whole shebang, aw'ight. If he can hang after that, then we ride or die with him. But if he freaks——I mind-stun him and we send him back into civilian population none the wiser. We clear?"

Damali lifted her chin, dismayed that the entire Guardian team was staring at them and the only one whose head was still bowed in prayer was Mr. Sinclair's. "Okay. Fine."

Monty Sinclair looked up into the faces of the full Guardian squad. His shy, humble manner of speaking kept the team's questions at bay and softened some of the hardness in their eyes.

"You see," Monty said simply and without apology, "my entire family was from here. I went to London to better myself, where I met my beloved wife. We had children and I worked hard. My son even joined the service there." He shook his head. "I have been praying for a miracle . . . and your Damali was that for me. She told me things that I needed to know before I die. She spoke to the spirits who meant the most to me." He stopped and swallowed hard and then his watery brown eyes searched the Guardians' faces. "For the last few days I haven't been listening to the television or radio . . . it was our anniversary. I played old calypso and our favorite songs. Today, after I turned on the news, I almost decided——"

Damali's hand on Mr. Sinclair's shoulder stopped his words. As she glanced around the group, she didn't have to tell them that a suicide had been averted. "We're here to let you know that there is good, there is Light, and that angels exist."

"Yeah, but so does the darkside, brother, no offense," Yonnie said, pounding Rider's fist. "I'm just being real."

"I keep telling my wife the same thing," Carlos muttered.

"Can I be blunt?" Rider asked, stepping forward.

"Why stand on ceremony, man—ain't you always?" Big Mike said, shaking his head.

"Thanks for the endorsement, Mike," Rider said with a sarcastic half-smile. "Did that lovely lady over there tell you that we're wanted dead or alive by about half the governments in the world . . . and that you could have your lovely hundred-and-ten-footer smoked by a U.S. destroyer cannon with you on it?"

Monty Sinclair lifted his chin. "She told me you were freedom fighters and that it was dangerous."

Shabazz slapped his forehead. "This ain't an adventure like you'd see in a Bond film, man. This isn't the movies."

"I am well aware. I trust this lady with everything that I am . . . she is an angel—I can feel it." Monty Sinclair squared his shoulders. "I grew up here, as I said, and I know these waters. I made money in my first jobs piloting ships to all the resorts, taking tourists around. I can navigate, and I joined the Navy for some years, and then got my British citizenship," he added proudly, "and then made my money on the Exchange. So if there's a question of my integrity to be able to get you where you want to go—"

"Show him the wings, D . . . I'll get you another tank top when you're done," Carlos said, annoyed. "Then when he passes out, we'll send him home. Okay?"

"Fine," Damali said, lifting the back of her white tank top, much to the chagrin of Mr. Sinclair. "Sir, we are—*different*. And, what we do to fight evil *can* get you killed. My husband is right. In the spirit of full disclosure, and out of complete courtesy for all that you've been through, and before you decide to go with us, since once you do, there is no going back, we want to show you so you can really decide. All right?"

"Madam, I assure you, you do not have to disrobe to show me your good intent!" Mr. Sinclair said, mortified. He turned away, but Big Mike reached through the huddle of Guardians and turned him back to face Damali.

"Yeah, sir, she does, sorta . . . and you do need to see this." Big Mike gave the man a slight shove as Damali covered her breasts with folded arms but allowed her wings to unfold from her shoulder blades.

For a moment no one spoke as Mr. Sinclair slowly sank to his knees and then covered his face with his hands.

"Send the man home, would ya, D," Carlos said, walking away.

"Hold it, hold it, give the man a chance to breathe and take it in," Yonnie said with a smile, chewing on a toothpick. "I had the same reaction when I saw my first pair—bet you did, too, boss. Besides, if he's cool and can hang, we could really use that boat right about through here."

Jose nodded. "I'm just saying."

Juanita shook her head. "Y'all are so not right."

Marlene and Marjorie knelt beside Mr. Sinclair, rubbing his back as he began to loudly sob.

"It's all right," Marlene murmured.

Marjorie laid her cheek against his back. "Let it out."

Damali dropped down on her knees and took up Mr. Sinclair's hands until he looked at her. "Sir . . . we need your help. But it's dangerous. I'm not an angel, just a . . . I don't exactly know what—a hybrid, I guess. My Guardian sister Val also has wings, and, uh, a couple of the guys have fangs." Damali motioned toward Val, who gave him a small wave.

Monty shook his head wildly and then squeezed his eyes shut. "Don't send me away from this miracle. I've seen this all my life," he wheezed. He promptly opened his eyes and pointed at a stained-glass window. "Out there, on the boats . . . I saw a caramel-skinned angel—one at the bow, and a darker beauty at the stern—that guided me through an unimaginable storm . . . but it was sunny and gorgeous out . . . pure blue skies, when they boarded my craft. And they said not to be afraid. I'd always have that little daydream in my mind while I was piloting, wondering if I was sheerly mad, or if it were just a metaphor for a guardian angel or two helping me to navigate all the storms of my life."

Monty scrambled up to his feet. "You say going with you is dangerous . . . have you watched the news? I could die from a rabid dog attack, from the plague, from random violence, or someone attacking me for a few groceries as food begins to run out here, like it has on the mainland."

"The man has a point," Berkfield said, gaining nods all around.

"Yeah, well," Carlos said, still unconvinced. "D just showed him the good stuff . . . let's see how he does when me and Yonnie show him a battle bulk and fangs."

Nuit strolled into his private, subterranean lair just off the corridors of the council grand hall, glanced at his wife, and smiled. The sumptuous Hell chamber was yet another prize, just like Lucrezia.

Surrounded by powerful black marble that emanated a constant, renewing dark charge, he touched the veins that pulsed in the walls and smiled. Just for sport he pierced a capillary with a sharp nail simply to watch the blood slowly ooze down the wallpaper before the wound healed itself. He licked his finger and returned his attention to Lucrezia.

"You have done well, Fallon," she murmured seductively. "The others are green with envy . . . hissing and spitting in outrage behind our backs."

He nodded with a sly smile. "Then be sure never to turn your back, *chérie*. Not even on me, at times."

She laughed softly, walking past the long onyx table flanked by high-backed, crimson, velvet-ensconced thrones, dragging her finger playfully along the gleaming finishes. Gazing around at the iron-held wall torches and the walk-in fireplace constantly being tended by enslaved Harpies, she sighed.

"I like the weaponry on the walls," she remarked, seductively glancing at the implements of torture strategically mounted against segments of granite.

"It is living art," Nuit said, coming deeper into the sanctuary. "Do not get too close or you might find yourself an unwilling captive. This was Dante's private haven. Lilith offered it as a prize . . . since she already has better than this on Level Seven."

"Better than this?" Lucrezia murmured, tilting her head to the side and tracing her jugular with a forefinger.

"Don't get crazy," Nuit warned with a laugh. "To go after Lilith's lair is to literally lose one's head."

"Just dreaming." Lucrezia offered him a pout and then smiled, letting him see just a hint of fang. "I love what he did with the serpents," she added in a husky voice, looking over to the bed that rose out of a black mist above a bottomless abyss.

Moving forward, she allowed her council robe to fall away and pool on the floor as she reached out toward one of the massive marble posts that held draped, crimson sheers. Curious, she waited until one of the huge adders slithered down from its perch to wind around her arm. Then suddenly the serpent yanked her to the post it had descended from, binding her to the marble in a writhing hold. Clearly jealous, the others left their posts and joined in the pulsing tussle for dominance of her body, striking her and one another until order was finally restored.

"Ah . . . they're trained," she murmured, and then held Nuit's gaze trapped within her own.

"Over multiple millennia, *chérie.*" Nuit licked his bottom lip as his fangs crested.

"You're not joining me?" she said, her expression crestfallen when he simply materialized a goblet in his hand and pressed it hard against the wall.

"In due time," Nuit said in *Dananu,* savoring a sip of blood while he watched the serpents close their eyes in ecstasy as they enjoyed rubbing themselves over Lucrezia's nude body. "But in order to keep this, I must be vigilant. . . Vlad would literally kill for this chamber."

"Can't you just relax for a little while?" Lucrezia gasped in *Dananu,* lolling her head back against a post as one of the large adders parted her thighs.

"Soon, *chérie* . . . but I must ask you a bit of business, first."

She lifted her head and hissed. "I am your *wife,* Fallon, not your competitor."

"Be that as it may—humor me."

They stared at each other for a strained moment and then she smiled.

"You know you love a man who exerts absolute power, you bitch, so let *les bon temps rouler.*"

Lucrezia threw her head back and laughed, beginning to undulate with her living shackles. "What do you want to know?"

"How is the poisoning of the current pontiff going, my dear?"

She closed her eyes. "Such a simple request . . . he'll be dead in a week. I would have disclosed that in bed."

"Oui," Nuit murmured in *Dananu.* "And I love you for that." He walked closer to her and offered her a sip of blood from his goblet but didn't release her, and then slowly took her mouth. When he pulled away he licked the residue of ruby stain from her lips, allowing his left hand to gently fondle her pale pink nipple as he absently took another sip of blood.

"I think you just like to watch," she murmured into his mouth in *Dananu.*

"You know I do." He smiled.

"Be honest, Fallon," she murmured in the bargaining language, beginning to squirm against her holds as his touch sent pleasure waves into her skin. "Just being in this chamber has filled you with desire that you can barely contain . . . having access to Dante's war room, feeling his strategies crawling across the walls, coating every surface in his old, dark power with an open power abyss all the way down to Level Seven beneath his bed, has made you blind with passion."

He briefly closed his eyes and turned his head away from her for a moment as though she'd slapped him, but then quickly composed himself to respond to her with a smile. "Now that the Dalai Lama has been captured and his replacement named by the Chinese government, and with the sealed fate of the pope . . . we must plan something equally as compelling for Judaism and Islam . . . or we could simply allow those two branches of human devotion to implode in the war of the region. What do you think?"

"I think you're afraid to fuck me in Dante's old bed above

the abyss for fear that the Dark Lord will ridicule you for lack of performance!"

Nuit laughed. "Is that what you think?" He wagged his finger at her and set down his goblet on the fireplace mantel, leaning on it and watching as she strained to break free. "I believe you are talking out of your head because you're so frustrated, my dear. All of that carnal power wafting up from the depths between your lovely legs. I am not the one welded to the marble that holds residual memory . . . and Dante was such a bad, bad boy."

"Fallon, that's enough," she said in a desperate whisper in *Dananu*. "Let me go—or come to me."

His gaze hardened, even though his voice retained a seductive *Dananu* croon. "Do not forget that with power comes privilege . . . I have been a vampire for so many years longer than you. And as desirous as I am of you at the moment, I own something right now that you don't—control." He took up his goblet and knocked the rest of it back, and then wiped his mouth on his sleeve. "Let's get back to politics."

Lucrezia closed her eyes and released a wail of frustration.

"Only Pope Alexander VI, your father and old lover, can bring back all of the Machiavellian politics and sexual corruption of the Renaissance papacy that is fitting for the end of days. With the new religious replacement in Asia, the Middle Eastern sects and religions at war, Christian televangelists and megachurch pastors falling from their pulpits, thus grace, like flies . . . all we need is a new pope in our hip pocket. That should please those I have to keep appeased in order for you to enjoy the finer things in death, my dear."

"I hold no sway over reanimation, only blood in my veins from my father's old line. I told Lilith I would avail myself!" Lucrezia yelled, straining toward Nuit and trying to reach for him. "Darling, what do you want from me?"

"Lilith is busy . . . the more I can bring her without disturbing her, before Vlad brings her something that will excite her, the better."

Tears rose in Lucrezia's crystal green eyes as a serpent struck her jugular. Her voice dropped low and husky as she arched. "Please . . . make love to me before I lose my mind. Only Sebastian can reanimate!"

"Exactly."

Lucrezia stared at Fallon for a moment. "Nooo. . . don't you dare!"

"The man has been relegated to a eunuch down here. The Harpies will barely give him any, and his only outlet has been fantasizing about you and Elizabeth and jerking off when he thinks no one is around. The bats tell all."

"No!" she screamed as Nuit began to head toward the door. "I will never forgive you for this, Fallon! How can you do this to me?"

"Because absolute power corrupts absolutely . . . you have heard the quote before, I'm sure." He stopped walking and stared at her for a moment. "In this state, do you really care who attends your needs?"

She looked at him and didn't immediately answer.

"When Lilith commends you on a job well done and bestows more power on you—which is what I am supposed to do as a husband, to ensure your success and your protection—will you hate me still or love me more for positioning you well, *chérie?*" He blew Lucrezia a kiss from across the room that made her close her eyes.

"Non," she murmured. *"Je t'aime.* When put that way, how could I hate you? But . . . after—soon after—promise me you'll return and finish? Sebastian is so . . . not you."

"How could I resist such a lovely offer?" Nuit said, genuinely torn.

"What will you do while you're gone?" Lucrezia's eyes rolled back in her head as her eyelids fluttered shut again.

"Take a walkabout to retrace some of Rivera's old ground."

Elizabeth's fingers dug into Vlad's shoulders to massage away the tension, but he shrugged her off and stood. "A granite cell in the caverns of Hell for me and my wife is sacrilege, after all I've delivered to the empire."

"Only for now," she said, crossing the small, Spartan space to fill a goblet from a dead Harpy she'd cornered. "This is temporary."

"*This* is unacceptable!" he bellowed, and flung the goblet against the granite wall when she handed it to him.

Rage consumed him as he paced within the rock-hewn space. "Look around you, Elizabeth. This is a replica of a mausoleum chamber. A death slab of stone in the middle of a cavern . . . no running blood facilities. This is what topside generals used to hide in below and regenerate briefly before going back to their more sumptuous lairs aboveground. And they expect *me* to waste illusion energy on outfitting my own chamber rather than use the dark core energy to save me the expense?"

"We will bring the Dark Lord and our Chairwoman something they want and have favor restored. Until then, rest, and save your attack for our enemies in the Light."

"Fallon is among my betrayers."

Elizabeth stared at Vlad. "He has made minions of masters while Lucrezia and I were convalescing. He used the time well . . . when Alaska falls into perpetual night, they will emerge. The masters he made in L.A. are feeding now with rampant abandon each night. From one end of North America to the other, his loyalists would blot out the night, if we attempt a coup . . . and our forces have been depleted from the wars with the Neterus. It was our armies that were ravaged, not his."

"And I need you to remind me of these failings?" Vlad said in a quiet, lethal tone, coming near her.

"Only so that we might develop a strategy for a bloodless coup, my love," Elizabeth whispered, backing up as his eyes glowed red and then went pure black. "If your wife was pregnant and you were being pursued, where would you go?" Elizabeth hurried away from Vlad and picked up the goblet with nervous hands.

Vlad slowly outstretched an arm and leaned against the wall with a flat palm, staring out into space. "We have savaged every continent, and still they hide. Sebastian's Berserkers will soon awaken and will ride hard on the four corners of the earth."

"I would go somewhere small, unchartered," she said quietly. "Away from dense populations that carry the contagion."

Vlad spun on her. "But they are hunted by the human authorities. Somewhere small, like an island, would be insane. There'd be no cover, nowhere to run. In Budapest there are mountain ranges beyond . . . in Russia, vast wilderness . . . in the old Ottoman Empire, the lands of Genghis Khan, there are—"

"Every place they know we'd look. But a small island in the Caribbean, or in the Pacific, or off the mainland of—"

"Could be wiped away with one tsunami!" Vlad yelled, and punched a large chunk of rock out of the wall.

"Let us work as a team, rather than allow our mutual frustrations to claim us," Elizabeth said calmly in *Dananu*. "You know how Sebastian feels about me . . . allow me to strike a deal with him to have the Berserkers search and destroy the lands looking for the sixth seal as he wishes, but give a small retinue of them to me to search the island clusters for the Neterus." When her husband simply stared at her, Elizabeth pressed on. "If I am wrong, Lilith will be none the wiser. You will be guiding the armies to trounce the land and find the Dark Lord's seal, as only you can do—Nuit is no military general, nor is Sebastian . . . what good is raising the Norse and Germanic tribes if there is no one to lead them?"

She filled his arms as his gaze mellowed and then she took his mouth. Turning her throat to him, she closed her eyes. "I will bring you a prize that you can trade for more power, trust me."

CHAPTER SIX

Damali and Marlene lifted Monty Sinclair up as Marjorie dashed to find him some clean drinking water.

"Sight of fangs will do it every time," Rider said, walking away shaking his head. "When are you guys gonna learn?"

"Naw," Yonnie protested, pointing toward Shabazz with a toothy grin. "It was the shape-shift that put him on the stones, yo. Don't blame it all on me and my boy, Carlos."

"Would you guys lighten up before you give this poor man a heart attack," Marlene warned, fanning Mr. Sinclair with a tourist brochure. "Sir, are you all right? These guys are weird but harmless."

"I take offense," Shabazz said, rolling his shoulders.

"He, he turned into a panther." Monty searched her face. "I must be hallucinating."

"Jaguar . . . Shabazz is picky about his phyla, and for the record, I'm glad you got that passing-out thing out of your system before you were at the helm of a ship with us on board," Rider said. "Sheesh, for the love of Pete."

"You still up for a *Pirates of the Caribbean*–style adventure?" Berkfield asked, examining the man for any injuries from his fall.

"But, but they had . . ."

"Fangs, yeah, we know," Jose said calmly, squatting down with an old jar of apple juice that Marjorie handed him. He looked up at her. "This'll kill the man for sure, sis . . . that's all they got?"

"Pantry is wiped out. Seems the clerics and staff stocked up and left." Marj chewed her bottom lip. "Sorry."

"Well, get him a splash for his face from the font—if holy water's gone bad, then we're all in deep caca," Berkfield fussed, glancing up.

"Knew we shoulda cleaned out the mini-bar," Rider muttered, walking by a pew and punching it. "Damn!"

"Ahem." Marlene gave Rider the evil eye and then looked back to Mr. Sinclair. "Sir, if you'd rather not go with us, we can see you safely home. All right?"

He shook his head and struggled to stand. "The two angels said it's all right and not to be afraid." Monty Sinclair looked around the team. "Something like this only happens once in a man's lifetime and only if he's blessed . . . if I die in this, I will have lent myself to something so much bigger than me."

Nuit folded himself into the cavern shadows and watched as Elizabeth frantically passed him. "A day late and a dollar short," he muttered with a chuckle as she left Sebastian's lair unfulfilled.

Confidence claimed him, as did the dark swirling power of the victorious. Once he was sure that his rival's wife had gone, he mentally called for a retinue of barrel-chested, international couriers. Australia was beautiful this time of year.

This had been a bad idea; he could feel it in his bones. Damali felt that taking Mr. Sinclair into an energy fold-away would be too much of a strain on the man's heart right after he'd seen the team unmasked. Now they had to walk!

It wasn't that it was so far, truthfully he and the team could have jogged to the docks. The part that he hated was the eerie quiet. Every now and again a dog barked in the distance, but it still had the normal tone of just a frightened pet. The wildlife here hadn't begun dropping from the trees or going mad. Graves didn't appear disturbed, and wholesale looting for goods hadn't happened yet. But it was all just a matter of time.

"You know we're gonna have to stock the boat with supplies, C," J.L. said, hanging back with a couple of the Guardians that were covering the rear.

"I know," Carlos said quietly so that Damali didn't hear. "Problem is this. If I take it from the church missions here, then when supplies on the island run out, local civilians will be ass out. Major institutions, like schools, hospitals, hotels, and whatever, are going to need whatever they have, too, for the population here."

Rider nodded toward the cruise ships. "They look awfully quiet to me, hombre. They came in from the mainland, ya know. They've got plenty of supplies in bottles and cans that weren't open to the contagion. What say a small group of us do a fold-away with you while the ladies get situated on Sinclair's boat . . . if there's innocents on there, we can bring 'em back alive. If everybody on the vessel is a goner, then it ain't technically stealing."

"This man used to be one of us for a few, right, C? 'Cause he sure sounds like a brother who used to have fangs," Yonnie said, laughing, pounding Rider's fist. "I'm down with the plan."

"Yeah, me, too," Carlos said, keening his line of vision on all the cruise ships that appeared to be dead in the water. He looked around the group as everyone came to a stop. "Yo, 'Bazz,

Mike, Berkfield . . . I want you guys to do a first pass on that boat before anybody gets on it. Could be some stray undead types infesting it—we need a sweep."

"Got you, C," Mike said, drawing out a handheld Uzi from the back of his fatigue pants waistband.

"Cool," Carlos said with a curt nod. "Then Bobby, J.L., Jose, and Dan, I want you brothers on security and communications to be sure we don't get accidentally blown out of the water by a nervous coast guard or military vessel . . . and I want a man with artillery at the cardinal points, top deck, to be sure we don't get pirate boarded by anybody else out there who's hungry and looking for fuel and supplies."

"Roger that, C," Bobby said, extracting a 9mm from his waistband.

"I'll see what else I can MacGyver up," J.L. said, "to protect the ship."

"Good man, good man," Carlos replied absently, walking up to Damali. He touched her face briefly and then allowed his hand to fall away. "I want you to check the galley with Marlene and 'Nez, and make sure there's nothing in there that can poison anybody."

She smiled. *So now I'm on kitchen detail—just barefoot and preggers, huh?*

He kissed her and then pulled away, his expression sober. *The last time I was on a yacht with you, we didn't have a good experience. Allow me this.*

She remembered all too well. The huge pleasure ship owned by the Australian master vampire with three more master predators and their vampire wives, all vying for a night alone with her and Carlos . . . trapped aboard with her Guardian team and nowhere to run. That's when Dante had found out that she was pregnant the first time. That's when Carlos had put himself between her and a tornado of Dante's Harpies. That's when Carlos had been unmercifully tortured and ultimately died in the sun. That's when she'd thought that she'd lost him forever. How could she forget? Worse yet, how could she have overlooked how bad a flashback all this had to be for Carlos? Damali briefly shut her eyes, nodded, and touched his cheek. "I'm sorry."

Turning to the team, she kept her memories to herself, her emotions in check, and her voice firm. "Monty, I want you to give us a brief spiel on how to steer this thing—in case . . . everybody needs to know how to crew this boat. Then I want a seer and stoneworker on the cardinal points with a gunner. Cool?"

Murmurs of agreement filtered through the group.

"Good," Damali said with a curt nod. "Once I get coordinates from Pearl, seers, we'll lock in on the sunken pyramid as our touchstone to keep us out of the dangerous Triangle fluctuations." She turned to Mr. Sinclair. "But the basic navigation and all the protocols of entering a foreign harbor with the right lingo is gonna be on you."

"Not a problem," Monty Sinclair said.

"Aw'ight, cool. We got a plan." Carlos began walking away from the group with Yonnie and Rider.

"Where're you guys going?" Damali's hands went to her hips out of reflex.

Carlos gave her a look over his shoulder. "To go get bottled water, uncontaminated food, and a coupla gas cans of fuel. We don't know how long we'll be at sea, so—"

"From where?" Damali folded her arms over her chest. "Why do you always do stuff like this, Carlos?"

"Might as well tell her, dude," Rider said under his breath. "You know how they are—this could take all day."

Carlos rubbed his jaw in frustration and then motioned to the cruise ships that were adrift just beyond the reef.

"You don't know what's on those ships!" Tara snapped, walking forward.

"Yolando, I said to be valiant and victorious, not foolish!" Val said, frowning. "It could be a death trap."

"Glad I ain't the only one who's being given the blues." Carlos let out a hard breath as he glanced at his two Guardian brothers.

Marlene folded her arms over her chest. "What about mangoes and pineapples, and fresh—"

"Anything not in a bottle or can could have been contaminated from the rain, the wind . . . we don't know exactly how they're spreading this shit, Mar. Might be airborne for all we know. Maybe not, but are you willing to gamble?" Carlos waited a beat, vindicated when no other concerns got raised.

Yonnie opened his arms wide as he spoke, looking among Val, Tara, and Damali. "We can't steal, because that sets up a negative energy trail right to us. We can't use up valuable supplies on the island that innocent civilians will need. They won't go on the cruise ships until they're really desperate, because, frankly, how will they board 'em? If we find people alive on the cruise liners, us going on board will be their salvation, because we can drop them on dry land. But, if we find anything else, us taking supplies off ain't stealing from the living—okay? Besides, any good supplies left on those five ships out there could be jettisoned back here to the cathedral we just left . . . a safe haven for it and for folks who, ultimately, could starve to death on this island."

"I think that about says it all. It's a screwed up job, but somebody's gotta do it." Rider hocked and spat, and then checked the magazine on his weapon before glancing at Yonnie and Carlos. "Gentlemen, shall we?"

Nuit stood in the courtyard of the abandoned Australian castle and drank in the night. This was what Dante had exiled himself from—feeling the raw power of the living planet. If his former Chairman had only left Vampire Council Chambers, he would have been able to track Rivera more closely, would have learned from his duplicitous style. But the old man was from the predawn era of vampires that hid in the caverns of Hell, soaking up power from the depths for power's sake alone and never enjoying their immortality to the very fullest—and that had been what had initiated his failed coup and alliance with the Amanthra demons.

Yet, he was still here . . . and the Devil's firstborn son, Dante, was not. The irony of that made Nuit smile as he gazed at another ruined vampire stronghold. He'd never envisioned the Chairman dead at the hands of the Neterus. Cain had even succumbed, and through it all he was still standing!

The awareness almost made him laugh out loud. Nuit waved off the thick-bodied, hooded messengers that had scythes at the ready to guard him. There was no threat here. Just feeding rats and meandering serpents. What had once been an opulent display of raw master vampire power had been reduced to dust at the hands of Rivera. That wealthy bastard, McGuire, had lost it all. Pity.

For a moment Nuit stood still, allowing the very night itself to soak into his bones. The majesty of the stars awash in a midnight-blue velvet sky made him open his arms wide and close his eyes. There had been so much waste . . . so much loss at the hands of the Neterus.

But rather than dwell on the outrage of it all, he squared his shoulders and walked up the steps, waving his security forces off. He wanted to feel the old trail of Carlos Rivera alone. He wanted to savor his archenemy's last steps as a vampire . . . to feel the burn of Rivera's passion for the Neteru female while he was still trapped as an entity of the night. *That* was true majesty. Passion and lust, dare he call it love, that transcended the grave and challenged the realms of Hell. How Rivera convinced the female Neteru to love him like that was still worthy of envy.

Nuit glanced up at the full moon, wishing he could have been an eyewitness. Now all he could do was shake his head as he entered what had once been a grand foyer.

Cobwebs, rubble, and fallen plaster greeted him. Nuit closed his eyes, sensing, seeing the castle come alive in his mind . . . a place that once held elaborate blood-gorging fetes. Delicately veined walls pulsing richly with fresh blood were now cracked and dried. Massive, sweeping staircases in shambles. The rare, leaded, beveled glass windows that still remained hung in piteous disrepair. Elizabethan-era knights, Louis XVI furnishings, Victorian treasures all rusted, stolen, dry-rotted, wasted . . . it was a travesty.

He passed the great room and the ballroom with his head held high, and then stopped and looked up at the vaulted ceiling. In a vapor fold-away, he immediately walked into the master suite two floors above that had been given to the then Councilman Rivera. Nuit looked around and chuckled softly. "You may have wanted to, but you did not love her here, did you, *mon ami?*"

Hands clasped behind his back, Nuit began walking. "With all those spies and treasonous bastards about, nor would I have bedded my bride here. Where would a man of your inscrutable strategy have taken her so that she could stumble upon the seal for you?"

Frustration claimed him as he sauntered through the room, but a gentle breeze drew him out to the balcony. The trail of Rivera's old vampire energy was so weak . . . but there was still something—a pattern that he couldn't ignore. A signature that he'd never in a hundred lifetimes forget: Damali. Her energy stained the crumbling stone rail.

Nuit closed his eyes and inhaled deeply. "She is your Waterloo, *mon frère*. You love her more than existence itself. This I fully understand."

Touching the air before him as though blind, Nuit turned and swayed, seeming to dance alone in the darkness . . . sensing where the couple had stepped, moving as they had moved on the terrace until a shudder of heat claimed him. He gasped as the sensation entered his chest and fanned out in a quickly spreading burn that contracted his groin and sent him stumbling backward against the rail.

His eyes slid closed as he surrendered to the passion and fell. Two hundred feet above the cliffs, jagged stone yawned up, and his hurtling form began to disintegrate into pure vapor.

He landed on all fours, panting and in a desert. Red iron ore stabbed into his palms and sliced under his nail beds as he threw his head back and howled. Her scent was everywhere, causing saliva-slicked fangs to fill his mouth, and his head to be thrown back in an agonized wail.

Nuit dropped to the ground, gathering dirt in his arms, washing his face with it like a madman. Damali's scent, her sweat, her feminine essence had spilled upon this barren land. She'd rained pleasure upon his rival so profoundly that even the earth wept, leaving crystallized casings of her sweetness behind.

Euphoric, trembling, he lifted his head, eyes glowing, need

carving his groin, and became wolf. There was no other choice. To remain man would leave him vulnerable to the longing. In his human form, he'd love the very ground imagining it to be her.

Time was of the essence. He had to move.

Massive sinew-laden shoulders replaced his athletic human body, and his ribs splintered and cracked to allow a barrel chest to form. His spine elongated with his howl and a dense midnight coat eclipsed his café au lait skin. Lowering his nose to the earth, he picked up Rivera's old scent, finding the edge of where Damali's scent left off and where only Carlos's footfalls could be distinguished.

Nuit moved like black wind. Rivera had loved her, then carried her for a distance. Excitement made him heady as he dashed to the edge of a strange gathering and then skidded to a halt. Carlos's scent went beyond the perimeter, but he could not. Nuit growled quietly.

An eerie blue ring of scorching white light blinded him and made him turn away, then become mist. Old, dark-hued men with strange white markings on their bodies stood and glanced around, on alert. Nuit watched from the nothingness, but then suddenly the sound of their collective mutterings and didgeridoos drove him away.

Dreamtime chants, twenty-thousand-year-old prayer lines—damn the shamans. But still he smiled from the subterranean caverns.

Nuit looked up. *He'd found it.* Vlad's armies or Sebastian's raised Berserkers would never find it—even if the old men died of starvation. The key was a human soul. That was the only way to cross the prayer lines that ancient.

Whirring in a black funnel cloud, he traversed time and space within minutes to return to Dante's old lair. It took all his acquired reserve not to blow the marble doors off their hinges, and to coolly open the doors, then close them behind him.

Lucrezia was alone, pouting, her hair tussled. She sat up in bed and folded her arms, glaring at him. He produced a goblet and pressed it to the wall, but had to hold it with two trembling hands as he greedily drank from it.

"You promised you'd come back to finish . . ."

"And I am a man of my word," he gasped between deep swallows. "As I promised you, *chérie*, you will not hate me for it, either."

"Sebastian will do my bidding," she said with dripping sarcasm. "Are you satisfied?"

"Non," he replied, instantly materializing in bed nude and flattening her. He brutally took her mouth with a bloody kiss and fisted her hair. "Anything but."

"This is *Eleanor's Dream,*" Monty said shyly, motioning to his vessel.

The team just gaped for a moment.

"You'll have to forgive all of us," Damali said, impressed. "We aren't up on nautical terms, and didn't mean to insult you by calling what you owned a boat."

"No, shit . . ." Berkfield said with utter appreciation in his voice. "What is she, a fifty-, sixty-footer?"

Monty smiled. "Sixty-eight-feet-six. She was originally designed to sleep ten, but I had the large main deck salons cut in half to add more bedrooms since that still allowed for considerable common space, and took a little off the galley to make another small bedroom, plus added a little pullout sofa to the pilothouse so that she sleeps sixteen privately, and there's still plenty of community space on the top deck. Someone could also sleep up there—you'll see. It's very comfy, and there's tables and chairs and whatnot."

"Well, just *dayum*," Jose said, peering up at the double-decker, white behemoth.

"What's she got under the hood?" J.L. asked with excitement, beginning to walk down the slip.

Monty eagerly followed him, rattling off specs with Berkfield right on his heels. "Twin three-hundred-and-seventy horsepower, Yanmar-diesel V-drives, twenty-five-kilowatt Westebeke diesel generator, a-hundred-and-thirty-six-thousand-BTU Cruiseair to keep things cool . . . furnace, cable, and satellite phone equipped, gourmet galley with stainless-steel appliances . . . holds six hundred gallons of fuel, has three bathrooms. With floor-to-ceiling solar-cooled bronze glass enclosing the main deck. Oh, yes, and music . . . a custom-distributed music system is also on board."

J.L. turned around with a wide grin. "You are *da man!*"

"Did I hear you say you had sat phones and cable on board?" Berkfield clutched his heart dramatically and swooned, making the others laugh.

"I heard gourmet galley, also known as a kitchen," Inez said, smiling.

"No—I heard three bathrooms," Juanita said, laughing, "and I've got first dibs on a shower, okaaay."

"This is what we'd always dreamed," Monty said, clearly proud. "This was going to be our floating retirement home where she and I would sail around the Caribbean, taking our friends, family, sometimes maybe allowing nice people to charter her, getting to know new people . . . having fun in our golden years, inviting the kids to come with our grands." He looked up at the yacht and then shielded his eyes as he looked up at the sky. "This is what she would have wanted, isn't that right, honey?"

Considerably sobered, the team looked at one another as Marlene walked forward and rested a palm gently on Monty's shoulder. "Thank you for sharing this sacred space with us."

Sebastian whistled while he walked back to his conjuring room. That was the thing he loved most about Hell, someone was always ready to cut a side deal to cut someone's throat. He couldn't wait until the next general council session where he could silently gloat and watch that pompous bastard, Fallon Nuit, be none the wiser that his own wife—the lovely, devastatingly sexy Lucrezia—had cuckolded him. It was too rich.

But he stopped midstride and gaped and then immediately went on guard.

"What are you doing here?" he asked cautiously, staring at the scantily clad Elizabeth. He looked around and pressed his back to the wall as she approached and then held up his hands, making claws. "Stay back! Assassinations on council are forbidden. My cauldron will tell, my, my spell books will testify!"

"Calm yourself, darlink," Elizabeth murmured, coming closer. "Vlad has lost favor . . . you are a valuable necromancer. The vagaries of fate have shifted alliances, and power is an aphrodisiac. Where have you been all this time, you naughty boy?"

Encouraged but still skeptical, Sebastian glanced around and moved closer, beginning to tremble. "I went to check on the locations of ancient graves . . . I must go to Europe and raise the Berserkers tonight for Lilith."

"May I join you?" Elizabeth leaned into him, pressing her body against his, and slid her tongue up his jugular and captured his earlobe.

"Vlad will murder me."

"What Vlad doesn't know won't hurt you," Elizabeth

murmured seductively in *Dananu*. "But I see that you've been in high demand tonight. Have you lied to me?"

Sebastian pulled back and looked at her. "I don't know what you mean."

"I smell Lucrezia on you."

Not wanting to miss this rare opportunity to bed both councilwomen in a single night, he hedged with a lie. "You smell a fantasy," Sebastian said, glancing away theatrically. "You know Lucrezia would never have me . . . and I doubt you would, so please don't tease me."

"A fantasy?" Elizabeth murmured.

Sebastian motioned to his spell room with his chin. "I . . . made her essence to surround myself with it. Just so I could . . ." He let his words trail off, giving her as innocent an expression as he could muster. "I am humiliated that you even know."

"I am hurt that you made her essence the object of your fantasy, and not mine," Elizabeth said coolly, drawing away.

"I only did that because I fear Vlad much more than Fallon," Sebastian said quickly, holding her arm to stay her leave. "You know what he'll do to me if he finds out that I've even dreamed about you."

"Then while in the Carpathians, you and I should take a long, hot bath after we're done so he'll be none the wiser."

Sebastian swallowed hard. "You would do that for me—with me?"

"If you do one little thing for me," she said with a wicked smile, and wide, innocent eyes.

Sebastian nodded. "Name it."

"Far be it from me to ask the question, but does it seem a little too quiet on this ship—or is it me?"

Yonnie looked at Rider. "It ain't you, Holmes. The hair is standing up on the back of my neck."

Carlos nodded and then made a fist, causing the men behind him to stop walking. His gaze scanned the deck and then he tilted his head like a hunting dog, listening. The sound of something wet, squishing, sent a shudder through his body. Using his forefinger and middle finger, he motioned to his eyes, and suggested a path for Yonnie and Rider to take in stealth mode. Calling the blade of Ausar into his hand, he waited until the warm, familiar metal filled his grip, and then he was a blur of motion.

In a shadowy corner behind toppled deck tables, four diseased humans were huddled over a dead crewman's body, eating. The sound of their gore made Carlos want to dry-heave as he watched them fight over entrails like scavengers.

They looked up with vacant black eyes and sallow skin, and hissed, but Carlos's blade took two heads before they could leap up and scrabble toward a new blood source. Hooked, yellow teeth and twisted, scaly talons reached out as knotted spines and double-jointed legs awkwardly propelled them forward across the smooth deck surface like fast-moving, diseased crabs.

Instantly, Rider got one in the center of the skull, blowing the back of his head off, and Yonnie made quick work of the aluminum frame of a deck chair—snapping it off and using it like a metal stake to hurl through the center of a young woman's head.

"Oh, fuck me . . ." Rider said, wiping his forehead with his T-shirt sleeve. "You know how many people a cruise ship usually holds? We go belowdecks where it's gotta be teeming with those things, and it's all over."

Carlos nodded. "Save your ammo, man. I ain't getting no life pulses off this vessel. Ain't no survivors. We're too late. I don't feel anything down below moving but death."

"Me neither, man—and you know vamps can feel the humanity thing going on . . . that's how we used to eat. But not like *that* . . . damn. Everything on this joint is as dead as a doornail, bro." Yonnie glanced around nervously. "I say we be out."

"Great minds think alike," Rider said, looking over his shoulder.

"Aw'ight, look," Carlos said, listening and keeping his gaze sweeping. "We fold-away down to the kitchen, jettison supplies back to Monty's yacht and the excess to the cathedral for survivors. The white-light blast I'll send it through should clean all the cans and bottles of all contagion, plus Mar knows how to make it do what it do. We go to the pilothouses on each ship— they've gotta have flare guns, weapons, and shit in the captain's quarters . . . and then we blow this joint so none of these creepy crawlers get back to the island and go hunting down innocent survivors. Same deal on the other four boats—on, sense, off, blow the sucker."

"Yeah, aw'ight, we got your six, C," Yonnie said, glancing around, "but hurry the fuck up."

Monk Lin took in a deep, cleansing breath. He sat perfectly still, an open vessel to the communication he sought. With his eyes closed and his legs crossed yogi-style, he sat on the floor of the safe house, waiting.

Soon, his eyelids began to flutter and images poured into his mind. He heard Cordell's voice, saw him open the maps. In each Templar location, there was a storehouse . . . grain, water, canned goods, weapons, cash, technology. Tears streamed down Monk Lin's face. The moment Cordell's image faded, he focused on the face of each seer in the twelve scattered tribes that he'd memorized by heart. And then he saw little Ayana's face.

"Tell your people that in these times, money means nothing. Goods are what will be treasured."

He opened his eyes. The Neteru team was still outside of his reach. He didn't understand it, but didn't question the Divine. The others now knew. Guardians would have a way to survive the difficult times, the darkness. They knew to go to higher ground. His job was done. The safe house was no longer safe. He bowed, and came onto his hands and knees and then pressed his forehead to the floor in front of his altar.

Tibetan incense swirled and danced, the scent of it mingling with death. The door burst open, and death ran toward him. He was up on his feet in a flash and had unsheathed two samurai swords that had been mounted on his altar. The whoosh and thud of heads being separated from bodies thrummed in his ears as he kicked out the window and somersaulted onto the fire escape.

The things that sought him crawled like fast spiders, but he slashed and cut, every fiber of his being remembering all of his ancient teachings. Winded, there were some on the roof above him, some scrambling over the hacked bodies he left below him. A military truck rolled down the street and he lifted a sword to hail it for help . . . but the soldiers only saw the carnage around him.

Inside the Bradley the terrified men made a snap decision.

"There's more of 'em on the fire escape, Joe. Hot those motherfuckers!"

Nirvana was close at hand. As he saw the flamethrower rise, Monk Lin let his swords fall away to clatter on the cement below, and simply turned into the orange-red sun. Bliss.

CHAPTER SEVEN

As the team boarded the yacht, Damali kept her senses sweeping. Isis blade at the ready, despite Carlos's concerns, she walked point, giving the sweep team the all clear cabin by cabin, closet by closet, shadowy corner by shadowy corner. Nothing crazy could debark with them—not on her watch.

She murmured the Twenty-third Psalm as she walked the lower deck, clearing out negative energy, blessing the vessel, and ready to kick anything's ass that was not from the Light. Time was of the essence and it was about efficiency.

But Montrose Sinclair's dream boat had the bright, clean feel of the uninhabited. The shame of it all was, it almost seemed as though the man had never even gotten the opportunity to ever take her from her berth. Damali stopped in the first bedroom she spied, checking under the queen-sized bed and along the sleek walnut finishes. Nothing. Just a bright and cheery room.

She met Jose on the steps on the way up. He gave her the all clear nod, and she could see Big Mike's huge shadow pass.

"We cool on the main," Big Mike said, walking with an Uzi cocked up toward the ceiling. "Nice digs, though."

Damali smiled and pounded Jose's fist as she passed him. "As soon as the away team gets back, tell Juanita that shower she wanted is hers."

"Thanks, D," Jose said, giving her a look that stopped her in her tracks.

Their eyes met and suddenly he hugged her.

"I really mean it, D. Thanks for everything."

"You aren't getting all sentimental on me, are you?" Damali said, trying to laugh off the deep emotions that had begun to surface.

"Yeah, I am," Jose said quietly. "I'm scared to fucking death that I might not be able to protect this kid or her, ya know . . . and when the money got blocked and all hell was breaking loose, I was like—shit. But then you and your crazy divining-rod senses found this real cool old dude who is about what we're about . . . and, like, I don't know what to say, D." He swallowed hard and looked away. "Our house burned down, we almost bought it in D.C. battling . . . my woman is pregnant."

He looked back at Damali, shaking his head. "*You're* pregnant. C is flippin' out like the rest of us, and we've gotta do war with the Nameless. Every man on this ship is feeling the same way, like, what the fuck, you know? How're we supposed to do this? How're we gonna raise kids in all this bullshit? This is much worse than when it was just us fighting monsters, D. I ain't never been this scared in my life—because it's not just *my* life, am I making any sense? I'm not the only one feeling like this; the team is buggin'."

Damali just nodded and let him get it out. She held Jose's hand tightly, trying to send as much love and peace into his system as she could through the vehicle of touch.

Suddenly Jose laughed nervously and looked up to the ceiling, blinking back tears. "Then you find us a luxury yacht to give us all a little hope, a tiny break in the action so we can get our heads right . . . where my wife can take a shower and lie down for a few hours—one with a gourmet kitchen. That's just like you, D."

There was nothing she could immediately say, and she didn't trust her voice to hold. She just pulled Jose into another hug and stroked his back. "Wasn't me," she finally said, listening to his moist breaths pelting her hair as he battled for composure. "Something way bigger than me found this for all of us."

"Clear," Rider shouted, running to the far side of the huge cruise ship galley, and opening the stockroom door, leveling his gun barrel at it.

Yonnie waited a beat, and went in quickly, and began flinging unopened boxes into the center of the floor for Carlos to jettison to the yacht galley. "Yo, C, send those huge watercooler bottles first. If we get jacked in here, the main thing is water."

"I'm on it, bro," Carlos said, keeping his blade at the ready, trying to keep a steady relay going without depleting himself too much on the first run.

But a quick swishing noise stopped all motion. Rider, Yonnie, and Carlos looked up at the same time. A pot fell from a partially opened cabinet and Rider shot it. Immediately a tide of rats poured out onto the counters, spilling onto the floor, and screeching in demonic outrage.

"Fall back!" Carlos yelled, kicking open the door behind him, giving Rider and Yonnie a narrow escape.

His eyes went silver, fury sending heat into his deadly gaze, cutting a burning swath in the wriggling, squealing flesh and fur that charged him. Then lowering his sword, he sent a white-light pulse from the tip of it to ripple pure energy across the floor. Everything from the darkside in its wake disintegrated as the blue-white nova nuked the area. But the sound of Rider's gunfire report and Yonnie's growls made Carlos spin to see the threat quickly moving down the narrow hallway.

"I shoot 'em and these bastards keep coming!" Rider yelled. "I'm running low, man!"

"Drop!" Carlos yelled.

"You crazy?" Yonnie shouted.

"Drop, man, or take a charge!" Carlos yelled again, rushing forward, and both Rider and Yonnie flattened themselves to the floor.

Tossing down a transparent shield of Heru on top of his men, Carlos lit the area with a white-light nova. Popping, crackling flesh splattered the walls with ash and grease from body fat, and yet Carlos could still see more diseased coming from behind the wave he'd just fried.

"We gotta go!" Carlos shouted, lifting his shield.

Within seconds the threesome dropped out of his fold-away onto the next ship.

Rider gave Carlos a sidelong glance. "Yo, dude, when you said we've gotta get out of here, I was thinking more like, we have enough supplies and we'd get on the nice yacht in the distance . . . not another zombie cruise!"

As Damali walked the main deck, a deep sense of melancholy wafted over her and then settled within her. Instinct told her the ship was clear, but habit and security protocols kept her moving. Instead of looking for nasty little beasties and the walking dead, she was looking at rooms—safe havens—for her teammates to fall back to for just a few hours on shifts. It was just as important as fighting, the business of watering one's horses. Jose had been honest. That was a cry for help that couldn't go unanswered. He was just the most forthcoming in the group, but she knew what he said echoed through all the male members of the squad.

She peered into the master suite, her eyes roving over the exquisite woods before she turned to go down the hall to the galley that had been sectioned off to create a smaller but comfortable guest bedroom with a queen-sized bed.

"Girl, look at all this stuff the brothers sent us from the ship," Inez said, laughing, holding up a huge box of pancake mix. "I don't know where I'm gonna put it all? Marlene said water jugs, like those big ones from office coolers, are up on the top deck. And I don't know what the heck I'm gonna do with all the frozen veggies."

Damali glanced around at the small breakfast table, six walnut bar stools that pulled up to the eat-in bar, stainless-steel appliances, and the Corian counters that were laden with dry goods, bottled juices, and flash-frozen freezer bags of green vegetables and fruit. She smiled when she saw items that would make Marlene pull her hair out—whipped cream in a can, frozen ice cream sandwiches, ice cream, and Jack Daniel's. "I hope Monty's got another freezer."

"Yeah, can you get Carlos to work on that while he's out?" Inez called behind her.

"Uh-huh," Damali said absently, as she continued her second pass patrols.

Worry nagged her gut in an insistent way that gave her pause. What was it? The distortion near the Triangle was the only logical explanation she could come up with. Maybe she was tapped into the general horror energy of the population here? Yet, it didn't feel like piercing danger, rather more like shattering sadness that gripped her. Then, again, was that unusual, given the circumstances?

Unable to put her finger on it, she kept walking, sorting things out in her mind as she went along the short, wide corridors that welcomed sunlight. Two large salons with comfortable, mint-green sectional seating, a bar, game tables, big-screen televisions, and thickly cushioned lounge chairs each shared a common wall that had been removed, per Monty, to make space for two additional bedrooms with queen-sized beds.

Large ferns added a sense of cool tranquility to the space. Small hutch window seats stored the overflow of towels and sheets and toiletries that wouldn't fit in the linen closet. Monty had created a floating hotel, a showcase home on the water. That had to be where the melancholy came from. Seeing all this that had been built with such hope, and to have those hopes destroyed, was in and of itself tragic enough to make her cry. Add pregnancy hormones and the end of days to the equation and it was a wonder that she didn't just stop, break down, and bawl.

Half jogging, half walking to get away from her thoughts, Damali scaled the steps to the top deck, where she found Marlene and the rest of the team managing water bottles and newly imported military weapons, gazing out from the rails, and lounging on the comfortable, white wicker sofa that sported fat, lemon-yellow cushions. A refrain pelted her mind. *Thank You, thank You, thank You, God.*

Bobby and Dan had settled into chairs around a glass and wrought-iron table, and had pulled out a deck of cards as though they were on vacation. Good. Damali released a quiet breath of relief and glanced over the rail to see Mike loosening the moorings as Monty coached from above. Berkfield and J.L. were in the pilothouse, as giddy as two little boys, oohing and aahing over the high-tech nautical controls.

She peeked her head into the large room that was covered in glass and winked at Berkfield, who was at the helm.

"Oh, maan, Damali . . . all my life I dreamed of being behind the captain's wheel of one of these." Berkfield tipped his new captain's hat to her, laughing. "Monty is all right—look. He had an extra and said that us guys with the horseshoe deserved to wear these."

"But, look, D," J.L. cut in. "The generators, the radio, aw, man . . . all the radar and sat gear on here is *ridiculous*. Monty's got his own server, too, so I can tap into what's left of the Internet. Even though the main service providers have collapsed, there're still independent guys out there trying to keep a pulse on the Web, trying to filter the bullshit on the Council Group Entertainment news. Bet I can rig a way to get secured Guardian transmission relays hooked up . . . and Carlos sent us all kinds of deep sea fishing gear, like harpoons and whatever, that me and Jose can retrofit for weapons! He must have raided the naval ships, too, D—you know our boy is insane. Look at this, shells and launchers, and oh, my God, D, sweet, sweet ammo." J.L. kissed a grenade. "I love you, man!"

"Carry on, gentlemen," Damali said, waving and quickly getting out of Dodge before J.L. could get too deep in technical explanations. But where were Carlos and company?

Trying not to panic, she went to a starboard rail and looked out at what still appeared to be a gorgeous, tropical paradise. Nothing moved between the moored vessels in the marina. The bar and bait shops sat eerily idle. There was no calypso blaring, no tourists, and no happy, honeymooning couples. No taxis or moped traffic could be seen. Pedestrians were nonexistent. It was as though everyone had simply vanished.

Beaches were strangely still; only the surf provided lapping sound. The gulls were gone. Huge cruise ships off in the distance loomed on the water like large steel shadows, nothing moving on any of the decks that she could see from where she stood. Even the wind seemed to hold its breath at times. And there was that sense of dread filling her again.

Damali wrested her mind away from the unseen and glanced

around at the only life she could wrap her mind around—her team and Monty Sinclair. Four couples would have to stand watch, one on each of the four cardinal points, while a fifth guarded Monty and learned navigation so he could rest, while the other four couples could sleep. That made sense. Four seer Guardian sisters could hold the Atlantis grounding and their navigation on course, sending energy to the submerged pyramid that Pearl had told her about, while the male at each seer's side could cover her with artillery, in the event something wasn't cool.

But something was still eating at her mind. Damali pulled her locks up tighter in her topknot and walked back toward the stern. What the hell was taking Carlos and the fellas so long? Before the thought had fully completed, a massive blast rocked their vessel, toppling Guardians onto the deck like bowling pins.

"Heads up!" Shabazz hollered, scrambling to his feet.

Mike was over the gangplank in seconds, kicking it away from the vessel and rushing to the top deck so he could see. Damali jumped up and strained at the rail as she watched a fireball consume the furthermost cruise ship. Everyone gathered on the top deck watched in horror as the ship listed and began to go down.

"We've gotta get her out of her slip and away from the dock!" Monty yelled, running into the pilothouse. "The waves coming in will batter her royal."

Another huge blast rocked the yacht again, sounding like distant cannon fire. Damali looked at her team. Her husband was crazy. "He's gonna blow 'em all." Disbelief claimed her as she craned her neck and shielded her eyes to the sun, searching frantically for any glimpse of Carlos, Rider, and Yonnie.

"Up anchor, they're all gonna blow!" Berkfield shouted, running back into the pilothouse with Monty.

"Yo, yo, yo! Three o'clock, hit it and quit it, man!" Jose yelled, causing Big Mike to pivot, then spray the marina planks with machine-gun fire. "The blasts woke something up, D!"

"Monty, get us away from that dock!" Damali yelled, suddenly noticing activity in the moored boats near them.

Quick moving shadows ran through smaller, docked vessels and then came out of hiding into the sunlight, bearing bloody fangs. Sallow-skinned predators with black, sunken eyes and mangled teeth scampered over decks onto the dock, running toward their yacht. Some still clutched the body parts they'd been feeding on in the lower decks of the neighboring crafts.

"Mike, where's your shoulder launcher, man?" Inez screamed, rushing to the pilothouse.

Berkfield met her with it, heaving a new launcher to Inez, who tossed it to Big Mike. As soon as it hit his grip, he took aim and separated the dock from the marina. The blast rocked the yacht, and a third cruise ship explosion put everyone down hard on the top deck.

"There's gonna be all kinds of wreckage and eddies out there!" Damali shouted toward the pilothouse, and then looked at her Guardians. "We have to get to deep water before those cruise ships go down and create a whirlpool!"

Krissy and Bobby jumped up, shock-charging the water with sibling-connected wizard skills.

"Keep all those jellyfish and seaweed out of the engines," Krissy yelled to her brother, causing everyone to scramble up and lean over the side of the yacht.

Millions of jellyfish had coalesced out of nowhere and bonded with deep ocean kelp, creating a mucuslike, thick, gray-green sludge that slowed the yacht's escape. Working with Shabazz, Bobby used his wizard strength to merge with Shabazz's tactical charge, jettisoning flotsam from the fallen cruise liners out of the yacht's path. Heather called the stones, her stoneworker skills merging with Dan's tactical current to propel beach pebbles, and any natural debris that would respond to her magnetism, at the speed of ricocheting bullets into the foreheads of the swimming undead.

Running from belowdecks, Jasmine clutched a sheet. Immediately Berkfield was at her side and he slit his wrist with a Swiss army pocketknife that he always carried and gave her his arm. Working at a frenetic pace, Jasmine quickly painted the sheet with Berkfield's blood, both father and daughter-in-law uniting in the effort to use the healing, life-giving blood that flowed through his veins with her ability to animate from pictures.

Jasmine hurled the bloody sheet to Tara, who flung it overboard into the water and then began firing rounds to protect it. Anything undead that had been on the smaller crafts that hadn't exploded dove after the bloodied linen as though frenzied sharks. Jasmine closed her eyes and a blue-white light rolled down her pretty face. Within seconds a huge water dragon formed out of the sheet, its scales glistening bloodred amid opalescent white.

Careening toward the misshapen bodies, it gorged, clearing a path. Krissy raised the strangling seaweed, craning her fingers, binding the undead and slowing their escape so that Jasmine's dragon could feast. Jasmine rushed to Krissy's side and slapped her five, both sisters-in-law momentarily jubilant as a fourth blast rocked the yacht.

Monty's hands slid from the captain's wheel as Val's wings unfurled and she took to the portside rail, running down it with perfect balance, a bow and arrow raised, headed forward to the bow of the ship. Intermittently Val would stop, take aim, and spear a demon with a dead-aim arrow.

"Keep that man on focus!" Damali shouted, taking the stern rail, wings spread, her eyes keened for predators or survivors.

"Incoming!" Marlene hollered, using her walking stick as a pointer the second Damali jettisoned it into her hand.

Crazed sharks broke the water's surface with massive gray dorsal fins, eyes gleaming red and teeth gnashing. Guardians were at the rails, firing to keep them back from the hull, but it was a numbers game that the sharks would soon win.

"Supercharge that exterior!" Damali shouted to her tactical members of the squad. "All hands on deck!"

Shabazz, Bobby, J.L., and Dan hit the decks with a fast-moving, blue-white charge that immediately spilled over the sides of the craft, exploding any demon body that touched the vessel's skin.

Inez, Juanita, and Marj had been firing into the water with 9mms, but then glanced up at the same time as Marlene, all women pointing in the same direction at the same time.

Damali lowered her Isis and released a white-light energy pulse that hit the water like a depth charge. A great white shark, four times its natural size, pirouetted out of the water like a marlin and slammed into the surface, creating a massive wave.

"Stop time!" Marlene shouted to Damali. "The crabs, fish, and barnacles in that wave are carrying contagion from the cruise ships. Don't let it onto the boat!"

Damali flung her arms open wide, her eyes glazed over, and suddenly she felt her body snatched through a rip between time and space where everything slowed down. She could hear Marlene shouting to Monty to bless the water . . . him arguing that he wasn't a priest. Then Marlene grabbed him by both arms as she entered the pilothouse and made Berkfield take the helm.

"Ship captains can perform clerical duties," Marlene said, her

voice slow and muddied in Damali's ears as she clutched
Monty's arm.

She watched Monty make the sign of the cross before the
slowly rolling, incoming wave . . . saw his mouth move, and then
watched tiny blinking lights go off within the translucent, blue
water as though a million mermaid paparazzi had gone insane.

Pops and crackles and white-light explosions cleaned the water. Shabazz and Dan were poised, hands craned, biceps bulging,
trying to reverse the momentum of the incoming wave and
send it away from the yacht. Then suddenly time snapped back
to real time and a fifth blast made Damali lose her footing, but
aerial mastery and a good wingspan kept her aloft.

The team hit the deck again, but this time they had three
more dirty members that tumbled to the surface of it with
them. Carlos and Yonnie jumped up, both pulling Rider's arms
to get him up. Val dashed down the rail as Damali flew over the
starboard side of the craft.

"Yo, man," Shabazz shouted, laughing as he saw Carlos.
"What the hell was that? You coulda warned somebody before
you started World War III!"

Elizabeth smiled as Sebastian stroked her arm. Darkness in the
Carpathians always made her nostalgic . . . if only it were Vlad
and not the sallow-skinned little weasel, who was unfortunately
gifted with superior spell-casting.

"This is what I do best," Sebastian murmured seductively,
trying to kiss her, but she turned her head to give him her
cheek.

"Let me see, first," she murmured in *Dananu* with a false
smile. "Then, if I'm impressed . . . who knows, I might become
aroused."

"I promise you will be," Sebastian said excitedly. "Watch."

He licked his fangs and settled himself, opening his arms wide so that his robes billowed in the unnatural breeze.

Elizabeth glimpsed up at the full moon and then down at the bloody pentagram he'd drawn on the ground. She would again watch and learn. Sebastian was such a fool. The thing that intrigued her most was that she never knew what elements or elementals he added to his black cauldron to bring it to life, to make it spit and hiss and do his bidding. However, one day, if she were careful, she would.

She watched him draw a long, onyx wand into his hand that held a crystallized human skull on the end of it. He drove it into the cauldron and began to stir, muttering words beneath his breath so that she couldn't hear. Her gaze narrowed . . . the little worm had learned something after all. No matter. The larger goal was at hand.

Then without warning he flung a handful of teeth and bones into the center of the pentagram, along with a Viking helmet and a German war horn.

"Arise!" Sebastian commanded, making the wind howl and the barren trees quake. "Awake and come to me, mad for conquest, lusting for battle, and I shall fulfill your desires for victory! Do my bidding and you will again war!"

Fascinated, she could not conceal her excitement as the teeth and bones drew together, and then the helmet and war horn melted with them into the earth.

"It didn't work," she said smugly after a few minutes. Everything had gone still. "I'm bored. I'm going back to—"

"Wait," Sebastian hissed, his black glowing eyes filled with anticipation. "All good spells take a setting time. Vlad cannot offer you this."

She didn't move when Sebastian's talon grazed her cheek. All she offered was a slight nod in response.

"And once I've raised them, let you see . . . what is my reward?"

He'd spoken to her in *Dananu*, but he was so eager that he didn't really need to say anything at all. She considered his small erection and the small beads of perspiration beginning to form on his pocked face. The fact that he was struggling to hold back the finale of his spell so he could bargain with her truly made her smile.

"I didn't come here for an evening parlor trick, Sebastian," Elizabeth coolly remarked.

He hissed and lunged at her, holding her throat in a threat. "Raising the dead of this magnitude and of this age is no easy feat!"

"All right," she murmured. "I'll grant you that. It is rather spectacular . . . but I was hoping you'd share them a little with me—maybe just a small retinue, since Vlad doesn't really believe in my ability to lead a small army."

"He is arrogant and pigheaded," Sebastian crooned. "Don't forget, we led some of his demon warriors together before he was reanimated."

"How could I forget," she murmured, stroking his fist in a very suggestive way.

But he closed his grip tighter on her throat. "And how could I forget the very fact that it was you who double-crossed me and raised him?"

She swallowed hard, feeling his claws dig into her flesh and an icy current of blood begin to seep down her throat.

"You owe me," he said quietly, and then took her mouth. "Not the other way around."

"Yes," she whispered. "But if you would do this one thing, I will always align with you against Lucrezia and Nuit—to make up for my earlier offense, plus make this night worth your while—if you'll allow me control over a small dispatch of your Berserkers. Deal?"

Sebastian licked the blood from her throat, trembling. "Deal."

Fallon Nuit lifted his head from Lucrezia's throat and then rolled off her body, peeling himself away from her damp skin.

"What's the matter?" she said, slowly sitting up as he paced to the war-room table and placed both hands on it.

"Come, see for yourself. Apparently Elizabeth wasn't choosy about taking sloppy seconds." Fallon spread his hands out onto the gleaming black marble, watching images on it come alive as though he were staring at a flat-screen HDTV.

Lucrezia came to him, wrapped in a crimson satin sheet, her gaze hardened to a glare as her arm threaded around his waist. Thousands of pelt-wearing, demon-riding avengers broke through the crust of the earth. Their massive bulk writhed with snakes and maggots, their faces mere flesh-rotted skulls that shrieked, each entity a nightmare unto itself with weapons raised.

Chains and maces, black swords of death, animal-headed horses with bat wings and monkey tails took flight, spewing an unending launch of vile manifestation against the bright light of the moon.

"They have no class," Lucrezia said, rubbing Fallon's back.

"Eastern Europeans . . . so baroque," he said, sniffing in disdain. "We, the French, have a style all our own. And those of us from the era of ladies and gentlemen that hail from the refined Creole families of Louisiana prefer politics and courtsmanship—versus brute force, which is very, very sloppy."

"I am glad that you were given Dante's old lair . . . which gives you access to seeing what is afoot and being plotted against you," she murmured, kissing his bare chest.

"A strategic advantage to be sure, darling . . . which is why I asked you to play along with me." Fallon kissed her slowly and deeply. "Your essence was a tracer. Thank you, darling. So now we know what they are up to . . . and I just needed to keep them diverted while I went on my walkabout."

She chuckled softly, nipping his shoulder. "I don't know what you found there, but I like what Australia does to you."

"Shush," he whispered playfully. "Mustn't let the cat out of the bag that I made my little trek. However, in the meantime, when you call in your marker to reanimate your father . . . I'll be working on another strategy. Let them have their fun and waste resources with the brutes he's raised. All that will do is piss Lilith off. I assure you, they won't find what they're looking for and it will not net results."

CHAPTER EIGHT

Billowing clouds of smoke were behind them and an uncertain future lay ahead of them. Guardians collapsed on deck chairs, each taking their turn to console a completely freaked-out Monty while Berkfield took the helm.

"What I have just witnessed is beyond the capacity of human understanding!" he said, pacing and talking with his hands.

Carlos just looked up at him from where he sprawled on the padded furniture. "You did good, man. You got us out of there in one piece."

Yonnie pounded Carlos's fist and got up to sling an arm around Monty's shoulder. He smiled when Monty squeezed his eyes shut. "I know, I know the fangs . . . but now you see why me and my good brother, C, have 'em?"

"Y-yes, yes, I guess so," Monty stuttered. "Glad you're on our side."

Team members swallowed smirks out of respect for the newest member of the team, but the thing that had been clawing at Damali's mind was back . . . then in slow motion she covered her mouth with her hand and turned away. Each team member's body tensed as their collective gazes bore into her back.

"Monk Lin," Damali whispered. "We lost him."

"Aw, man!" Carlos was on his feet. "How?"

She couldn't even look at him. "Friendly fire . . . local patrols didn't understand." That was all she would say in front of the group, especially in front of Monty. No one needed to be further demoralized, and having lost the last living member of the Covenant would have done just that.

"Kiss my ass!" Rider got to his feet and began to pace. "The man was a complete pacifist . . . I mean, how could that happen?" Rider raked his fingers through his hair. "I just don't get it."

Tara gave Damali a look and soon the other seers closed their eyes and turned away.

"What? What are we missing here, ladies?" Rider said, sounding indignant.

"There is a reason why during this period, you gentlemen are blind," Marlene said calmly, grounding the group. "The male and female energies are balancing as they should . . . if Monk Lin was here, he would tell us that according to the Ayurveda science of life, the *mahabhutas*—the five master elements of space, air, fire, water, and earth—are realigning within each person and on the team as a whole to accommodate change. There are things that we seers can see now, being of the space-air *dosha,* that are easier for us to communicate calmly and with purpose." Marlene stood and walked as she talked, holding the group rapt.

"Space holds all the aspects of unlimited potentiality; air has the qualities of movement and change. These ladies have this *dosha* that is called in the tradition *Vata,* and they have infinite possibilities growing within them and are experiencing significant change. That would be Val, Tara, Jasmine, Krissy, and Juanita . . . although she's still a little fiery, that is mellowing."

Marlene looked around at the group. "We are also evenly divided between those of us, like Marj and I, and Damali, plus Inez and Heather, who carry the *dosha* of water-earth now, or *Kapha* energy. Water is cohesive and protective; earth is solid, grounded, and stable. It's not just about sun signs; that is a different matter. I am talking about energy here."

"And you gentlemen at present are fire," Damali said calmly. "Fire is hot, direct, and transformational. *Pitta* energy. Right through now, if images of what was going on came to you guys directly, as ready for war as you are, you'd burn out your adrenals. Seriously. And, later, as we all get farther along, we're gonna need you in one piece. It just makes sense."

"Now that's deep," Big Mike said, nodding. " 'Cause it's been bothering me lately that I feel like I'm a step behind in getting gut hunches and information . . . you know what I'm saying?"

"Word." Jose nodded. "Usually the hair is standing up on my neck or—"

"I get a vibe," Shabazz cut in. "And those have been coming slower."

Dan rubbed the back of his neck. "I thought it was just me."

"Naw, man," J.L. said, pounding Dan's fist, and then Bobby's.

"Well, shit," Berkfield said, yelling out from the pilothouse. "Then now you guys know how I feel all the time. I'm always late to the party."

"You know what's so odd," Monty said, his gaze sweeping the team. "My wife used to get . . . *impressions* all the time. That's why I sank my life savings into this yacht. She specified everything on here—she was the one who insisted on the sleeping quarters being as they are, everything. And as she was dying,

I was going to sell it, but she begged me to keep it and to hold on to it."

Monty stood and shook his head, walking off a bit to look over the rail. "She knew, or felt something miraculous would happen. She said, 'Monty, promise me you won't give up before the miracle happens.' I never knew what she meant." He turned around to face the group, eyes shimmering. "I felt cheated. I thought the yacht would give her something to hope for, something to cling to so she'd get better. When she didn't, I was so angry. But after what I witnessed today . . . never in a million years could anyone have ever told me I'd be a part of something so unfathomable."

"We're glad you didn't give up before the miracle, man," Carlos said, shaking his head. "We owe you, big time, because as you can see, without your escape hatch, we would have had our backs against the wall in Bermuda."

"It's mutual," Monty said. "If I had not come to know you, I would be trapped back there," he said, pointing to the island. "How long before those things slithered over the rails and into the water to swim ashore? I would have been caught unaware like all those poor people at the marina. I only pray that we created a barrier and none of them got past the docks. So, it is I who owes you."

"Naw, man, it's mutual," Yonnie said. "We got an old saying, 'Fair exchange is no robbery.' "

"Don't teach the man that," Carlos said, giving Yonnie a look.

"Why not?" Monty asked, seeming confused. "It makes sense."

"Don't it just," Yonnie replied with a sly smile. "But listen to C-los; we don't use anything from the old empire, if we don't have to. Brings back memories."

"Old empire?" Monty's gaze went from one Guardian to the other.

"Hell," Shabazz said flatly. "These brothers died and came back, so they don't really like going there."

"Like a near death experience?" Monty hung on Shabazz's gaze, innocent, open, and absorbing everything.

"Naw, more like a real-death experience." Yonnie produced a toothpick in his mouth and gave Monty a wink.

"Okay," Damali said, throwing up her hands. "Convo for another day, another time. Let the man absorb this much first and maybe over a beer, later, you can get deep and esoteric, Yolando. For now, I don't want our ship captain having a heart attack."

"My bad, ma," Yonnie said, grinning. "You're right, ma. Okay, I'll chill."

"Thank *you,* Yolando," Carlos said, shaking his head. He stood and walked over to a five-gallon, sealed watercooler bottle and brought it back to set it on one of the glass and wrought-iron deck tables. "This right here, Monty, is salvation. Not only is it something we'll need if we're stranded out here indefinitely, but it's a weapon. So before I return you to the helm, with Berkfield and J.L. on your flank, I'ma need you to bless these. If we get in a tight, this is like C4. One brother can hurl this up while another blows it with ammo for maximum impact, and it'll fry anything it splatters without deep-frying you."

"I saw that with the ocean," Monty said, excited.

"Me and Mar are gonna fill you in on lots of little details like that," Shabazz said. "But meanwhile, we're gonna have team members watching your six who need to also be learning how to navigate this sucker." Shabazz's hard gaze went around the seated group. "Everybody's gotta be able to fill in for everybody else. We don't know what we're facing out there or how deep this contagion goes."

"I hear you, 'Bazz," Dan said, leaning forward on his forearms and clasping his hands. "Like, if we happen to pull into a marina in Puerto Rico and we're low on supplies, but it's a ghost town at the docks—is it stealing to salvage from the gift shops? Seriously. This isn't like all systems are normal . . . isn't like we're ripping people off that could sell their merchandise and have kids to feed, blah, blah, blah. The systems are gone. The monetary system has collapsed."

"Dan's got a point," Juanita said, her gaze going from Jose to Carlos, and then to Damali. "When we were at the hotel, this mess hadn't reached that far inland. In fact, the manager was still functioning in some kinda crazy denial, like business was as usual. But I'd bet an hour into the morning, homeboy probably took off and went home to hole up with his family, if he had any sense."

"Dan does have a point, you all do," Damali admitted. "I was just trying to be on the safe side." She turned and looked at Carlos. "Look, I may have been overzealous, but I just didn't want anything we did to draw havoc our way."

"Hey," Carlos said. "I feel you. I ain't mad at you, boo. In fact, it was a good thing that we went on those ships and didn't just jack supplies from the hotel—because we wouldn't have realized how bad it is. They ain't showing zombies on the news. All they are talking about is rabid animals, that freaking dengue fever."

"What?" Monty glanced around. "What the heck is dengue?"

"Mosquitoes carry it," Jasmine said softly. "It's formally known as Dengue Hemorrhagic Fever Virus. In developing nations, roughly ten million people get it annually, and it gives you a high fever, aching muscles, vomiting, and only like 1 percent of the population dies from it . . . but this year it broke out in Rio de Janeiro first and then swept South America, Central America,

Africa, India . . . my home in the Philippines, Indonesia—a hundred million people with a 75 percent kill rate."

Monty sat down slowly.

"You know what I think is happening?" J.L. said, talking with his hands and then springing up out of his chair from tension like a jack-in-the-box. "I think that every plague that was already out there just got tougher. Period. And everybody who had been susceptible to the shadows from before is getting hit with whatever part in their spirit the contagion lodged in."

"Oh, snap," Damali said, beginning to walk in a circle. "So, like, if the person had greed and avarice in them, they might become a feaster—one of those things that gets up and walks and eats flesh."

"Yep," J.L. said. "Or, if they were depressed or jealous, maybe they got the bubonic thing, or, I don't know, Ebola?"

"That's freakin' genius," Carlos said, "but I'ma tell you what it is."

"Preach," Yonnie said, going to a rail to lean on it and chew on a toothpick. "My boy knows Hell. Watch him deconstruct this shit. Mr. Chairman, you have the floor."

Carlos couldn't address Yonnie's theatrics and think at the same time. With his hands behind his back he closed his eyes and began a slow pace in front of the team.

"They mirrored the levels of Hell, topside. Well, I'll just be damned." Carlos stopped walking. "Anybody whose spirit was foul and was going to them anyway just manifested whatever level they were gonna bottom out on when they died. That's why some folks didn't catch jack. . . Monty ain't coughing, because he wasn't headed south. Some of those good folks on the ship that wound up as breakfast, yeah, they died, but they weren't contagious. That's why it's bullshit that this thing is spreading through the currency. It might be if you ain't righteous in your soul—but for anybody else, uh-uh. You can't catch it. You can't catch none of this mess. It's not about your physical immune system being strong: it's about your spiritual immune system being able to take the weight."

Yonnie pushed away from the rail and flung his toothpick down onto the deck with conviction. "Genius! That is some wicked smooth shit if ever I seen it! Damn!"

"Whoa," Damali said quietly, staring at Carlos. "That is pure brilliance."

Her compliment made him stand a little taller but he fought not to show it. Carlos looked at Damali and then Yonnie before staring at the team. "I hope I'm wrong, but this is the fourth quarter for life as we know it."

"But what about the rats, the animals?" Inez said, unsure. She glanced around. "They're innocent, like kids."

"Those were demon-possessed creatures," Damali said gently, going to her Guardian sister. "And all this time, through all the chaos, I never saw any kids turning."

"But on the news they're showing children bitten by rabid animals. Their little bodies can still get whatever normal diseases are floating around, and especially with dirty food and water supplies, they can be poisoned." Inez hugged herself as Damali's arms enfolded her.

"We're gonna go get your boo, that's why we're headed to Miami so we can get back into the States . . . just gotta go around the edge of the Triangle, girl. You keep her in your mind surrounded by white light—your momma, too."

Inez nodded and swallowed hard.

"Yeah," Carlos said, running his fingers through his sweat-damp hair, "first wave of it got anybody infected by the shadows from before. They were your first to fall. Then, they ramped up the diseases, and I'd place even money on it that Lucrezia has an all-out poison campaign . . . so we do have to watch what we consume, water supplies, and things like that—because you can still die of regular shit like cholera, that's more prevalent now than ever before. That's what's making the kids and innocents sick who didn't go down on the first wave. Then they have the demon bats as street sweepers, literally attacking folks who are still standing because they have strong mental, physical, and spiritual constitutions . . . case in point, they threw everything they had at the moment at us."

"They know where we are now?" Val asked in a horrified murmur.

"No, I don't think so," Carlos said. "Because if they did, they wouldn't have stopped with a coupla walkers, some bad-ass sharks, and jellyfish. Hate to break it to you, but some ridiculous shit would have come up from the ocean. Think tsunami, typhoon, *Poseidon* kinda drama. What went after us was just general, regulation demon energy on autopilot to take down people who ain't diseased."

"That makes me feel better," Rider said, and then got up to hock and spit over the rail. "You're just full of comforting anecdotes." He cut Carlos a glare. "But the ladies-in-waiting . . . c'mon, dude. Not so graphic."

Berkfield laughed. "Go easy, Carlos, it's Rider's first."

"My bad, just trying to keep it real," Carlos said, weary. "I can't tiptoe over some of this. It is what it is."

"But maybe that's why they said the world is gonna end by the fire this time, C," Bobby said out of the blue, making all eyes go to him. "Like . . . before, in Noah's time, it was the Great Flood. But this time, they're talking brimstone and whatever. So, water wouldn't get rid of all the diseases, but fire would burn it out."

"If we make it that far," J.L. said, slumping in his chair and closing his eyes, "we only got like a few more years, if that. Our kids will be toddlers when everything goes black in 2012." He sat forward quickly and held his head in his hands. "It was in the Bible code, the Mayan calendar ends on that date, December twenty-first, 2012, Nostradamus predicted it, and the sibylline prophecies said so . . . the *I ching* called it the end of history, Lakota Sioux ghost dancers have it orally in their tribe—"

"Black Elk spoke on that," Jose chimed in. "The Hopi—"

"Albert Einstein predicted the polar shifts at that same time," Dan said, his gaze nervously ricocheting around the group. "The prophecies of Malachi, even the oracle at Delphi—"

"Okay, okay," Damali said, walking back and forth waving her arms. "Stop! Energy is going in a *real* nonproductive direction. Carlos figured out the key to this—so now we know how all the contagion has really been spreading. Genius. Half the battle is knowing what you're up against and how it's coming at you." She motioned to Yonnie. "Do me a favor and open that water, Monty you bless it, and lemme dunk my pearl."

Although the process to bless the water jug, get a bowl, and submerge her necklace at a top deck table only took a few minutes, it felt like it took forever. Marlene sat across from her with Carlos on one side and Shabazz on the other, with everybody else closely crowded around.

Damali waited as her pearl got acclimated to the spring water, her rosy pink glow finally lighting and a small stream of tiny air bubbles made their way to the surface.

"Pearl, you there, you okay?" Damali asked gently.

"My word, Damali," Pearl said, sounding breathless. "What just happened?"

"Long story," Damali said, letting her breath out hard.

"Horrible and I already know," Pearl murmured. "You all feel like you need rest—your energy isn't good at all."

"I know," Damali said, glancing around. "The stress is wearing on people."

"Very dangerous at a time like this. People must heal."

Damali's gaze met Marlene's. "Yeah. I know. But before we draw straws for who gets the first shift and showers, we need some navigational advice. You said to lock in on the pyramid that's in the center of the Triangle, right?"

"Yes, but draw your lots first," Pearl replied. "Those ladies have to be clean, bathed or showered, so that nothing from the recent battle goes toward the Atlantean crystals within the pyramid. The stone structure will give you a steady compass point, but the Guardians will get back one of the healing rays. I cannot specify what ray any particular individual will receive, but it will sense the child she carries and give her crown chakra vibrations of Divine insight, or second-sight intensity, or charismatic speech from the throat chakra, or a lion's heart, or something from the chakras of gall and indignation over the injustices of the world, hence courage or gut instinct, or significant primal reflexes. Each female will come away from her post with her child's gift amplified, as well as her own."

"Whoa," Carlos murmured. "Pearl, that's some serious mojo."

"Indeed it is." Pearl giggled. "But may I make a suggestion?"

"You are the oracle, sis," Damali said, growing peeved at the way Pearl always flirted so outrageously with Carlos.

"If it's not too much of a hardship, why not allow Marlene and Shabazz, Marjorie and Richard, and Mike and Inez to take the first watch with Mr. Sinclair at the helm. Those are the only couples not expecting, even though the strain on Inez is great . . . but tell her not to worry, her mother and baby are in solid Guardian hands. I would not make this suggestion if it were a time for Inez to grieve."

Inez covered her face with her hands and breathed into them, as Mike rubbed her back and then pulled her into a deep hug,

"Those mothers-to-be need to bathe, to wash any possible contagion from them, as do their mates," Pearl said pleasantly. "Use the additional salons as bedrooms for now . . . pull out the sofas and use them for rest. Everyone should be hydrated and eat while they can, sleep while they can, so they are refreshed in the event of emergency. Marlene and Marjorie and Inez can hold the trinity polarity of the vessel, guiding it past all calamities, while Richard and Shabazz and Mike can learn to pilot it, as well as provide security. Mr. Sinclair can take brief breaks by dozing on the pullout sofa in the pilothouse, if the other gentlemen simply hold his course. Once the night falls, Mr. Sinclair will need to be at the helm as the most experienced captain, and the seven couples can relieve the three. This is my advice, take it or leave it."

Damali was so grateful to her pearl for her advice that once in a cabin alone, she simply kissed her necklace repeatedly until it giggled. Fatigue made her entire body feel as if she were walking through molasses, and after an insane morning, her stomach was growling and her eyelids were so heavy that she could barely keep her head up.

She didn't care who got what room, as long as she could shower and then fall down on a soft mattress. Carlos had ransacked the hotel gift shop back on the island with a straight energy jettison without leaving the yacht, bringing in clothes for everybody, except Big Mike—for him he just pilfered the British Navy's base, and even then, the pickings were slim.

But she should have known that her husband would have

wrangled the master suite out of the deal. Part of her appreci-
ated that he did, while the other half of her felt slightly guilty.

When she stepped out of the tiny shower, she was surprised
to see him leaning against the door with a smile.

"You feel better?" he asked, not going near her.

"Have you been standing there the whole time?" She
squeezed her freshly shampooed dreadlocks out, and gave him a
half-smile.

"Yeah, I figured I was on those foul-ass cruise ships, no
telling what funk splattered me. Didn't wanna sit on the bed
with it or touch you to get it on you, so, if you're done, lemme
jump in real fast, change, throw our duds overboard, and I'll go
get you something to eat."

"How about you go get washed and I'll go get you something while you're in?" she said, loving him for just suggesting
that he'd do that. "I wasn't on those ships, and I didn't see half
of the gore, or fight it. I'm just glad you guys made it out alive."

"You're gonna make me kiss you and use up our sleep time
on something else," he said with a grin. "But, seriously, why
don't you just go lie down and I'll go. In fact, I insist, because as
it is, I've gotta light blast this door where I've been leaning, just
in case."

"You drive a hard bargain," she said, yawning as she sat down
heavily on the side of the bed.

He motioned toward the wicker chair in the corner of
the room with his chin. "Brought you a cotton sundress . . .
thought it might be comfortable to sleep in. Some more jeans
and a couple of tanks, some sneakers, flip-flops, undies . . . I
wasn't sure what all you wanted. Pretty much cleaned out the
store for everybody and left that on the top deck for them to
sort out—so if you don't like what I picked, there's more stuff
up there."

"If you weren't dirty, I'd kiss you," she said with a gentle smile.

"Then lemme go clean up," he said, pushing off the door with a sly grin. "Be back in a flash."

She followed him with her eyes until he closed the door behind him, but the moment he did, she realized just how exhausted she was. The sundress now seemed sooo far away. All she wanted to do was lie down for a few moments, shut her eyes, and curl into a little ball.

He was in and out of the shower like greased lightning, but by the time he opened the door, Damali's peaceful breaths made her chest gently rise and fall. His poor boo was wrapped in a damp towel, hair all over her head, nearly passed out from all the drama, and hadn't even been able to change into her sundress.

Carlos kicked his soiled clothes to the side, walked over to her, and placed a delicate kiss on her forehead. How during the extended war of the Armageddon did he keep that serene expression on his wife's face? He couldn't even begin to figure that out. Rather than try, he walked over to the chair and found his sweatpants and a pair of flip-flops. At least while she was asleep, he could find her something decent to eat. The bitch of it was, she was vegan and everything good, like fresh fruit and vegetables, was potentially tainted. So he'd have to concoct a meal for her from frozen stock . . . maybe some kind of stir-fry, who knows.

On a mission, he light cleaned the door, the doorknob, and any surface he'd touched, just for good measure, taking their soiled clothes out with him to fill in a garbage bag and then dump. As he stood at the bow rail alone, holding the plastic over the pristine blue sea, the political incorrectness of just dropping it into the ocean made him jettison it back to the already destroyed marina.

"Be kind to the earth," a familiar male voice said. "You'll need her one day, so will your children."

Carlos whirled on the sound, his heart beating hard. "Father Pat," he whispered, emotion catching in his throat.

"We didn't forget about you," Father Pat said quietly, his translucent form moving with the gentle Caribbean breeze. "It has only been three days since D.C. The Neterus will return to your side."

"But, you were the one I missed the most, man. I'll get them back for what they did to you—you know that, right?"

"I do . . . but not at the expense of your family or team. It is glorious here."

Carlos nodded and briefly looked away. "They got your boys, too. The other clerics."

"I know," Father Pat said softly. "Son, I know."

"But what do we do now without you?" Carlos hadn't meant for his voice to waver or for his tone to sound so forlorn, but the sight of the man who'd been like his father tore open a wound in his soul and poured salt into it.

"You go on," Father Pat murmured, producing a Templar blade. Slowly, before Carlos's eyes he became younger, his clerical robes turning from black to royal blue. In the center of his chest was a large silver cross with a medallion centered in it, a bleeding heart pierced with a dagger and a crown of thorns.

"Easier said than done," Carlos replied quietly after a moment. But then he lifted his chin and squared his shoulders. "You look good, though. I'm glad all the suffering is over."

"I will never, ever leave you, son," Father Pat said quietly. "And you know old warriors never die."

Carlos smiled and shook his head. "That's what I always loved about you, man. You were a tough old dude."

"Had to be—to go out and find a young vampire to turn into a Neteru, yes?"

Carlos's chuckle deepened as warm memories poured into

his spirit. "Yeah. You were crazier than me. I'da left my ass in the desert at the first sight of fangs . . . and I was ornery and bloodthirsty, too."

"I recall," Father Pat said, coming closer. "Do you trust me now?"

Carlos raised an eyebrow. "Sorta, but the blade in your grip is making me nervous. If I messed up with the Light, can you give a brother warning?"

"I know this isn't your style," Father Pat said, chuckling. "But can you go down on one knee?"

Carlos just stared at him for a moment.

"So I can knight you?" Father Patrick let out an exasperated breath.

"Knight me?"

The deceased priest walked away shaking his head and then came back to Carlos. "You have always asked too many questions and that, my friend, has always gotten you in trouble. But, if you must know—I cannot share any Templar secrets with you unless you're one of us."

Carlos slowly dropped to one knee and looked up with a sheepish grin. "My bad."

"Listen to me," Father Patrick said, laying the transparent blade on Carlos's shoulder. "Right now, goods and weapons are what you need. Money is worthless. But we also have gold and diamonds, other means of exchange. Wait to trade these until the time of the mark of the beast. Right now, be sparing on your use of grains and water . . . when the economy comes back online, you will have resources. It's in the tunnels . . . our consecrated tunnels where no demons can enter."

"Thank you," Carlos said quietly, looking up into Father Patrick's wise, aged eyes. "I'm gonna miss you not being here like old times, you know?"

"I will be here to christen your children, to follow you in battle. I will never leave you, that is my vow."

Carlos nodded and held Father Patrick's line of vision as his wisp of phantom blade touched each of Carlos's shoulders.

"I am proud of you," Father Patrick said quietly. "I watched you go from an angry kid from the streets into an honorable man. See with my eyes where your resources are hidden when you need them. I have also shared this with Cordell so your teams on the mainland and around the world can eat."

As Father Patrick backed away, Carlos stood. "I don't know what else to say but thank you." The urge to hug him was so great that Carlos had to ball his hands into fists, lest he made a fool of himself by trying to give a warrior hug to thin air.

"The honor is all mine," Father Patrick said, obvious pride glimmering in his eyes. "To watch your development, Damali's development, was the greatest gift of my life. Remember these words from Revelation, son, 'and I will give power unto two witnesses, and they shall prophecy a thousand, two hundred, and threescore days . . . these are the two olive trees and the two candlesticks standing before the God of the earth . . . and if any man will hurt them, fire proceedeth out of their mouths and devoureth their enemies.' Carlos," Father Patrick whispered.

The fading priest stepped in closer, his words urgent as his form began to disappear. "Your wife carries the strongest Neteru ever born. Go to Megiddo after you collect Ayana, her grandmother, and the Weinsteins. Find the place of Revelation 16:16, the water tunnel southwest of the mound. There is an underground spring there with water that is untainted, and the tunnel is a one-hundred-and-five-foot drop cut into bedrock by the sheer will and bare hands of people with no modern machinery—that is what humans can do, Carlos. The iron tunnel that leads from it is two-hundred-and-ten-feet long. This place is packed with things you must know in the final battle—ask Solomon, it was his center of administration. Ask Akhenaton, there were six letters sent to him from there, and it is spoken of on the stele at the Temple of Karnack. This place that overlooks the Valley of Jezreel in Israel is prophesized. It is called Tel Megiddo in Hebrew or Tell al-Hutesellim in Arabic. Ask the Neteru Kings of old, they will guide you. Be well, my son . . . I must go."

Carlos turned away from the now-empty space before him and stared out at the endless blue surrounding the ship and closed his eyes. A single tear rolled down his cheek. Even in death, the old man had his back.

CHAPTER NINE

Deep, soak-into-your-bones warmth surrounded her. Heavy exhalations painted the back of her skull and the nape of her neck with moist heat. Damali stirred and snuggled in closer to Carlos's spoon of her body. A perfect fit; a divine design. Heaven on earth, if just for rare glimpses of this peace that surpassed all understanding. She'd learned long ago never to take something so profoundly simple and so wonderfully exquisite for granted.

His hand loosely cupped her breast, causing the sensitive nerve endings at the tip of it to tingle every time his palm gently grazed her tightening nipple. She'd become so relaxed that her body felt like a lump of clay, molded by the shape of his, and now dampened by his touch. She didn't know how long she'd been asleep, nor did she care at the moment. Tranquility permeated her senses, melted her bones. They were adrift on an azure-blue sea, and with her eyes closed she was floating on a sea of comfort, navigating between semiwakefulness and the depths of heavy REM.

But soon the throb between her legs nagged her to full consciousness. Carlos's all-pervasive warmth pressed to her bottom enticed friction . . . just a slight undulation like the gentle waves that lapped the ship's skin. Then her long, deep breaths hit sudden shallows, causing her to sip air through her mouth. He felt so good and smelled fantastic . . . clean with just his natural scent. His thumb absently slid past her nipple, making her breath hitch. She wondered if her personal captain heard her. Damali smiled with her eyes closed and willed herself to allow the man his rest. A gentle kiss against the back of her head told her he had.

They lay like that for what felt like a long time, him slowly waking up, her enjoying being surrounded by his endless sea of warmth. Talking would have ruined it. Sensation, skin contact, was the only form of communication needed. They stretched as one, her legs slowly lowering from their sleepy bend, his seeking a space between them without breaking the integrity of their spoon.

His hand was a slow, steady stroke of pleasure-filled heat down her arm, then her side, and over the swell of her bare hip and back again. The towel was gone, lost in the sheets he'd covered her with while she was asleep. His breathing didn't change, but his body did, responding to the tautness of her nipple and the slight shudder his calm ministrations had caused.

Somehow during her sleep, she was sure her joints must have dissolved. Her body felt like liquid heat as his touch flowed over her in gentle waves. And yet everything about him, other than his touch, had become solid mass. To ground herself, she slowly reached for his hip, flowing touch down it, taking sweatpants with it, washing away fabric with the insistent surf of her hand.

His breathing stopped for a moment as her warm, wet waves pelted pure stone behind her. Just as water wears down rock, it was only a matter of time. She could feel him begin to dissolve into sand . . . his erosion started with a quiet moan that he swallowed to preserve her dignity. Then a quick feral kiss that he pressed against her temple, his arms gathering her closer to brace against the inevitable.

A storm of passion had arisen out of nowhere from what was otherwise calm. Deepening, building, torrential . . . slick, wet rhythm, the sound of pelting rain, his breaths gale force in her hair, there was no way to stop rushing water. He wasn't even in her ocean, just lapping against her shore and feeling her smooth, engorged pebble. That alone had devastated him . . . had ruined her. And yet a storm was still building, one that looked innocent enough from the onset, but had category five written all over it.

She felt the unspoken question in his mind—the tension in his body transmitted it, his openmouthed breaths wind-chanted it. Yes, it was going to be a big one, hold on.

No one could fight the ocean, the element of water, not even her. One swirling eddy, one deep spine snap, and he was engulfed, plunging into drowning heat that put fangs in his mouth and her face into the pillow.

He turned away from her throat, survival instinct making him cling to the last vestige of sanity he owned, but she was caught up—building, climbing, a wall of raw power and water and intensity that fisted the sheets as she bit her lip, neither willing to cry out to betray personal tsunamis.

The moment she went under, he succumbed, let go, and drowned hard . . . convulsing into breath-stopping shudders that bloodied his lip. Panting, holding on to each other tightly, they washed ashore to a place of calm, not opening their eyes for a long while.

Slowly, as their breathing normalized, his hand found that same lazy pattern that had started it all . . . like an ancient mariner's nautical sight, he knew her sand shoals, her eddies, her deep water. Understood her storms and respected them, just like her cloudless, crystal-blue days. His kiss had charted her long ago, and yet she was still a mystery, so much of her unknown by man. Depths that had yet to be explored. Her heart a siren's call to his, two souls inextricably linked. He'd been seduced by her since forever; had given up the struggle not to drown in Damali . . . it was what it was. He would gladly die at sea.

He kissed her damp shoulder and nuzzled her hair, his mouth now hungering for hers in the worst way. She turned to him to offer what he sought; it was a ritual between them. Her beautiful brown eyes smoky, her expression serene, sated. A soft, graceful hand caressed his cheek. Her turned his face into it and kissed her palm.

"*Te amo,*" he murmured, tracing her collarbone with a finger.

"I love you, too," she whispered before she took his mouth again.

"We need to get another shower." He smiled and closed his eyes.

"Yeah," she murmured with a smile, closing her eyes. "In a little while."

Damali gently caressed the pearl in her choker necklace with deep reverence as she and Carlos took plates of stir-fry veggies and rice to the top deck. From this point forward, she would stop giving her oracle the blues. Pearl had obviously grown, had become more subtle in her prognostications and predictions. Damali swallowed a private smile—time that Pearl had spent with the Neteru Queens had clearly infused wisdom and a lot of grace. The group nap she'd suggested wasn't as much about physical rest as it was about emotional release and comforting damaged spirits through the healing art of touch, love sublime.

"Hey, everybody." Damali gave the group a relaxed smile,

searching for room on the table to add her bounty. People had made crackers and cheese, tuna sandwiches, peanut butter and jelly, hummus and chips, and steamed dumplings from the frozen food bags. She chuckled softly. "I guess Inez is crashing, because this sure doesn't have her stamp of coordinated grub on it."

"Hey . . ." Juanita said, laughing. "Did the best we could under the circumstances."

"Yo," Carlos said quietly, smiling wide. "Brought some grub to add to the party. I found some vegetables down there in the freezer. Don't make me get Mar on you, eating dinner with nothing green on your plates."

"Tell me y'all fixed Monty a plate?" Damali began filling a clean plate with grub for their captain.

"You know we took care of homeboy," Yonnie said with a yawn. "Sinclair is *da man*."

"Good, but I hope you didn't give him all of this and made him something that makes sense," Damali said with a skeptical grin.

"See, now you hatin'," Juanita said, laughing. "We gave him a little of everything as we brought it up from the kitchen."

"Oh, maaaan, you'll have him sick as a dog with all that rolling around in his gut." Carlos shook his head. "Y'all trying to put our captain out of commission, or what?"

"Dang, C, we ain't think about all of that."

Damali and Carlos stared at each other for a moment and then burst out laughing as she quickly took Monty a sensibly arranged plate anyway. To her surprise, Carlos went with her, bringing some bottled water and juice.

"You cool?" Carlos asked, offering Monty something cold to drink.

"Good as ever; I'm too excited about this adventure to sleep yet," Monty replied with a big smile, and then motioned with his chin to a small table where they could leave his food. "Your hospitality warms my heart. I feel so useful, so alive . . . like I've gotten a brand-new family."

"You have." Damali hugged Monty and then quickly stood aside so Carlos could welcome him, too. "We *are* family now," Damali said, truly meaning it in her soul. "There was a reason we all came together. Believe that."

"I do, with all my heart," Monty said. "I haven't been this happy in a long time, isn't that odd?" He looked from Damali to Carlos, eyes beaming with delight. "Now, go, relax, and leave me to my thoughts. This is my time when I just daydream and watch the sea . . . very calming."

"I can appreciate that, man," Carlos said, threading his arm around Damali's waist. "Thanks, again . . . seriously, for putting it all on the line."

Easy salutations and waves met Damali and Carlos with laughs when they returned. Folks were sprawled out across the comfortable seating, looking like it was an effort not to fall asleep where they sat.

As she glanced around the top deck, every couple that had been given so-called R and R was holding hands, touching in some way, their gazes gentle, expressions serene. She watched their auras mingle in the waning, orange-red sunset haze of Caribbean dusk, opalescent hues shimmering against a background of pale purple and darkening blue. Lovers engaged in a private dance. It was written all over their faces; they'd all used the time the same way—to bond, strengthen the cord of man and wife through touch and skin reverence, deep soul-level appreciation. Each had brought a portion of a meal to the top deck, an offering for their fellow teammates and their spouses to break bread and cherish whatever time left them that God would allow.

The pure synchronicity of it all was wonderfully eerie. Oddly, and yet perfectly, without discussion or previous coordination, each woman had selected a sundress that complemented a chakra point. Every man was in white shorts or sweatpants with a T-shirt of a complementary hue, laidback and chilling. The color thing was deep. She couldn't have planned it consciously if she had tried—and her team daggone sure wouldn't have gone for it if she had. They never dressed that way as a group.

The norm was combat fatigues, jeans, or leather, with Tims, not flip-flops and shower shoes. Not potentially about to go to war. But the group was so fluid, so relaxed that it blew her mind. Given all that they'd been through and what they possibly faced as the sun dropped, they were cooler than she'd ever seen them going into a battle.

Every woman looked radiant and every color gave off a vibration; Marlene and Nefertiti had taught her that. She could see it dancing in each woman's aura and then commingling into her husband's auric field. The sound of each color gave off a definitive pitch, a barely audible harmonic that was soothing.

Later, when she and her Guardian sisters would finally stand at the yacht's rails to begin the pyramid meditation, all of their color vibrational choices would matter.

She had on a strapless, white, flowing gauze shift—which made sense for her to be the crown chakra as the team's female Neteru. Heather had chosen a pretty violet wrap, and as the stoneworker third eye for the group, and therefore the one most closely aligned with the submerged stone structure, it was logical for her to have been drawn to the hue of the third eye. Lovely Tara, the group's voice of reason, had gravitated to her Native American turquoise, which was also the hue of the throat chakra.

Damali picked at one of the platters she'd set down earlier on the large glass and white wrought-iron deck table, straining not to shake her head at the simplistic perfection of the Divine hand at work.

Quiet Jasmine had chosen a jade-green slip of a dress that framed her long, jet-black hair and gorgeous Asian eyes. It made sense for this delicate soul to have chosen the color of the heart chakra—the bridge between worlds. Her blond sister-in-law, Krissy, had picked a lively, canary-yellow dress, and her constant upset at the injustices of the world and her cry for equity made that solar plexus chakra color naturally hers. Audacious Juanita, a streetwise Latina sister from the 'hood like her, had picked a fiery orange, off-the-shoulder tie-wrap, whose hue was all about the gut hunch. But she would have never guessed in a million years that innocent Val would have chosen the deep reddish fuchsia, spaghetti-strap mini she'd picked. That color was so powerful . . . primal, and Val was . . . Damali allowed the thought to dissipate. Yonnie was a definite influence, so, yeah, it made perfect sense.

Damali glanced at Carlos, not even needing to say it. He shrugged and answered her message as they picked up plates and utensils.

Did you know? Did you pick the colors and sizes with specific Guardian sisters in mind?

No . . . just pulled in things based on estimated size. At the time, I was rushing, wasn't picking out styles and colors, D. C'mon, now, baby. Did I mess up? Tell me you aren't trying to be the fashion police during the Armageddon—they all look nice to me, and you're stunning, baby . . . what?

Damali kissed his cheek as he set a huge mound of brown rice on each of their plates.

No, you didn't mess up, she mentally shot to him, laughing. *Everything is so perfect that it's freaking me out.*

Oh. His mental murmur contained a caress. *Glad I did something right.*

He smiled; she smiled, not looking at the others for a private moment as they continued dishing up their plates of food.

You did more than something right. She allowed her sidelong glance to catch his and trap it for a moment like a caress.

He brushed her mouth as they found a space on an empty sofa and sat down. "Eat," he said quietly, his knee skimming her thigh.

There was nothing else to say, the companionable silence said it all.

"Where are you, where are you, my troublesome Neterus?" Lilith muttered, staring at the slowly rotating globe that hovered in her empty chambers. "Plagues haven't driven you out—demons haven't flushed you out to help your beloved humans," she added with a sneer, and then flung her goblet of blood at the transparent image.

She released a shriek of fury and balled her talons into a fist. "Your deaths haven't registered, the deaths of your beloved Covenant haven't even brought you out—not even the destruction of your Guardian team hideouts or hostage attempts! Damn you, where are you? We've covered the lands far and wide, every place on the globe, even the Arctic, sending the undead to feast on the living."

Lilith raked her talons across her scalp, parting her jet-black hair and leaving trails of blood. Ignoring the injury that sealed immediately, she began to pace. The puzzle was an enigma. They'd opened the bowels of Hell to have them mirror reflect the psyche of the human population. Plagues tortured people like the phantoms of Level One, succubae and incubi possessed the unwitting and made them commit heinous acts of violence against humanity and the earth like that of Level Two.

Her Level Two poltergeists were running rampant, terrorizing any soul they could find. Serpentlike Amanthra demons, and all of the wetland demonic forces from huge spiders and pests to rodents and maggot infestations, were running amok— Levels Three and Four had gone topside. Her most cherished were-creatures from Level Five, everything from werewolves to massive were-cats and anything in between, had been belched to the surface to infect and take over humans . . . and her vampires from Level Six . . .

Lilith just closed her eyes. Fallon Nuit had demonstrated such mastery with his subliminal attack on mankind through the airwaves of Council Group Entertainment, and then had created so many gorgeous, powerful entities of the night. His master vampires were going to be the stuff of legends, rivaled only by Vlad's armies and Sebastian's necromancy. Her councilwomen had been treacherously flawless—poisons and feeding frenzies, jealousies and greed. All of Hell was topside, and now manifesting in the entire human population based on the sins of the individual and the world. Only those destined for the Rapture would escape . . . so why hadn't the Neterus surfaced?

She opened her talons to accept a new goblet of blood and retracted her huge bat wings, folding them into her shoulders as she retracted her spaded tail. Fury without direction was getting her nowhere. Her husband, the Dark Lord, would not accept excuses at this time in the empire. Lilith placed a forefinger to her crimson-stained lips, studying landmasses.

"Where in the world are you, my sweets?" Then suddenly she smiled as a hunch clawed at her mind. She chuckled and walked around the globe several times. "Nooo . . . oh, tell me that it isn't that easy! If you're not on land, then you have to be on the high seas!" Lilith threw her head back and cackled loudly. "I cannot believe the Light allowed you to take such a perfectly insane risk! They must really be getting desperate."

Frank Weinstein turned away from his stricken wife. Stella just stared out into the nothingness of the mountains, refusing to accept food or water from the Guardians, and he knew that if she could have, she would have refused to breathe.

War robbed humankind of its humanity and lifted the veil of innocence from the eyes of children . . . and adults. It was a monster in and of itself that was no respecter of age or gender. His wife was alive but her spirit had been shattered. Their son, Daniel, was most likely dead, and the potential of hope, a reason to keep going, would lie with him in some unmarked grave . . . or on the streets, his body savaged by rats and starving dogs.

It was this reality that, more than anything, kept his Stella frozen in a dark abyss of terror. They held guns—people who had lived a life of nonviolence, oblivious to the horrors of global atrocities. Yet, this was what their parents and grandparents had warned of, this was what Rabbi had given his life for . . . a devil was a devil, evil was evil. Did it matter if it was embodied in a human shell or in its hideous supernatural form? The truth was an avenging angel, which declared that no one, no people, could allow it to happen again, anywhere, to anyone.

But what was real, what was a mind fractured into hallucinations? So-called rebels had saved their lives and secreted them away into the mountains; their trusted government had hunted them down and tried to round them up. Everything black was white and white was black. He was now an outlaw; his honorable son had given his life without even a decent burial. Synagogues, temples, churches, mosques, had all been burned to the ground. People were eating one another! He'd seen demons eat a man alive in the tunnel . . . *a holy man*. And now he had a gun? To do what with—turn it on himself and his wife, if their Spartan sanctuary was overrun?

Frank Weinstein covered his face with his palms, completely unable to process the events of the last twenty-four hours. He wept silently, thickly, beginning to rock. "Come back to me, Stella," he whispered into his damp hands. "There's no one left to understand who we were but you."

A concrete beam had knocked her out but had saved her life. It had blocked her body from the other falling debris that would have surely killed her, and then, according to the baby, it had kept a monster from eating her alive.

"Jesus, take me now," Delores Filgueiras whispered, her eyes shut tightly in prayer.

A gentle hand at her back made her open her eyes. "Ma'am, He ain't gonna do that because it would break your daughter's and granddaughter's hearts."

Delores looked at the Guardian whom they called Dragon Rider. "You're safe for now up in the mountains."

Another Guardian came to her and squatted down. She owned an intense gaze, but there was gentleness in her voice. "You did good back there—was the stuff of Guardians. The baby said you ran against panicked humans, threw your body in the way to cover her when the blast hit." Quick shook her head. "If you hadn't fallen on Ayana, the demons would have found her right off and taken her hostage—that's some love. She was so tiny; she crawled out and then boo saved you. So, ma'am, stay with us, and we'll get you back to your daughter or die trying. We promise."

Dragon Rider nodded. "And for the love of God, lady, don't wish for an untimely death . . . because the one thing I know, if you haven't figured it out yet, He answers all prayers."

Relaxed and completely open, each couple took a position at the top deck rail, choosing one of the four cardinal points. Two couples stood at starboard, two portside, two at the bow, with Damali and Carlos at the stern.

"Tell me when you feel that rock, lady," Damali called out to Heather.

"Aye, aye, Captain," Heather said with a wide smile, and then sent her gaze out into the starlit night.

Guardians waited like silent sentinels, listening to the night and the ripples of water caressing the vessel. Then Dan's voice broke their private communion with the vastness of the sea.

"I think she's got something, people," he said nervously, his line of vision going between Heather and Damali.

Heather's eyelids fluttered violently and her once-calm breathing became a labored pant as her head dropped back.

"What should I do, D?" Dan paced behind his wife, not sure if he should touch her or allow her to descend further into the trance.

Carlos looked at Heather as he spoke to Damali. "D, she's going in really deep . . . is it cool?" When he turned around, Damali was in a heavy trance state that mirrored Heather's. "D!"

"Don't touch them," Marlene said, walking up and onto the top deck. "Now it begins. Just watch."

Shabazz was on Marlene's heels. "What's going on, baby? Look at 'em! It's like they're all—"

"Drowning," Marlene said calmly.

Every male on deck yelled the same word at the same time: *"What?"*

"They have to let go and stop struggling," Marlene said, moving to the center of the vessel, opening her arms and using her ebony walking stick like a lightning rod. "Once they die to what they knew, they will be emptied of the old and filled with the new."

Carlos pointed at Marlene, challenging her, but with respect. "Marlene . . . don't you let one of them die or hemorrhage. I don't want them emptied, none of the brothers do—we clear?"

"This is feminine energy, baby," Marlene said gently, her wise eyes beginning to glow white. "The energy of peace after the fire. Trust it."

"I trust *you*, Mar," Carlos said, beginning to pace.

"Trust something much bigger than me," Marlene said, starting to whirl in a circle as an iridescent shimmer began to overtake each female Guardian standing at the rail.

Damali clutched her throat with one hand while holding on to the rail with the other, suddenly gasping and convulsing until her wings tore through her shoulder blades with such force that rivulets of blood coursed down her back.

"That's it!" Carlos shouted, heading toward his wife.

"Touch her now and you'll injure her!" the pearl in Damali's necklace shrieked. "Don't, Carlos!"

Every man backed up from his wife, panic and adrenaline making the muscles in their biceps twitch.

"They must die," the pearl said more calmly as the winds began to rise with roiling waves that summated out of nowhere. "Go home to the source . . ."

"She's not dying—fuck all that," Yonnie yelled over the roaring winds. "C, do something, man . . . you know all this spiritual shit!"

"We wait," Carlos said, glancing between Damali and Marlene, who nodded.

"Wait for what? A fucking tsunami to take our wives overboard!" Rider shouted as a huge wave in the distance headed toward the craft.

"Have faith," Marlene said quietly. "Wait."

"Atlantis is rising," Pearl said in an eerie echo. Her voice had taken on a hollow tone like that of an amplified seashell. "Every old, highly advanced civilization came from there . . . this was where the tree of knowledge was replanted. Every reincarnation of advanced empires comes from that tree, and it flourishes as long as the leaders adhere to the principles. But those empires will go into instant decline and obscurity when the laws of the Divine are violated . . . and their civilizations will turn to dust. It has happened cycle after cycle, until there can be no more cycles after this."

"I don't care about that ancient history shit," Carlos said, going toward Damali. "There is a wall of water about to hit this ship, Pearl, and I need to know where the closest landmass is on this side of the Triangle—stat!"

"She'll capsize!" Monty yelled frantically from the pilothouse. "She wasn't meant to withstand anything like this!"

"C, we can't fight the ocean!" Big Mike shouted, bracing Inez in an iron grip.

Berkfield began flinging life vests into the center of the deck. "Marjorie—don't just stand there! Help me!"

"It isn't a wall of water, Carlos. It's a wall of energy from Atlantis," Pearl said in a soothing but firm tone. "Do not touch your mates, they are almost dead, and they will be washed away. It is prophecy."

"What!" Carlos was pure motion.

Every male on the ship broke his position and made a dash toward his wife, but a bullwhip of white light that came up from the depths like the tentacles of a giant octopus separated them from their objective.

"Do not interfere!" Pearl warned. "The children they carry must be infused with all the insights they need to rebuild the next world after the Fall. It is their role to protect the future. They must have all of the technical advancements of Atlantis, plus the wisdom that was lacking in subsequent empires . . . there will be no more cycles left after theirs for humanity to finally evolve."

Before the male Guardians could make another desperate lunge for their wives, the wall of jewel-blue energy hit the craft, washing over the deck, and radiated a sparkling, opalescent charge over every surface. Each female Guardian stopped struggling, stopped breathing, her eyes wide and glassy as the hue of her chakra color slowly overtook her irises.

Beams of colored lights danced beneath the pristine water's surface, connecting to the fingertips of each woman as she opened her arms and then gasped in a soul-shuddering breath. The light swelled from the ocean's depths, covering them each in blue, violet, orange, red, every color that was worn spilled onto the deck, overtook their hair, lifting it from their shoulders, and creating a halo around their entire bodies.

White light spiraled up from the great sea beyond and entered Damali through the crown of her head, lighting her eyes in glowing, white-hot energy that lifted her from the surface of the deck, arched her back, and then suddenly sucked in every color her sisters emanated. Her gasp cut through the night, and her exhalation sent the light toward them, lifting every other woman off her feet in a color orb of the chakra hue she wore. Then Damali's Guardian sisters turned to face one another, still in a trance, each opening her mouth and releasing the sound of her hue. Damali's voice blended with theirs to ring at a glass-shattering pitch.

The harmonics fused, creating a spiral of multicolored light that became denser and denser until it was an opalescent staff that rose from the deck and then exploded into glittering, iridescent pinpoints of light energy.

In the shimmering wake, a hologramlike image of a magnificent crystal pyramid filled the center of the all-female circle. Each woman's eyes glowed a different hue, and the writings through the ages moved in a blur in her irises. Languages never recorded, symbols lost in antiquity . . . then Kemetian hieroglyphics, Sumerian, Aramaic, Greek, Chinese, runes, wall art, so many so fast that it was impossible to catalogue, and it all passed through their eyes as male Guardians stood in awe, paralyzed with reverence.

Then, one by one, each woman dropped to the deck, washed away by a current of energy that left her sputtering and trembling. Damali collapsed, her wings still glowing with energy, her eyes flickering as the last of the current abated. She looked up first as footfalls neared the circle.

"Don't!" Damali said, her voice foreign, older, and sensually husky as it echoed through the night. She stood with effort, her gaze unfocused. "Atlantis had to sink. Its knowledge was too powerful and vast for the undeveloped human spirit. The avatars of old, however, reincarnated, time and time again, each remembering some of their time in the chrysalis of pure knowledge . . . and time and time again, their human condition, eventually, was overtaken by the temptations of the darkside in the world."

She opened her arms, golden tears filling her eyes. "Just as Kemet rose to great heights and knew a long reign of advanced science, beauty, art, and grace for centuries . . . after thousands of years without incident, the later pharaohs forgot the Divine principles and fell into decadence, they lost all that they had once owned . . . as has every empire in the world after them. These children we carry must not forget. This time when they rebuild, they will hold the collective consciousness of the old avatars of Atlantis . . . but will also contain the spiritual lighthouse—once the darkness in the world is vanquished. Just like you must not forget . . . everything that you are, the dark and the light within must be used for the Ultimate Good and for the protection of the final empire."

Damali let out a hard breath, blinked twice, and just that quickly her eyes were normal brown again. Slightly disoriented, she looked at her Guardian sisters who were stirring on the deck and then looked at the stricken expressions on the rest of the team.

"You guys okay?" she said, giving Carlos a curious glance. "What?"

CHAPTER TEN

Lilith craned her fingers in, black energy swirling in the centers of her palms, and then in a fit of fury, she hurled the orbs at the hovering globe so hard that it nearly tipped off its axis.

"Waters arise—empty your depths! Bring them to me! Sweep the shores of all life. Swallow everything in your wake!"

Raging dark energy plunged into the blue oceans of her globe, sending tidal waves inland toward North America to crash into fragile crusts of land. She shrieked with mad glee as Manhattan submerged and New England disappeared. The length of the eastern seaboard, except Washington, D.C., disappeared under a blue eclipse. Florida broke off and sank, along with Cuba and all of the West Indies. The Gulf of Mexico spread inland like a deep blue stain, a wall of water that made Lilith screech and clap, and then form another orb to explode in the Pacific. Immediately, from Portland to La Paz, encompassing all of California inland to the Sierra Nevada, disappeared beneath a roiling blue carpet of death. Central America was gone.

"You're in North America, I know it! Why won't you *just die*?"

Nuit stood in the desert, wearing black fatigues, with a look of cool satisfaction on his face. He stared at the human mercenary soldiers before him, admiring their Bradleys and military arsenal.

"One clean sweep," he said calmly. "Twelve dead old men, Aborigine insurgents, terrorists . . . and you bring me the artifact that they stole from my corporation long ago—and you will be handsomely rewarded."

"The contract still the same, mate?" the commanding officer said, flashing a dazzling white smile against ruddy skin.

"Yes . . . one hundred million of recently recovered monies for each of you . . . and eternal life." Nuit rubbed his jaw and chuckled, looking at the six men who were mounted on unstoppable weapons of destruction. "And you do this of your own free will?"

"No worries, mate. For that deal, who gives a shit about a bunch of crazy geezers?"

The Unnamed One looked up from his large black marble war board, standing slowly as a commotion drew his attention to his outer chamber. His hooded demon sentries shielded their eyes from a white glowing object held by the charred human remains. The blackened bodies of six men stuck to the surface like gooey tar, which was the only part of the large disc his demons could hold by skewering the bodies with their scythes.

"My darkness," the lead demon murmured, nervously genuflecting. "Councilman Nuit sends his regards and has brought you an unusual offering. He requests an immediate audience, after having the audacity to send you something with the dreaded Light embedded in it. We have detained him to prevent what could only be an assassination attempt, this close to the—"

"Send him in!" the Unnamed One thundered, quickly walking around the war board to further inspect Nuit's unimaginable offering. Pure ecstasy coated his dark heart and then he closed his eyes. *This was what he'd been waiting for.* Now he could release his full torment on the world, and the moment the Light retaliated by breaking the fifth seal, he would trump them with the sixth!

As Nuit was thrown forward and hit the sizzling cavern floor, Lucifer bent and offered Nuit a helping hand up. "Come, my new Chairman . . . talk to me. . . ."

Carlos quietly stepped back from the group. From a very remote place in his mind he saw Damali commune with her sister Guardians and Marlene. The brothers were listening to the women's experiences with complete focus. But he watched the water.

Something very deep within him was still coiled tight like a serpent ready to strike, needing to strike. It was something that went well beyond gut hunch. It was a knowing.

The night was darkening, the stars seeming to go out one by one like someone was blowing out birthday candles. He had at one time been the very night itself. He understood the slow, seductive creep of darkness. Yonnie gave him a sidelong glance and left the central gathering on the deck to join him at the stern.

"Yeah, I know," Yonnie said, confirming Carlos's suspicions while chewing hard on a toothpick.

Carlos nodded, motioning toward the water and then the horizon. Distant lightning flashed, making the group stop talking. Within those few seconds of illumination he saw that it wasn't stars going out above, but the water rising to eclipse the horizon.

"Oh, shit!" Yonnie yelled, jumping back as the two men at the stern stared into a demon-infested wave.

"Battle stations!" Shabazz shouted, jumping up and heading toward the pilothouse with Big Mike.

Carlos held up his hand and didn't move. One could fight demons, but couldn't fight the sea. Viking war ships numbering in the thousands painted the rising surf black. Carlos pulled Mike and Shabazz in with the others and then covered the team with a shield of Heru, ignoring Damali's shouts to let her fight with them. Carlos stared at Yonnie.

"How many of these motherfuckers you think we can take before it's all over, man?" Carlos asked calmly, watching the tsunami-size wave continue to build.

Yonnie shrugged and spat out his toothpick. "Couple hundred, if your shield holds . . . maybe you should jettison the team to anywhere you can dream of now before we capsize." Yonnie let his breath out hard. "I mean, what the fuck? They definitely gonna die here."

Carlos nodded, the absolute impossibility of what faced them making him become eerily calm. The problem was, no image would come to his mind of where safe could be. His fingertips didn't tingle, no energy surge pulsed through him enough to lift and jettison the entire team safely in a fold-away. He knew he'd drop them in shark- or demon-infested waters—something was siphoning his power, sucking him dry. He was still too close to the Devil's Triangle and it was as though it had become another entity to laugh at him.

"So, whassup, man?" Yonnie finally said, beginning to pace.

"Triangle's got me shot-blocked," Carlos said as calmly as possible.

Yonnie nodded. "Then we do this old-school. Go out swinging." He pounded Carlos's fist as Carlos's line of vision remained on the building wave.

From his old Vampire Council life, he remembered what the Vikings were capable of . . . rape, pillage, plunder. The bloody death—cracking open a living being's rib cage and pulling out their lungs. Torture refined to a spectator sport. Quick raids and hits on unsuspecting villages by sea, from North America to Africa, raining down hell on every continent in between . . . always by sea. Decimating Europe and the Middle East, even as far as India and Asia.

And now these raised barbarians stood on living dragon ships bearing glistening fangs, propelled by demon surges. Eyes glowing in hollowed sockets, weapons raised. Bloodlust crackling over the black ghost ship hulls . . . and nowhere to send his wife and child, his brothers and sisters and their children, panicked to the point of numbness, he wondered what the innocents had felt when their villages were attacked. Many probably took their own lives rather than succumb to what the Berserkers had in store for them. And he was now the member of what amounted to a floating village.

Seconds had clicked by, but it felt like many long minutes. Carlos snapped out of the daze, Damali's call a refrain in his ears. He turned to see a rainbow of lights dancing under his shield and then something in her eyes made him open his mind, open a channel to her telepathy, and agree without words to lift his paltry protection.

She was right, his fellow Guardians were right, if they were gonna die, they had the right to go out swinging. The shield he'd erected to keep them breathing in an air pocket when the wave hit, and to keep the demons off their backs, would only hold until his energy waned in the battle—which wouldn't take long given the circumstances. Carlos reluctantly dropped his shield of Heru. The very instant he did that, the vessel became encased in shimmering light.

Guardians held on to anything they could as the huge wave finally crashed into the ship, swallowing it. But they gradually stared up as though moving in slow motion to see the dragon hulls pass over them. Bright light from their vessel illuminated the crystal-blue water that surrounded them, but they didn't feel wet and could oddly breathe.

Weightlessness soon lifted them off the deck and they found themselves moving their arms and legs to hold the relative position they'd been in. Guardians touched their bodies, their billowing clothes, one another while watching their hair lift and sway in an underwater dance. Silence blotted out panic as they all took in the deeply surreal scene.

Damali stared at Carlos and simply touched her pearl at her throat. He nodded, understanding but yet still confused. The demons couldn't see them. Yonnie stared up at the passing legions in awe. Slowly Guardians stared up to watch the majesty of being passed over as ship after demon ship lurched forward above their heads while schools of sharks swam right past them, chasing the bloody vessels for a sure after-carnage meal. Then suddenly as the wave passed, their vessel broke the water's surface and everyone took a huge air breath. Sound came back. The yacht bounced a bit and then steadied, leaving Guardians sprawled on the deck floor.

Carlos reached out and clasped Damali's hand and kept his voice quiet and reverent. "Whoa . . . what a ride. One day you've gotta tell me all about Atlantis."

A few Guardians rose from the deck and Carlos looked around the yacht and then to Monty.

"Where are we?" Carlos asked. "Your navigation equipment is going nuts, Monty. What did getting hit with that energy wave from the lights and that crazy water do?"

Frantic, every Guardian with sensory capacity tried to hone in on a landmass, to no avail.

"J.L., you get that communication connection up yet?" Shabazz paced back and forth on the deck. "How's Damali's pearl?"

"Spent," Damali said quietly, "like the rest of us."

"It's cool, it's cool," Carlos said. "We'll figure this out. I just want J.L. to get some kinda communication going, because the last thing we need right now is a run-in with a protective battleship or a coast guard patrol, ya know."

J.L. looked up. "Dude . . ." he said in a far-off tone. "This can't be right. . . ."

"What can't be right?" Yonnie said, going to the pilothouse.

"Manhattan is gone . . . Philly is gone, ain't no Miami . . . no Cali, no Boston . . . it's gone."

"J.L., what *the fuck* are you talking about?" Dan shouted, jumping up from Heather's side to bang on the glass outside the pilothouse. "Motherfucker, my parents are in Manhattan! Stop freaking us all out by tuning into those bullshit, Apocalyptic, fraudulent sites! Find us some real news!"

"Man, I'm sorry," J.L. said gently. "My bad. Lemme try some other sources. But they said meteors hit in the Atlantic and Pacific sending in—"

"See, right there!" Dan yelled, pointing over the deck rail. "That's how you know it's bullshit! We are in the Atlantic last I checked, man. If a meteor hit here, large enough to create a giant tsunami to wipe out the eastern seaboard, we'd be floating toothpicks right now!"

Quiet seized the team as Carlos slowly went to his wife and gently took off her necklace. She caught his hand for a moment and then kissed him before letting him walk away with her oracle. He rubbed his thumb over her pearl and found an opened water jug. All eyes were on him as he tipped it to pour freshwater over the pearl's dehydrated surface. A soft, sad coo drifted up into the wind.

"We need to know," Carlos said.

"The rising wall of Atlantis energy saved you by pushing you through the Strait of Gibraltar right into the Mediterranean Sea. You must go to Megiddo."

Carlos just stared at the pearl as Dan's back slowly hit the pilothouse wall and he slid down to the deck floor. Heather was at his side in seconds as he covered his face with his forearm.

"Oh, Dan . . ." Marjorie and Berkfield rushed forward toward Dan and Heather with Bobby.

Krissy ran to the couple, and then seemed at a loss for whose tears to attend to first.

"I should have gotten to them," Dan said thickly. "My mother and father . . . how could I leave them?"

Heather's arms gathered as much of him as she could, but Inez's slow, agonized wail tore the team members in two. Mike tried to hold her but she fought like a woman possessed.

"My baby girl and my momma! No, no, no, God, no, not my baby girl! Oh, my God, my baby was just three years old, Jesus!"

Female Guardians tried to run in to assist Mike, who took every blow she hurled at him as though he'd drowned the child himself.

"You promised me!" Inez screamed, fighting the arms of female warriors as Mike finally walked away to break down against the rails.

Pandemonium erupted. The brothers broke off into small squads of support, half going to Dan, and the other half going to Mike, who wailed like a huge, wounded bear.

"She was just a baby," Mike sobbed. "A little precious baby!"

Carlos and Yonnie both had to box Mike in to keep him away from the artillery stash, each talking to him quickly in staccato pants. Rider tried to get a leg and almost got knocked out from Mike's flailing.

"Wasn't your fault, man—we couldn't get to 'em . . . woulda lost 'em in the pull through the Triangle," Yonnie said, working with Carlos to wrestle Mike to the deck.

"Look at my woman!" Mike hollered. " 'Nez, baby, I swear to God, I'm sorry!"

Carlos felt his body lifting as Mike broke free, his insane strength now a liability as Yonnie lost his grip on one of Mike's massive appendages. The only thing he could do was take the full body charge by getting in front of Mike, and then roping him down with an energy lasso.

"Let go of me!" Mike shouted, still struggling as a dazed Carlos tried to sit up.

"No, 'cause we love you, man," Carlos said, panting.

Damali had Inez in her arms, rocking her with Juanita as piteous wails sliced through everyone's skeleton. Guardian sisters ran between the fallen, trying in any way they could to touch, heal, and cry with those who'd experienced such visceral loss.

Dan sat in a curled ball of humanity, his arms gripped tightly around his knees, his head tucked in, rocking, while Shabazz and Berkfield tried their best to rationalize the incomprehensible. Finally Marlene parted the gathering of men, dropped to her knees, hugged a young man who'd just lost his parents, and let him wail. Shimmering tears rolled down her cheeks as she held him shaking her head, unable to bear going to Inez—the loss of her own daughter palpable to each Guardian with Marlene's every ragged inhalation.

The storm of hurt and pain that hit the ship was so violent that no one spoke for what felt like hours. Mike lay on the deck face down, panting from the fatigue of struggling against his binds, energy-tied down for his own safety. Inez lay on a sofa, covered by Damali's healing wings, having cried herself sick. Dan had finally accepted Heather's hugs, and his head was in her lap, his face to her belly, as they both rested on the deck floor numb.

Carlos stood at the stern, looking out at the water all around them. There was no naval presence guarding U.S. ports now. Pearl and Father Pat said to go to this strange land with the walking wounded, spiritually destroyed Guardians, and he didn't even know where that was. Four days, and the Neteru Councils hadn't surfaced . . . nor had any warrior angels . . . and a little baby girl had died—for what?

He hung his head, wishing he'd tried to pull them through the Triangle. Seeing the pain, hearing it, crawled all over his skin. And this was just his tiny family. What kind of human suffering was the world experiencing at large? All of this because of a deal forged eons before he was even a spark of conception. His Neteru Kings held back from going down to Hell and blowing the doors off it, all because the Devil was granted a period of time to corrupt the human soul. All because some of the Kings on the Neteru Council had to wait until the end of days, and had to let human nature, human karma run its full course . . . Carlos squeezed his eyes shut tightly. It was all so wasteful, so blindly wasteful, and if he was lucky, this was what his kid would inherit.

Hearing Inez's wails reminded him of just how powerless he was in this entire dance of life. Hearing Mike's wails made him want to put a gun to his own head. The only reason Dan's pain didn't carve at him as deeply was because, in some way, he could rationalize the loss of an older couple, people who'd lived, loved, raised a family, and had died together quickly. If he were honest about it, even the loss of Mom Delores didn't tear his spirit from its housing within. She'd gotten a chance to see her child grow up, marry a good person, and have a child of her own, knowing her kid and grandkid would be with good people that loved them. But the loss of that baby girl, little Ayana . . . that was what had rocked the entire team. That was what had stabbed him in the heart.

"Where is Megiddo from here?" Carlos whispered into the wind. He looked out at the glass-still surface of deep blue water. "Father told me, but I can't picture it in my mind," he said in a weary tone. "Can't picture none of it at all. My team is bleeding to death . . . Heaven help them. I don't know what to do."

"Bring them in first," a deep, unfamiliar voice said. "There is no more Triangle barrier here. I will help you so that you do not deplete yourself."

Carlos slowly straightened, drawing the blade of Ausar into his grip as he turned around to meet the threat.

"My father's sword suits you, Neteru brother."

A dirty-faced warrior stepped out of the folds of nothingness, a younger Ausar look-alike the size of Big Mike. He grabbed Carlos's left forearm before Carlos could react, bumping their chests hard enough to knock the wind out of Carlos as he gave him a hearty warrior's embrace and then let him go.

"Heru?"

The Neteru prince nodded with a wide smile. "We have

laid siege to the Berserkers, and then have been trying to move civilizations from the floodplains," Heru said, using a Neteru blade to paint a vivid war report on the deck floor as mesmerized Guardians looked up from their private pain to watch.

"Heru . . ." Carlos drove his sword into the deck and gaped, for the first time in his life actually starstuck. "I carry your shield, man. You are *the one!*"

"No, my brother—this time, you are *the one.*" Heru laughed deeply and gave Carlos another warrior's embrace of friendship, crushing the air from his lungs again before he released him.

"How . . . where . . . what happened to the Kings—I've got a million questions," Carlos said, awe making him tongue-tied.

"Warrior angels have chased the infidels to the borders of darkness, and have put pressure on the Antichrist's healing dens. Twice we almost had the bastard," Heru said, frowning as his charismatic voice enthralled the team.

"But you didn't save my baby girl!" Inez screamed, up on her feet and rushing forward before Damali or Carlos could grab her. She barreled into Heru's midsection, drew a blade from the back pocket of her jeans, and held it to his throat. "I just want to know why?"

Heru smiled and glanced at Carlos with approval. "Good warrior; excellent reflexes. You will need that on the battlefield against the darkness."

" 'Nez," Damali said softly. "Don't."

"He's on our side, 'Nez," Carlos said carefully.

"Let her," Heru said calmly. "But there isn't just reason to . . . your daughter lives. I will bring her here. There isn't much time. What is left of the North American teams must join the Middle Eastern teams before the fifth seal is broken."

The blade fell away from Inez's hand to clatter on the wooden floor. Carlos caught her before she dropped.

"Medic!" Carlos hollered. "Need some water, man!" He slapped Inez's face until her eyes rolled toward the back of her head and her eyelids finally began to flutter.

Berkfield was trapped mid-deck on the way to get water when Dan slowly pushed himself up to stand and began backing away from the pilothouse. Damali covered her mouth and then stifled a scream. Monty's frantic shout made Carlos loosen Big Mike's energy binds as Dan staggered forward.

Frank and Stella Weinstein clutched each other trembling. Delores held on to the door frame, as Ayana broke free and ran straight for her dazed mother's arms. Inez's screams and the toddler's shriek, "Mommy," put Mike on his feet and sent him hurtling toward Inez and her daughter. Monty staggered out of the pilothouse, clutching his chest.

"They came out of thin air. They—"

"Berkfield, take the helm," Carlos shouted. "Somebody tend that man before we have a cardiac case!"

Heru crossed his chest with his forearm and stared deeply into Carlos's eyes. "We would never forsake you at this hour, brother. The Kings have heard your petitions."

"What do you mean, *Co*-Chairman?" Lilith said in such a quiet, deadly hiss that even the Devil slowed his exit, not sure that he should actually turn his back on his wife.

"Your efforts have not produced the Neterus. But I got something equally as strategic. Therefore, Nuit earned it," the Unnamed One said with a sly half-smile. "I now have the sixth seal." He gave her a wink, backing out of her chambers, laughing. "Carry on."

★   ★   ★

"The rest of your teams are at Megiddo," Heru said, using the tip of his sword to draw on the deck floor. "Here is where you are needed. It is also the safest place. The released armies of darkness, the raised Berserkers and all else that joins them, will spew catapults of brimstone to look like balls of fire in the sky."

"Meteor showers," Damali said, her voice capturing Heru's attention.

He bowed deeply from where he sat. "Yes, Queen." Then he checked himself, cleared his throat, and landed a solid hand on Carlos's shoulder, shaking his head. "My brother, you are gifted and highly favored."

Carlos couldn't fight the smile that tugged at his cheek. He didn't care what he had to fight at the moment; sanity had been restored as quickly as it had been taken. Time was speeding up, the roller coaster moving so fast that no one had a chance to recover from one mental breakdown before the next one hit.

Inez sat with her child clutched to her chest, Big Mike holding both of them. Monty and Delores sat huddled together with Marlene and Shabazz offering them reassuring hugs. Dan sat between his parents, wiping his eyes, with them bookended by Heather and the Berkfields.

"Here's my question, though, man," Carlos said, bringing his focus back to the young Neteru prince. "We've got civilians this time out."

"It is the only way. You must go to the tunnels. The Middle Eastern team is made up of Guardians from the entire region. Every country is represented, yours blended with it reunites the scattered Twelve Tribes. They will be able to show you the ancient escape tunnels used to elude the Romans when Jerusalem was ransacked two thousand years ago. There is an escape in the south end that terminates at the Temple Mount, which is known to Muslims as Al Aqsa Mosque—a disputed holy shrine—it also leads to the Kidron River, which empties into the Dead Sea."

Carlos stood and walked back and forth, dragging his fingers through his hair. "But we've got civilians, man. Babies, older people who have just come through God only knows what. The water cistern at Megiddo is a hundred-and-five-foot vertical drop into ancient tunnels, and then you're talking about a full-team jettison into the hot zone, downtown Jerusalem, man . . . c'mon."

"Megiddo," Heru said, standing, his gaze beginning to glow silver as he lost patience with Carlos, "will require an excavation. There, the Neteru Kings of old hid something written that came out of Ethiopia."

Damali tilted her head as she craned her neck upward. "Coptic text. Part of the prophecy."

Heru nodded. "She is—"

"Married," Yonnie muttered under his breath, gaining a glare from Heru.

"You, the Neterus, must go beneath this hallowed ground in Megiddo to get the text and, from it, the implement that can stop Satan's Thirteenth—his most cherished demon that will lead his armies of dark angels out of their Euphrates containment."

Carlos and Damali stared at each other.

"Okay, I've heard enough," Rider said, standing and walking across the deck. "That name is a showstopper with seniors and a baby on board—*and my wife pregnant*."

"How do you rule an army of warriors under democratic processes?" Heru yelled, losing patience as he stared at Carlos and Damali. "The insubordination you accept would not have been tolerated in the ancient empires!" He spun on Carlos. "There is a dagger that was hidden in the juncture at the disputed holy site beneath Jerusalem. That is one-half of what you need—the dagger used by the Roman Guard to pierce the side of the Christ. But you also need to be armed with the actual name of the demon, which was hidden in the Valley of the Kings' text, the Gospel of Judas. But the darkside stole the manuscript . . . however, we buried a copy in the spring tunnel at Megiddo."

Carlos wiped his palms down his face. "Okay. And we're supposed to take everybody with us?"

"Yes," Heru said flatly. "Time is quickly running out. Everyone here has a role." He spun on Inez and pointed to Ayana. "Only she is small enough to get into the crevice that houses the sacred dagger." He leveled a blade at Dan's parents. "Rabbi will come to them to lead them through the streets of Jerusalem. They will remember the way from their pilgrimages and fluently speak the language that you stumble over. They will get entry to places you cannot easily pass. But you, Carlos, must focus on *Kupigana Ngumi Aha*."

"Whoa, whoa, whoa," Carlos said, now walking in an agitated circle. "Hand-to-hand Kemetian martial arts with hombre's worst demon, using a dagger? Not a long blade to put a little body distance between me and—"

"It must be dead aim in the heart, and to do that, you must use the form of grappling and boxing used by Kemetian priests for felling the unholy." Heru turned to look at Damali. "*Ma'at Akhw Ba Ankh* is your weapon, Queen."

"Meditation and breathing? While my husband does hand-to-hand combat with the Thirteenth, I'm supposed to just chill and deep breathe—with a baby in the tunnels and a civilian couple trying to run through the streets that will send all of Hell after them?" Damali raked her locks. "I have much respect, don't get me wrong . . . but let's just say this strategy has the ring of real crazy to it."

★   ★   ★

Confused, the team looked around at the barren hill that was no more than a vast, crusty ruin site. Completely razed, the rock-studded terrain belied the fact that twenty-seven metropolises and the center of significant trade and commerce had passed through the gates here at one time in history. Just seeing a past cultural epicenter that was thought to be the center of the then-modern world reduced to dust gave every person on the trek pause.

"I know your Neteru homeboy was busy and all, and did us a favor by letting you save your energy, C . . ., but couldn't he have just dropped us off in the tunnel?" Yonnie shook his head as they searched for the southwest section of the mound that was supposed to house the tunnel entrance.

"In case you hadn't noticed," Rider fussed, kicking stones out of his path as he hiked up his M-16 shoulder strap. "Easy, straightforward, any of those adjectives, just erase them from your vocabulary when dealing with the Light. They like to err on the side of the mysterious."

"Do me a favor, Jack Rider," Marlene said, giving him a hard glare. "Blaspheme on your own time when alone, huh? I'm not trying to get anybody smoked by a lightning bolt because you're having a bad hair day. We got some real important folks back. I'm grateful."

"Okay, okay, Mar, I'm sorry," Rider said, jogging to catch up with her. "You don't think they'd really send a lightning bolt for an offhanded comment, do you, Mar, seriously?" He glanced around and tugged on her arm. "For real, because I was just joking."

As Marlene turned to answer Rider with a smile, a huge fire-ball tore across the sky.

"Get down!" Carlos shouted, and then created an energy dome over the group using his shield of Heru.

The impact of the blast sent up clouds of dust and rocks fly-ing like razor-sharp pieces of shrapnel that pelted the shield. The ground beneath them violently quaked, and the moment it stopped, machine-gun report echoed in the distance.

Mike turned his head to the side, listening like a giant hunt-ing dog while he body-shielded Inez and Ayana. "You hear that?" He lifted his head to stare first at Yonnie on his flank and then Carlos, who was a couple of feet away.

"Gotta be an American team," Yonnie said. "Talking about, 'it's on to the brink of dawn.'"

Carlos lowered the shield, glanced around quickly, and held his fist up. "Let me—"

"Yo!" a female voice shouted in the distance. "Get out of the open, people. The Berserkers are on the move!"

"Dat's Miss Quick," Ayana said, talking around her thumb. "She took us to the mountains."

"Go, go, go!" Damali shouted, scrambling civilians and push-ing the team from behind.

Carlos had the front, she had the back, sandwiching the team between them for maximum safety as they ran the treacherous two hundred yards.

But every instinct within her told her something else had happened. Heru's appearance was so out of the blue, so very, very strange—the Kings and Queens were gone, otherwise en-gaged? They'd raised a crown prince? They'd brought the east and west together and had left Guardians stationed in other parts of the world for later?

Familiar Guardian faces came into focus as she ran, pushing the group to be sure they got everyone into the tunnels alive. New York, Detroit, Chicago, D.C., Atlanta, L.A., she almost wept to see who'd made it, just as much as it broke her heart to see who hadn't.

Then she saw them. Father Patrick. Father Lopez. Rabbi Zeitloff. Monk Lin. Imam Asula. The Covenant.

Carlos had stopped and turned, pushing past people to double back to stand by her side. They looked across the barren land in awe, and for what seemed like miles, all they could see was an army of saints. Hannibal rode in from the left flank, Adam and Ausar from the right. Steeds pawed the rock-hewn earth as Nzinga's and Eve's mounts joined the front line with Aset and her Amazon warrior sister. Seth pulled up next to Abel, as Heru rode in close to his father.

The ancient empires had risen, royal warriors in every hue, their regal carriage and wise, exotic eyes deep-set with intense knowledge. Larger-than-life, they loomed massive like their monuments, as though they'd stepped right out of the Egyptian hieroglyphics on their tombs and into the world.

Heru lifted his sword, touching it to Ausar's and Adam's, creating a silver trinity as he stared at Carlos. "Lead! The fifth seal has been broken! Today, once and for all, we dethrone the unholy!"

A Neteru war cry went up as every sword pointed to the ground and opened a fissure in the earth.

"Take me to Lilith's lair!" Eve shouted to Damali. "Together we shall stand victorious!"

"Get those civilians down in the tunnels, and seal it off with a prayer!" Damali shouted over her shoulder to the Guardians that stood transfixed.

"Now!" Carlos yelled, as a fire-snorting, winged steed came to him, ready for war. He mounted it when Nzinga caught Damali by her arm and swung her up high to take flight.

As she rose from the momentum of Nzinga's hard pull, the air around her became still. The sun felt close and bright, warming her face as all sound muted and her head dropped back.

Arms at her sides, she careened up, up, rocketing in a blur, and then somersaulted to face the earth, blade pointing toward it, wings pressed in tight to her body. Then Hell vomited.

Out from the cavern, millions of demon scorpions poured onto the landscape, causing steeds to rear, but united Neteru blades sent a scorching carpet of white light to incinerate them.

Her target remained the yawning pit of darkness that was growing as her hurtling body got closer to it. She saw Carlos look up at her, timing his descent with hers to avoid a collision— and then their energy locked. Both over the edge as one, an army flooded in behind them, slashing, burning, cutting at demon bodies, and severing screaming heads.

United blades delivered white-light mortar fire, blowing open levels, and sending the unholy into the sun. Phantoms, poltergeists, succubae, and incubi dissolved, slaughtered by the millions. Demon limbs littered the caverns, and innards-splattered rock walls dripped with demon gore. Neteru Kings went back-to-back with their Queens, gutting the entrance levels of the pit, and then razing the third and fourth levels by white-light infernos. Were-creatures in mangled transition were caught by dreaded sunlight. Hulking werewolves howled at the piercing beams that blinded and dismembered them, huge heads thudding to the burning floor in a sulfuric wash before combusting into putrid ash. The martyred fallen chased any fleeing demons into deep caverns, routing them out, knowing they could never be held captive again.

But the deeper Damali and Carlos dove, the quieter it got, until soon it became apparent that Hell had emptied onto the earth, en masse.

Damali and Carlos dropped into an empty Vampire Council Chamber. Thrones were gone. The pentagram-shaped table was gone. The doors had been left wide open with no fanged crests or hooded messengers. Harpies were nonexistent. Transporter bats were careening up and out of the vaulted ceilings. The Neterus looked at each other—Carlos grabbed Damali's forearm and gave her a heave to ride with him on the back of his mount as the huge white steed reared and opened its massive wingspan, spooked.

"Punk bitches moved." Carlos glanced around at Hannibal, Adam, and Ausar, who'd caught up to them with Eve and Aset.

Eve released a war cry of frustration and pointed her blade toward the floor, sending multiple pulses of white-light rage into it. "Then open the Devil's lair—I've always wanted to meet that sonofabitch!"

A dispatch of warriors circled back with Nzinga. "The warrior angels said to retreat. Something is wrong," Nzinga said breathlessly. She pointed to the vaulted ceiling, breathing hard as the light began to diminish above them. "You two must leave now!"

"Where's the sunlight?" Damali said quietly.

Carlos kicked the sides of his steed. "We're out!"

Rock and thick, grasping roots with tendrils of dark webbing began to pull the earth back together. Combined Neteru blade pulses were the only thing that opened the quickly closing passageway out above them before the earth snapped shut.

Damali and Carlos hit the ground hard as their mount's leg got caught in the fissure as it sealed. Warriors surrounded the shrieking white horse, trying to keep the panicked animal from beating its wings and cracking bones while it pawed the earth. Furious Neterus shot the ground with blue-white novas attempting to free it. Then, suddenly, something pulled hard from the underside of the earth, sending blood splatter from the animal's mouth and nose as its hide peeled up its back. Hannibal leapt forward and beheaded the creature under the fast-moving eclipse to put it out of its misery, and then spat on the ground in frustration.

"The sun is going as black as sackcloth," Aset murmured, gazing directly into the eclipse as the ground began to rumble. "And the moon is bloodred in the sky, now seen with the sun."

Damali watched the meteor shower for a moment and then offered another verse as gale force winds began to swirl. "The stars of heaven fell to earth . . . and the fig tree cast her untimely fruit."

"And the heaven departed as a scroll when it is rolled together," Carlos muttered in disgust. "When did these motherfuckers get the seal, that's what I want to know?"

Adam and Ausar stared at him.

"Does it matter, young brother?" Ausar said, touching his blade to Carlos's. "We fight until the last man stands."

@ CHAPTER ELEVEN

Carlos never had a chance to respond. As complete darkness fell over their armies the sound of Ayana's high-pitched scream told him that his worst nightmare had come true.

Pure darkness had coalesced a hundred yards from the water tunnel entrance, almost seeming to be reaching down into it to pluck Guardians out of it. All he could determine was, either the prayer barrier hadn't gotten laid down fast enough, or when the team hid, the site wasn't cleared. Not knowing twisted his mind and practically seized his heart—if anything happened to the innocents on his watch . . . if anything happened to his brothers' wives . . .

A child had scrambled to freedom with machine-gun report behind her. The other Guardian teams were on fire, fighting like every man and woman was ready to make this place their Masada—their last stand.

His team went ballistic; Big Mike was diving headlong into untold numbers of beasts; Damali was in forward motion to save the child; Inez was swallowed by a wall of darkness. Marlene's yell cut through the night. Mounted Neterus tried to encircle Damali to keep her from what was clearly a suicide mission, but

Damali would not be hemmed in . . . and then something fragile within him snapped.

His wife turned toward him, her eyes glowing white. Everything felt like it was suddenly happening in slow motion. That same fragile cord had apparently popped within her, too. A black claw reached out for the child and then exploded as Ayana's voice hit a decibel beyond his range of hearing.

Furious transporter demon bats lost sonar navigation, crashing into one another and attacking their own in a feral frenzy. Gargoyle-bodied Harpies became instantly disoriented by the light-frequency of the sound as the voice of pure innocence turned them one upon the other in vicious attacks that culled their numbers.

Carlos released a Neteru war yell, fangs lengthening, silver sight scorching everything in its wake. Battle bulked, his arms and legs felt as though forged from steel cable, his night vision pure laser, his intent singular—save the baby.

Every footfall felt like it took an eternity to propel him forward, yet it was only seconds in real time. Save the child— Ayana locked into his focus. Her face was his visual mantra.

Warriors slashed and cut their way forward as the darkness filled in all around them. And then he heard Damali's breaths above the din. Slow, individual inhalations and exhalations of *Ma'at Akhw Ba Ankh* separating out her signature from the pure chaos of wanton battle.

Opalescent light around her broke the oppressive darkness that was closing in like its own entity. The luminous aura created a guidepost, bathing a thirty-foot circumference around her in scorching white light. Demons fried, popped, and sizzled, screaming to their deaths while her powerful aura shielded human Guardians and gave them a living lighthouse in the darkness.

Damali opened her mouth and released a long, sustained, nasal cry that sounded almost like a cross between a muezzin call to prayer and the harmonic sound lines of the dreamtime shaman.

The sound hit Carlos like a depth charge, arched his back, stripped sanity from his brain, and sent him airborne into pitch-blackness. He couldn't see what he killed, not because he was night-blind, but because he was moving too fast. Soon his sensory precision adjusted to bring him flashes of awareness from the vibration within each entity he slaughtered. He could tell humans from that which he dismembered by their aura of light and lack thereof. If it didn't shine, it had to die.

Icy cold entrails filled his hands. Gook splattered his face, sending sulfur up his nose. Demon legions had formed, legions had been decimated. Neterus and armies of the Light cut their way through the erupted contents of the Sea of Perpetual Agony while the sky rained brimstone and angels charged.

Covenant clerics appeared, fighting back-to-back with Neteru Guardians, keeping the living alive, circling the child and civilians in protection. Carlos's gaze swept across the bloodied battlefield. His wife had stopped running and slashing demons with her Isis blade to open her arms under a shaft of inner light, her sword lifted, pulling down rays from the sky, and exploding out a white-light nova carpet from where her feet met the ground.

Suddenly colored shafts of light could be seen in the distance, each of her Guardian sisters lit to produce a hue and harmonic that blended into Damali's. The genius of Atlantis and Marlene's and Pearl's words stabbed into his mind; his wife had become a living crystal, the main pyramid that drew down Divine light and refracted it to her sisters.

Their light shafts gave human warriors cover and night vision, incinerating any demons that came near in a one-way shield of energy that allowed projectiles out and none to come in. Gathered in a semicircle, pushing back armies of darkness as they advanced from the mouth of the tunnel entrance, they were a walking light and sound weapon. Neterus and angelic forces boxed in the demon legions from the flanks and rear. Hell was surrounded. Let the total annihilation begin!

Carlos slashed his way forward as he ran toward the child. Then Ayana was at Damali's side, protected by Father Patrick wielding a Templar blade. The small angel from Nod body-shielded the child, too. Sara and Hubert were here?

He could only process what he saw next in flash-frames of bewildered consciousness. The longer Damali held the note, the stronger the beams of light became. The stronger he became. The harder the Neteru Councils fought . . . the more determined the armies of martyrs were.

Big Mike surfaced from a pile of werewolves and Level Five were-demons, arms bulging, holding bodies by the throat. His old werewolf fang wound across his knuckles was bleeding. A section of the deceased, Brazilian were-human Guardian team leapt out of the morass of bodies with appendages in their jaws. If ever there was a squad that had given their lives in the name of On High, it was Kamal and his men. For a few seconds Carlos watched, rapt, as their translucent spiritual energy deftly slipped between Mike and fatal harm, fearlessly fighting with him, death no longer their issue.

Carlos quickly sent a blast from his sword to assist, but watched stupefied as Mike's rib cage cracked, his chest became more diesel, and he gutted a huge alpha male werewolf with his bare hands. Inez had thrown away her 9mm when the clip ran out and was charging toward her child, severing any demon appendage that reached for her with a bowie knife in each hand.

Imam Asula followed through with a machete, hacking demons out of her way, going in and out of astral projection to frustrate the unholy that couldn't destroy him.

Monk Lin's face melted into J.L.'s as phantom samurai blades filled J.L.'s palms. Krissy's harmonic tone bathed him in yellow-gold light, allowing that Guardian brother to actually lift and propel himself from it as though it were a solid object. Slain Tibetan monks, student protesters, and eons of innocents fell from the sky like golden-clad ninjas to decimate the darkness around them. Huge Amanthra serpents attacked, but J.L.'s double-sword agility and his fast-moving spiritual backup dropped heads quicker than a serpent's strike.

From his peripheral vision, Carlos caught a glimpse of the team's youngest male warrior. Bobby's body became awash in jade-green light, then X-rayed into dreamtime shaman images, his wizard skills locking into the sound of Jasmine's call, white lighting a swath through a legion of scythe-bearers. An Aborigine army encircled the young couple in prayer sound lines, their Light-poisoned darts taking down targets of darkness until the ground smoldered.

Rider threw his head back and yelled as turquoise light folded him away into nothingness, releasing him behind unwitting vampires to blow their brains out. Native American wind chants blew in ghost riders wielding glowing battle-axes and Light tomahawks, taking heads as they cut through grounded demons that could not get airborne under the Light-frequency sound.

Padre Lopez moved in and out of the darkside's vampire columns, a phalange of holy water blinding them as he flung last rites with a hard gaze. Nubian warriors melted up from the earth as druid warriors melted out of the stones. Kemetian ground troops rode out of splinters of Light on golden chariots.

Light hit their shields and spears and within seconds they'd broken formation to join with fallen Spartan armies to war against the darkness of ancient Rome.

Every male Neteru Guardian's past wounds, every weakness he'd owned, now surfaced with the harmonic tone echoing through the war zone. But those old darkside-inflicted injuries were no longer a liability; this time they were a source of strength. Carlos saw it with his own eyes, old wounds that should have crossed a man over to the darkside, the Light was now using it to reinforce their warriors—just like Damali had said. If he made it through this battle, he would never question her again. He spun and took off the head of a massive demon Roman soldier with one swipe of his blade, ducked to avoid a mace, and then halved the foolish entity that had swung it.

A ground blast dropped Jose, who was so battle-crazed that he stepped beyond a pool of protective light. Before Carlos could get to his Guardian brother, Yonnie covered Jose's body, only to be rushed by huge international transport demons. Carlos tore toward his fallen men, but Val's red energy flowed over Yonnie, her voice a sustained chord of deep sensuality. Yonnie lifted his head, eyes gleaming black, holding attacking messenger demons paralyzed in the bands of crackling energy that radiated from his fingertips.

Confused demons genuflected, hesitating too long as they mistook the camouflaged Yonnie for a Council-level vampire of their own. Yonnie slapped Jose five as he pulled him up from the ground and an orange rush of energy claimed Jose from Juanita's tonal wail, putting fangs in Jose's mouth.

"My line brother, let's do this shit!" Yonnie whooped.

"My councilman, my line brother," Jose said through fangs, whipping out a fresh 9mm loaded with hallowed earth shells.

The two Guardians locked arms and took a running whirl to

become a huge black tornado emitting a black Vampire Council charge and bullets, slaying everything in their wake.

Nearby roars made Carlos pivot, missing a flying demon barb to his head, only to see that Shabazz had upper and lower canines presented, his dreadlocks lifted in blue adrenaline static, hands a razor-blur of instant death. Kamal and Hubert from Nod were right at his side. In the distance Carlos could see Light forces and winged cavalries rolling over dark legions, practically wading now through ash.

Marlene had worked her stick so mightily that she stood in ashes that reached her shins, white-light heat rippling down her locks and keeping entities back. Slave ship chants surrounded her, along with the chants from Trail of Tears captives, and the cries of concentration camp victims—all were now replenished with fluorescent vitality as they fiercely fought against imperializing powers of evil, devastating their ranks.

Dan was covered in a purple haze, his tactical energy rolling out in concentric circles, incinerating demons in a depth charge that shook the earth. Peoples from native lands too numerous to count stood with him, their shackles raised, their indignation against injustice a powerful force that lit the region as they lifted their fists and their collective cries exploded demons beyond the hillside.

Marjorie was a madwoman, magnetizing demons to lift and send into the path of Berkfield's single pump shotgun shell to the head. It was as though the two were playing coordinated target practice, and the only thing missing was Berkfield's cry "Pull!" A sea of clerics surrounded them from every nation and every religion; all those persecuted in the name of the Most High now stood their ground to obliterate dirty emperors, Inquisition participants, barbaric clerics, and dirty politicians who had innocent blood on their hands.

Breathing hard, and glancing around, the teams slowed as an eerie quiet settled upon them in the howling wind. The lighthouse Guardians stopped harmonizing; nothing blew across the landscape but demon ash. Sulfur rose from the ground and wafted away in spirals. Heaven yawned open her charcoal-gray clouds and suddenly shafts of light, which seemed like a million flashbulbs, had gone off all at once, pulled the martyred off the battlefield. Angels nodded and swiftly followed their battalions to a victorious retreat. But Adam, Eve, Ausar, and Aset rode forward with Hannibal and nearly the full Council of Neteru Kings and Queens. Never before had Carlos seen them so fatigued. Their bodies were dirty, exhausted, but bloodlust was still in their eyes.

"Go," Ausar commanded. "Heru and Adam's sons are at the new front, holding off an onslaught with our Amazon Queens and Nzinga's warriors. We have done well and it will take them a long time to replenish what we have devastated. Solomon will guide you from here with Akhenaton. But you must move quickly to be in position before the Rapture."

Without another word, the Neteru Councils turned their mounts toward the darkness, their steeds opening massive white wings as they rode hard into the night.

A fresh wave of demons poured out of the trembling earth that quaked with fury. Berserkers lurched out of fissures that had begun to connect like ever-widening spiderwebs. Instantly, Damali drew a deep breath, the light around her and her Guardian sisters lit quickly and then blacked out like someone had flipped a switch, and she scooped up Ayana as Val covered her back with a volley of arrow fire.

"Fall back!" Carlos hollered, assisting Guardians to get to the safety of the tunnels.

Warrior angels swooped down and blocked the Berserkers'

pursuit using blinding white light to hide the Guardians' retreat position, but huge chain and mace balls released like cannon fire behind them.

Never in his life had he or Damali been ordered to retreat that hard that fast in a battle, but there was more at stake this time than ever before. They'd literally cleaned out Hell, and now what was left of it was topside.

Clerics' spirits sealed the retreating team in protective prayers that rendered them temporarily invisible to the darkside as they fled. Covenant forces ran down into the tunnels first, ensuring their safety as angels drove back the hordes of beasts. But he still didn't understand why, with all the military support out there, the Neteru Councils had pulled back. Although he'd never question them, his expression must have transmitted his confusion to his wife.

"The darkside is saving their ruling Vampire Council strength for the final battle," Damali said privately, catching her breath for a moment on the long descent down the wooden steps inside the tunnel shaft.

Carlos looked up at the prayer-shielded opening guarded by angels. Bloodlust had definitely affected his strategic thinking. If the Antichrist hadn't been revealed yet, and the Messiah hadn't come yet to step to that rat-bastard, then this was only phase one. And if he remembered his biblical texts correctly, the martyrs would go home and be given final rest, peace, and joy . . . scraping throughout the Armageddon wasn't that—so, yeah, it made sense that after this one assist so that everybody could be vindicated, the Light was taking them home. That meant, most likely, from this point forward, he and the squads would have to rely on their own skills, some random angelic intervention, and the Neteru Councils. But full-scale armies of Light, maybe not. Deep.

Too winded to speak, Carlos gave Damali a quick nod and tried to retract his fangs for the sake of Ayana, who kept her little face pressed to Damali's shoulder.

"Didn't you notice that not one Vampire Councilman was on the battlefield—and that isn't like Vlad's army," Damali added, still winded and holding Ayana high up in her arms while hustling the combined teams to safety. "The Thirteenth leads them, and we need that sucker's name and a dagger to put him down hard. Without it, they can go like this forever. We kill them and they replenish their forces. We have to hit their leadership, the guys that can reanimate and make more . . . the brains behind the brawn, just like old times, Carlos."

All he could do was nod. What she was saying was strategically sound. Adrenaline mixed with testosterone had made him temporarily insane.

The Unnamed One stared at the war-room map, watching his armies being decimated. He made a tent with his fingers in front of his mouth as his Vampire Council sat in silent terror awaiting his response.

"They have finally gotten the courage to rout every demon from Hell. Bold. Unpredictable . . . and so very modern-era Neteru." He stood, allowing his impressive leather wingspan to cast a shadow over the table as his withering, black, glowing gaze slowly studied the faces before him.

Lilith didn't blink, assessing her chances for an escape if things turned deadly. Judging from her husband's cool demeanor and his choice to present fangs and leather bat wings rather than his normal handsome image and gleaming raven feathers, it did not bode well.

She glimpsed Sebastian without ever moving her head or eyes. He was trembling, trying to take shallow sips of air so that their Dark Lord couldn't hear him breathe. But he didn't need to worry, unless he made a fatal false move. He'd done as much as could be expected—working feverishly behind the battlefield lines, reanimating demons as they fell, replenishing the troops as fast as evilly possible. Those felled by a blade of Light or Neteru sword were history, and even the Devil himself had to concede to certain supernatural laws.

Nuit was golden now. He'd brought her husband his cherished missing seal after millennia, and although she would one day pay the ruthless bastard back . . . it would not be today. She would give credit where credit was due. However, Vlad had cause to worry. Lucrezia got a pass from her husband's treachery, as well as her own deft handling of poisoning the human population's food and water sources. Elizabeth was on very shaky ground. As for her own longevity, her ability to continually nourish the heir and to give her husband insight about what made the current living Neterus tick ensured that.

Her husband began a leisurely stroll around the table. Every vampire around it stopped breathing.

"We have had minor border breaches in the past, but none so thoroughly devastating as this one." He placed his hands behind his back as he stopped briefly behind each councilman's chair in a silent threat, terrorizing them by his sheer presence near them. "They came to my door, Level Seven, walked right through your Council Chambers . . . and no one has a suggestion about our next steps?" He roamed to the war board and stood staring at it with his back to the assembled vampires. "The losses of my legions are incalculable at this time. When the fifth seal was broken, according to what is written in Revelation, martyrs were to be taken up—*period*."

He spun, fangs glistening, his voice rising to a thunderous roar on the last word of his sentence. "The only thing that could have inspired martyrs to participate in all-out warfare after a full Neteru Council Light-devastated my realms was that they were galvanized and emboldened by a *living* Neteru team. Hope is dangerous; it is a virus that must be stamped out in the end of days! Human hope, love, compassion, empathy, I want it routed out! Wiped from the face of the planet! There's only one way to do that, and that's to show these warriors, and anyone who would follow them, that they are mortal. I want the pregnant female found, gutted, and whatever is in her womb ground into a black ink spot under your boots."

Nods of agreement immediately followed the command and eyes lowered in submission.

"These two have rushed my hand since they were born," the Unnamed One grumbled. "I was not prepared to unleash my Thirteen until after the Rapture. But, now, to ensure that the resources of the Berserker armies will not be vanquished, allowing time for us to rebuild for the period of Tribulation where we will grow strong and my heir will rule, I must place them under the capable leadership of my most cherished."

His gaze narrowed on Vlad. "I want you to rebuild the human army of my followers, those living and whose souls I own, as a secondary layer of protection around my heir's interests." Sending his dark-current gaze toward Elizabeth, he leaned across the table. "Make yourself useful, or you will be cannon fodder for my son." As he drew back, his expression mellowed as he gazed at Lucrezia. "Your father, Pope Alexander, has been raised and is in position. Finish the job on the currently installed."

"Yes, my darkness," Lucrezia said, prostrating herself against the table.

"Job well done, Fallon . . . but do not let that go to your head. You are only as good as your last game, and I want the

Neterus. I believe you are the only one here capable of finding them."

"I exist only to do your bidding," Fallon said, prostrating himself against the gleaming surface.

The Devil chuckled. "I like a man who has clear priorities. . . Vlad, you could learn from him." Whipping his attention to Sebastian, he sneered. "Not particularly bright, but hardworking. I want my ranks replenished. I only have scattered forces topside now, there is only Hell on earth, no Hell subterranean, and I do not like being so exposed."

"But this is a perfect arrangement," Lilith said with a sly smile, attempting to draw her husband's attention away from his desire to murder one of her valuable council members.

"You test my patience with riddles today, Lilith."

"No, on the contrary," she murmured seductively. "I think this sends a clear message of confidence. We are not lurking in the darkness, hiding from you-know-who in the caverns, any longer. We are out in the open, confident of our win . . . Hell running rampant topside. We do not have to seek the darkness— we are the darkness and brought it to the surface with us." She glanced around and smiled. "I like the new office décor. I like its layering system and it goes very deep underground into our tunnel system, should we need a last-minute escape . . . and, darling, it is heavily fortified. This man-made facility was a wondrous choice you've made. Allow me to do some interior redesign as Fallon and Vlad search out the Neterus. I'm close to our heir's healing dens here, too." She stood and went to him as his eyes flickered with pride and the subtlest hint of pleasure.

"Think of it," she murmured, stroking his ego in front of his powerful inner circle of commanders. "The Light was so desperate that they threw their own martyrs at a war zone. To me, that represents weakness, not military strength. Once we assassinate

the Neterus and destroy any last glimmer of hope humankind has
for salvation during the Tribulation, what remains of the human
population is completely ours."

He gave her a sly half-smile as she passed him to go stand by
the globe, glancing around his new accommodations. "You'd
better hope you are right," he said with a casual chuckle. "Otherwise, know that I will kick your ruthless ass."

Dirty, bloody, nicked, and bruised warriors hustled down the
two-hundred-and-ten-foot tunnel to the main spring reservoir.
Breathing hard, some helping the Weinsteins, Monty, and Delores, they gathered by the underground freshwater source,
awaiting instructions.

The sound of constant bombing overhead made small rocks
and gravel fall. People cringed against the larger blasts, but began to relax as the sound of war overhead began to move farther
and farther away.

"Roll call!" Carlos shouted, his gaze quickly assessing the
group for casualties.

"New York team, intact," Phat G yelled out.

"Atlanta in da house, all present and accounted for!" Quick
said, stepping forward and then back into the group.

"D.C. . . . at least what's left standing from before," Cordell
said, his voice flat, sadness weighting his words. "Philly team took
the kids from that compound up into the mountains and is
guarding them there. Last I saw, everybody made it past the flood
and the contagion. Didn't lose nobody this time on my watch."

"We're good," Craig said. "D.C., we'll rebuild."

"Cool, Cordell. Thanks, man," Carlos said. "Thanks for having our backs, Craig. Y'all were crazy out there."

"Yeah, we appreciate everything you gave and sacrificed,"

Damali said, her tone gentle as she stared at the elderly seer and then glanced at Craig.

"Detroit, still standing," Alicia yelled out.

"Chicago, representing," Barbara hollered, jumping up so people could see her in the back.

"L.A. . . . just one, but I'm still strong," Leone said, leaning against the wall.

"Philly in da house," Quick said, winded and then pounded Sasha's fist.

"Philly had to represent," Sasha said in a breathless rush.

"And you've still got one bloody Scot who will ride the dragons back down into Hell with you, sir!"

"Good," Carlos yelled.

Carlos and Damali gave each other a glance. The Midwest and Texas teams didn't make it. Most of those Guardians were lost in the battle of Cuernavaca at La Casa in Morelos, Mexico, along with the Brazilian team that helped them against Cain.

"Net squad?" Carlos looked around.

"Everybody's good, C—civilians ain't even nicked," Big Mike hollered from the rear.

Carlos's shoulders slumped with relief as Damali came to stand beside him, holding on to Ayana.

"We've got the baby, 'Nez," Damali called out.

"I know," Inez called back to her, moving to the front of the group. "Why you think I still ain't up top fighting and hunting for her?" Inez opened her arms for Ayana to fill. "Come on, pumpkin," she said softly, kissing Ayana's cheek to take her from Damali. But Ayana just clung tighter to Damali's neck.

"Aw, boo, don't you want to go to Mommy?" Damali said, trying to coax the youngster to let her go, not wanting to hurt Inez's feelings.

"Let her stay with you for a little bit," Inez said after a moment, dropping her arms, clearly too battle-fatigued to take offense. "My kid is a quick study. She's got the safest seat in the house right now, D. Bet half of us wish we could do the same thing."

Nervous, post-battle laughter filtered through the group, opening a release valve for the tension as Guardians pounded one another's fists and slapped one another five.

"There're new team members the Neteru squad never met," Carlos said in a loud, booming voice, casting a gaze over the large group. "Don't know your names, but thank you. Will get everybody acquainted as soon as we get basic logistics out of the way."

A tall, handsome, olive-toned man with a rush of dark brown hair and wearing ripped, olive fatigues parted the group with his wide, athletic shoulders. He reached out a hand to shake with Carlos and Damali and offered them a strong grip. His face was smudged, his piercing gray eyes hard, but his voice was welcoming.

"Hi, I am called Tobias. I'm the lead tactical on the Middle Eastern team—Israeli-born. My wife, Habiba, she is a seer, Palestinian-born, and I will introduce the others . . . from all over: Syria, Turkey, Kuwait, Iraq, Iran, Yemen, Egypt, Oman, Pakistan, United Arab Emirates, Afghanistan, all over," he said, waving a thickly muscled arm. "Muslims, Christians, Jews, Greek Orthodox, Armenian . . . we know this holy land and are here to do our part at the end. Peace must come. Innocent people are dying, while those in power manipulate war for profit."

"Good to meet you, brother," Carlos said, giving Tobias's hand a hearty shake. "Your team was awesome out there, and this ain't our yard . . . we could use strong guides and serious warriors at our backs."

"And we could use men and women of honor like your team at our fronts. Our mission is united. We are all humans who bleed red blood," Tobias said proudly.

"Couldn't have said it better, man," Carlos replied, giving him a warrior's embrace. "It's all good."

"It is, how you say, all good."

A beautiful woman with large, exotic, Bedouin eyes stepped forward. Her hair was covered, but she wore army fatigues. "We are honored and have heard much through the underground networks about the Neteru team and its legendary Neterus. You all give us hope . . . you even travel with your parents and children. Families beyond soldiers." She turned and gazed at Damali and then suddenly hugged her. "You have done what we all hope to do, live unmolested like normal people, if there could be peace."

"We all hope for that," Damali said, returning Habiba's warm embrace, and squeezing Ayana between them. "You are not alone. Everybody who's sane in the world wants that."

Carlos glanced around and then settled his line of vision back on Tobias. "Is the water source safe? Because if so, we need to water our teams, close up some of these demon nicks before we have any internal group problems, and figure out how to keep nonwarriors safe. Don't know if you heard, but we're looking for an ancient manuscript down here, and gotta go into Jerusalem into the tunnel system there."

"I can show you the tunnels in Jerusalem—but the city has been severely bombed, things are not what they once were there. It is dangerous, crawling with confused troops. Contagion is rampant. It would be best to take a small search party, rather than a full squadron to draw unwanted attention. However, I have never personally seen a manuscript here." Tobias pointed to the tunnel interior, sending his gaze around it with a puzzled frown. "The walls are iron ore . . . there isn't a place where it looks like someone dug into the walls to hide something old and fragile."

"The water is untainted, though. First things first," Habiba said, going to the edge of the reservoir and dampening the tip of her khimar. "Let the little one and your civilians drink." She came close to Damali and wiped Ayana's dirty face, but Ayana took the edge of the wet khimar and wiped Damali's pearl.

"Pearl doesn't like to be dirty," Ayana said quietly. "She doesn't like fighting and loud noises, and me neiver. But she wants to tell Aunt Damali where the book she's looking for is . . . you're nice and you're pretty."

With a look back at her mother and Damali, Ayana went to the female Guardian's arms.

"She's a seer," Habiba said in an awed rush.

"Yeah, a real serious one, too," Damali said proudly, taking up Inez's hand. "This is her mother." She nodded to Delores, who was leaning on Monty. "That's her grandmother."

"Three generations, all alive?" Habiba said, surprised, causing the Middle Eastern team to murmur appreciatively. "You are blessed."

"We are, indeed," Damali said, kissing Ayana's cheek.

Ayana gently tugged on Damali's hair. "Aunt 'Mali, Pearl wants to tell you somepfin, but she needs more water."

Damali smiled as the youngster took off her necklace. "She's too dirty, boo. You can't dip her in the drinking water . . . then all that demon gook will make people who need freshwater sick."

"Pour some on her den," Ayana said, frowning.

An Israeli Guardian from the rear tossed a canteen forward and those closer to Habiba passed it forward to her.

"Out of the mouths of babes," Damali said, holding her

necklace over the ground so that a clear stream of water could wash over it.

Within moments the pearl coughed, gagged, and sputtered. "Damali, oh, have mercy . . . that was horrific!"

Habiba and Tobias gathered in closer, mesmerized as their team members craned their necks to watch with the others.

"Yeah . . . that was pretty bad," Damali admitted. "I'm sorry you had to be a part of it."

"Quickly," Pearl said in a breathless wheeze, "gather your sisters around the water. Raise Atlantis down here."

"I don't understand." Damali glanced around at the female Neteru Guardians, and they stepped forward at the ready, but not sure what they were supposed to do.

"The lights, the lights," Pearl squealed anxiously. "Bring the lights together over the holy water, so you can raise what has been submerged!"

Reading each other's thoughts quickly, the Neteru Guardian females joined hands in a semicircle around Damali.

"The Scot," Pearl called out. "The stoneworker, Heather. You must raise the stone at the center. Ask the other Scot for help."

"Yo, Dragon Rider," Carlos called out. "An assist on some stonework."

"I will raise Stonehenge, if you need that, too, just say the word." The group opened so Dragon Rider could get through. She landed a hand on Heather's shoulder and Heather turned to hug her.

"Thank you," Heather said, giving her a quick hug before going back into formation.

Marlene walked close to the edge of the cistern, staring into the pool, her walking stick in one hand starting to glow, and the canteen that had been passed to her in the other hand held midair. "We ask the ancestors for permission to begin," she said, pouring libations as she began to wave a white-light wand of energy over the water. "We ask for protection, guidance, and strength as we complete these important missions, Ashe."

Marlene lifted her stick at the same time Damali lifted her Isis. White light passed between both women, one a pillar to the past, one a pillar to the future, with each color of the chakra system slowly covering the Guardians between them. Each woman's aura expanded, spilling over the edge of the pool into the water, and soon both Heather's and Dragon Rider's eyes rolled into the backs of their heads. Small beads of perspiration dampened their foreheads and made their clothing stick to their bodies. The sound of stone grating against stone filled the tunnel, as though their efforts were moving a huge slab off something.

Soon the surface of the water broke with a large, square-shaped object that floated to the edge of the cistern as the colored lights dimmed.

Carlos stooped down and fished the badly tarnished object out of the water, holding what seemed to be a black box in his grasp. He set it down on the rock floor and stared at it, burning away the black tarnish.

Pure silver gleamed as thousands of years of stain slowly melted from the deep, Kemetian etchings to reveal a sealed box that had been soldered shut, containing the same markings as on Damali's Isis blade.

"Open it," Damali said, squatting down with Carlos. "Somebody went to a lot of trouble to seal that manuscript in a box, surround the waterproofed box with blessed symbols, and then hide it in holy water for a coupla thousand years."

"You telling me," Carlos said, trying to sense where the precious contents were and therefore where he could go in. "This has Akhenaton written all over it, a Neteru King's silver mind box."

Team members gawked but no one said a word as Carlos

found the solder seam and slowly, gently, sent a penetrating silver gaze around it. Wiping his forehead with the back of his forearm, he carefully lifted the top. Inside was a large scroll made of papyrus on a silver rod with indecipherable hieroglyphics.

"Now what?" Carlos said, releasing his breath in frustration. "I know the old dark throne stuff, but not this. The Kings and Queens are long gone, and I can't read—"

"We can . . . I can," Damali said, touching his arm.

Marlene knelt beside Carlos and nodded. "You saw it in their eyes on Monty's yacht. This is why I said, let the process unfold. They have all the languages of Light within them—the languages of ancient wisdom—they being feminine energy of air and water."

"Mar, you are so deep you scare me sometimes," Carlos said with earnest reverence. He looked up at Damali. "Be careful, boo . . . from my old days I know that having the name of a powerful demon in your head ain't nothing to play with. In fact, the more I think about that, the more I'm not down with that."

"He has a valid point," Marlene said, standing. "I want everyone in here to turn around, except Carlos." She grabbed Carlos's hand and then Damali's. "Husband and wife, you are of one mind, one flesh. Give him the language and then let him open the scroll. Damali, do not touch it. You're carrying precious cargo, and if this demon is the Unnamed One's most cherished, then this is a *bad* mofo. Understood?"

"You don't have to tell me twice," Damali said, backing away from the scroll.

Carlos sidestepped it, too, and came close to Damali, placing his hands on her shoulders. "You let me take this one for the team, all right, baby? Then, once I get a name in my head, I'll seal the box and submerge it again—and it can stay down there for another coupla thousand years, for all I care."

She nodded and melted into his embrace, laying her head against his shoulder. "You be careful messing with this stuff, Carlos. Promise me."

"I promise," he murmured, brushing her temple with a gentle kiss. "Now give it to me."

Damali closed her eyes, her hands sliding up his back until her palms fanned out against his shoulder blades. It so reminded him of the old days when this was a form of foreplay that he had to keep his mind focused on accepting ancient languages rather than reminiscing about the past. He felt her face smile and landed another slow kiss against her temple to let her know he remembered, too. Then her agile mind seized his hard, causing him to release a slow hiss of air between his teeth. It hurt so good, felt so good, and the information she began transmitting broke him out in a cold sweat.

Silver filled his irises as she pulled back from him and stared into his eyes. Damali looked at her husband hard to be sure the transfer was going directly to him and not accidentally sent to an innocent member of the group. But as Carlos's eyelids fluttered, she could see glowing silver etching in every language from a time before recorded history whirring by his pupils, and then came the hieroglyphics. She pulled out of the transmission with a hard snap—he had the other later languages from after Dante's time, had that from before. But they didn't have time to stay for all of that.

Carlos fell forward and caught himself, fangs ripping his gum line. "Damn, baby," he said in a private murmur, trying to quickly compose himself. "Couldn't have brought me out of it smoother than that? Do I treat you that way?"

She laughed softly and caressed his cheek. "I'm sorry, will make it up to you later."

"I'm gonna hold you to that." He waved her off. "Give me

some space, turn around with the others, and lemme see if I can get a name. Cool?"

He was glad that she didn't argue. The title of the scroll alone gave him the willies. *The Gospel of Judas.* Carlos shuddered and lifted an end of it to begin skimming the text. It wasn't long before he quickly rolled up the scroll, slipped the lid on the silver scarab and symbol-covered box, sealed it, and flung it back into the deep reservoir.

"Is it okay if we turn around now?" Damali asked.

"Yeah, yeah," Carlos said, pacing back and forth along the water's edge. He had the heebie-jeebies and needed to chill out. Old dark throne memories were bludgeoning his mind as the name of Lucifer's most evil fought within the silver-lined space.

"You cool, C?" Yonnie called out, his gaze intense on Carlos.

"I was gonna ask you the same thing, baby," Damali said quietly.

"Yeah, yeah, I'm good, just a little freaked-out, but I'm glad I read it rather than you." He ran his fingers through his hair. "Would also make me feel a whole lot better if I knew where old Lu and his Vamp Council had relocated Hell."

"Oh, that's easy," Cordell said offhandedly, pushing off the wall. "They took over the Pentagon in D.C. Seen 'em do it."

CHAPTER TWELVE

Clean water, K rations, clean fatigues, and a place to lie down on pallets until the shelling stopped was what everyone needed. It was amazing to watch the human spirit at work—people from different languages and cultures all huddled together, trying to learn about one another, trying to socialize, sharing stories and pictures from pockets, playing with a friendly little girl, and honoring frightened elders as though they'd known one another all their lives. Differences melted away. It was so obvious to them all that pain was pain, joy was joy, love was love, and humanity was all connected by one source of Divine Light. Hope for the future was the fuel that kept them from giving up. Watching Ayana visit lap to lap offered them a glimpse of the tomorrow they'd never be sure they'd witness.

"In a little while, I'ma have to get with Tobias, and then me and him gotta get inside those tunnels in Jerusalem," Carlos said quietly as he leaned on an elbow next to Damali. "I just don't know about Heru's advice about taking the Weinsteins—and forget about taking Ayana into a potential demon hole to retrieve a blade. The couple is pretty shook up, but Ayana might be psychologically scarred for life behind everything that kid has seen . . . all of 'em have been through the wringer . . . and I don't want anything happening to that little girl or Dan's people, you feel me?"

"I'll consult Pearl again," Damali said quietly, her gaze trapping his. "As circumstances change, so do forecasts and predictions. Nothing is set in stone."

"Yeah, well, that's just the thing . . . it might really be in stone, or under stone, somewhere I can't see like that stone slab that Heather and Dragon Rider rolled away from that underwater burial chamber. This is Jerusalem, D. Old world and *everything* was done in granite, stone, marble, okay."

"Heather can't go," Damali said in a nervous rush under her breath.

"I know. I know," Carlos replied in a hard whisper. "I ain't trying to take her any more than I'm trying to take Frank and Stella, or Ayana for that matter. I really wish I could just go myself, not have to risk any Guardians getting near that thing, do the hit, and be out."

Damali gave him a blank look. "You are *so not* gonna go up against the Thirteenth by yourself, Carlos. Stop playing."

"Just a passing thought."

Her hand found the side of his jaw and she stroked the five o'clock shadow that roughly coated it. "*Please,*" she murmured, closing her eyes. "I know you don't want anyone's loss on your hands, but can't you try something that will give you all a fighting chance to get out of there in one piece?"

"Like what, baby? I've been going over this in my head and no matter who I recruit, chances are, they're not coming back."

"Then, I'll go," she said, withdrawing her touch from his cheek.

"That ain't gonna happen." He sat up and leaned against the hard wall.

"All right, then," she said quietly to keep their conversation private. "Maybe see if Dragon Rider will go with you?" Damali cupped his cheek. "If she travels with you posing as your wife . . . and Tobias and Habiba know the route, that's a small squad of specialized skills with no pregnancies or civilians in the mix. I'll be here to keep the teams safe on this end. Once you have a name and the dagger, you *all* get out of there . . . then we can figure out as a team how to get the target to come out of hiding."

"Yeah, I know," Carlos said, glancing around. "It all sounds so simple, so logical, but you and I both know it never works easy like that."

"I think you are right, Lilith," Nuit said, choosing his words carefully after the Dark Lord had left the war room. He stood slowly, looked around, and then walked to the war board rubbing his chin. "This is not idle, sycophant trivia to gain your favor or to kiss your lovely ass." He pointed to the Middle East. "What could they have possibly gained, personally, from taking their precious Neteru cargo there and exploiting all their forces in Megiddo . . . essentially blowing their loads, and then having nothing left to battle with?"

"What do they care?" Vlad said, standing to pace and nervously avail himself of a goblet of blood. "The Rapture is imminent. They will join the Neteru Councils in Mid-Heaven and become our nemeses from the astral plane, taking their unborn child into that realm—no different than Aset did with the birth of Heru. Why wouldn't it have been in their best interest to gut all of Hell and scatter her dark forces to the four corners of the earth, just like we'd scattered the twelve tribes of humanity?"

"I can see we are at philosophical odds, gentlemen," Lilith

said, pursing her lips, striding up to the war board to study it next to Fallon. "But you both bring up intriguing and very plausible points."

"Whether they turn left or right at this crossroads, Lilith," Sebastian said, demanding to be recognized, "I will ensure that, well before the dreaded Light-inspired event they call the Rapture, I will have replenished much of our forces."

"While I appreciate your charming attempt," Lilith said with a hiss, narrowing her gaze on him, "most of our casualties happened with weapons of Light, not the normal beheadings and such. If you study the ground, the ash, most of it contained unrecoverable losses. They even nuked the caverns, hence why we cannot return."

"Then I will raise for you whatever you ask of me, milady," Sebastian said in a forlorn tone.

Lilith's gaze softened as she glanced around the war room. "Things have indeed changed. I'm not sure I like the direction of that, either."

"Madame Chairwoman," Lucrezia said, her green eyes filled with dread, "I will also do the dark empire's bidding, but after these catastrophic losses, I am not sure what you would have me do?" She chewed her bottom lip as Lilith's paralyzing stare captured her. "After the Rapture, when we break the seventh seal to bring about the Great Tribulation . . . we will unleash six great plagues, yes? Could I be of service devising a poison for one of those?"

"Yes," Lilith said, drawing out the word and giving Lucrezia her full attention.

"Thunder and lightning, and earthquakes, in plague one," Lucrezia said, counting off the events on her fingers as she spoke. "Then that followed by hail and raining blood, then fire to burn away one-third of the trees and grass. The third plague, also called Wormwood, brings in the comet and mass destruction that will bring on human deaths by bitter waters. I could assist in making the waters bitter. From there, plague four, a third part of the sun and moon and stars will be smitten." Lucrezia let out a hard breath to blow a stray red curl off her forehead. "For all intents and purposes, any light left in the sky will go dark, permanently—not like this temporary condition now."

"Yes, yes," Lilith said, growing impatient. "We have been over this time and again. The fifth plague at our disposal will unleash smoke from the bottomless pit, otherwise known as Hell . . . and we'll send up demon scorpions and locusts to eat the flesh of humans for . . . oh, I don't recall exactly, but something like five or six months."

"What has any of this got to do with our problems at hand, Lucrezia?" Elizabeth screeched leaning down the table, irate and impatient.

"I don't know," Lucrezia said coolly, "but I am a Borgia, of the House of Borgia, where politics and refined games of treachery are well beyond the average caste . . . perhaps this is why Fallon and I are so well suited for each other. But since the Light allowed their martyrs to assist in battling our force, blurring the lines, and did not immediately remove them after the fifth seal was broken, hence allowing them to interfere with our breaking of the sixth seal . . . perhaps we could make the one thing that humans need more than anything else, beyond air, become prematurely bitter? Water, milady. The Light was late in taking up their martyrs so perhaps we can be early in poisoning the water?"

Nuit chuckled softly and returned to the table with a goblet of blood for his wife, "Brava, my dear." He took up her graceful hand and kissed its cool, porcelain surface. "This is why I love her so . . . her mind is an amazing instrument of deception. Vlad, I suggest that rather than brute force, you employ your wife to the more refined arts."

Vlad and Elizabeth responded with a violent hiss as the Nuits laughed and dismissed them with a wave of their hands.

"It might help if all of Heaven was very, very busy sorting and saving the dead and dying," Lilith said in an approving tone. "Humans cannot live long, especially in arid climates, without their elixir of life."

Lucrezia offered Lilith a deep curtsy of respect and then turned her fawning gaze on Fallon Nuit. "Mr. Chairman," Lucrezia said, noting her husband's newly elevated status to rankle her competitors. "If the sixth and final plague that will alter the balance between our side and the Light is the release of the Thirteenth to call the four bound dark angels now shackled beneath the Euphrates . . . and those fallen angels would be able to call forth a fresh, new army, one not yet vanquished or turned into unrecoverable ash, numbering two hundred thousand thousand . . . or better stated, two hundred million—which matches the number of angels allegedly in Heaven . . . hmm."

Lucrezia placed a delicately painted French-manicured nail to her ruby lips for a moment as she stared at the world map. "Before I left to live happily ever after, I could envision a parting shot being the assassination of my archenemy's most trusted general." She turned to Vlad with a narrowed, mocking gaze. "You, sir, are not him."

Lilith's gasp sent a shiver through the assembled council. "That is *precisely* what I would do . . . and then I would bear my heir and set him upon my weakened rivals."

"I told you she was deliciously wicked," Nuit said with pride, his seductive gaze raking Lucrezia's body. "*Très bon, ma chérie.*"

Lilith swept to Lucrezia and held her face, kissing her deeply.

"I will send a dispatch to Lucifer at once. We may not know the Neterus' exact location, but we can place spies everywhere in search of them. We will monitor their movements, we will see if they have found out anything that could lead them to our most-cherished demon. I have been so consumed with niggling details that I had not even considered the sheer recklessness of such a plan . . . which fits their arrogant modus operandi perfectly."

Nuit touched both women's cheeks with a deeply satisfied smile. "And now, dear Lilith, do you see why I love her so?"

It was eerily quiet above them. The brutal shelling had stopped, but nobody trusted that as a sure sign of safety. Tobias knelt on one knee while reaching forward and using a bowie knife to draw in the loose gravel and dirt on the tunnel floor at the edge of the reservoir. Neteru Guardians had gathered around Tobias and his wife with Damali and Carlos, while the others waited, hanging back to hear the full scope of the plan once the lead team nailed down logistics.

"If you were told to go into the tunnels," Tobias said, etching in the ground, his intense gaze going between the drawing he made and Carlos, "you have miles of potential disaster." Tobias wiped perspiration from his forehead with the back of his forearm and then released a breath of frustration.

"You have not seen what has happened to Jerusalem," Habiba said sadly. "Military is everywhere—some don't understand . . . but also there are demon spies everywhere. Human pawns have been manipulated to keep innocent people away from the holy places . . . so if you try to enter the tunnels beneath *il-Mabka*, you could be shot or detained by a person who still has a soul."

"*Il-Mabka?*" Carlos glanced between the couple for clarity, trying hard to make his brain quickly sort through the volume of information within it.

"The Kotel," Tobias said, seeming impatient. "The Wailing Wall."

"Know it, been there," Carlos said, nodding as he immediately recognized the third name given to the holy site. "Now I understand why the Covenant clerics made us learn all the sites."

"It's also called the *Western* Wall," Damali said, emphasizing the word *Western*. "We're from the west."

Tobias and Habiba shared a look.

"The Western Wall is on the western flank of the Temple Mount," Tobias said cautiously. "It has the Western Stone, which is the largest piece of unbroken stone . . . about thirteen-point-six meters. It's massive . . . weighs they say five-hundred-and-seventy tons. That part of the wall is underground and heavily guarded."

"That's more than one western reference," Damali said. "Then oddly the weight of it was cut to weigh in at five hundred-and-seventy tons—which reduces to twelve . . . a holy number . . . because that reduces to three, the trinity? *And* it's heavily guarded. C'mon."

"I only wish that your Templar seer had been more specific," Tobias said, looking at Carlos and Damali. "You are talking about a long length of tunnel leading to one of the most bitterly disputed holy sites on the planet. The Temple Mount is built on a hill, but the side walls are hidden behind what is left of residential buildings on the north," he pressed on, beginning to draw again. "Then the southern portion of the west side is the Western Wall, which is only half-visible aboveground. If you enter from the southern end near the Kotel you can walk the tunnel's length and come out on the northern end to escape being trapped underground—but the tunnel passage is narrow in places."

"That's just it," Carlos said, glancing between Tobias, Habiba, and Damali. "Heru mentioned the Temple Mount. He said to ask Solomon and Akhenaton about this tunnel, so—"

"Well, it makes sense the reference to Solomon," Habiba said excitedly, holding the Neterus' gazes. "Solomon's Temple was first on that hill, but it was destroyed by the Babylonians."

"Lilith," Damali said, sucking her teeth and then standing for a second before she settled back down.

"We can only speculate," Tobias said calmly. "But it was overrun by Babylon. The second Temple was build by Herod after that, but then that was destroyed by the Romans with the rest of Jerusalem, which they razed to the ground, leaving only the Western Wall standing. This is why it is so sacred."

Carlos nodded and stood stretching his legs and back. "The clues are all there, I just hate riddles under pressure." He cracked his knuckles with his fist as Tobias, Habiba, and Damali stood. "Looking for a Roman dagger or sword or spear that pierced the side of Christ . . . reference to Roman destruction ties in— as does Heru telling me to ask Solomon, since the ground was originally broken there for his temple."

"Not to mention, an escape route to the north—we're from North America," Damali added. "I would try to get more from Pearl, but she's spent—just like all our seers are."

"Right," Carlos said, smoothing his palm over his hair. "They want me to go find it in Temple Mount, just not out in the open—because like Tobias said, that's a hot zone. Probably gotta have all sorts of ID to get in there, if it's open at all."

"You are correct, brother," Tobias said, leaning over to stretch the tension out of his back.

"But I do not understand why your guides would tell you to

go by way of tunnel," Habiba said, frowning. "It would be much easier to slip through the abandoned buildings, rather than be trapped—and there's no opening in the stone there that could hide such a relic you seek. The stone wall hasn't been chiseled. I have seen it so many times, I could close my eyes and see it now."

"That's just it, though," Carlos said slowly as awareness filled him. "Check it out. If a diversion was created aboveground, it would be far easier to do an energy fold-away into a place that's vacant. Dragon Rider is a class-A stoneworker from Scotland. Aboveground, she can't do her thing, leaning against the Wailing Wall in the open, since that's now off-limits. But if I get her in the tunnels, she might be able to get a GPS on where what we're looking for is hidden in the Temple Mount."

"Oh, boy, here comes the fun part—the diversion part," Rider said sarcastically, now standing as the other Neteru Guardians slowly got to their feet.

"Nah, man. Not this time. Full squad stays here as the fall-back position to be the front line of defense for innocents and our away teams. Just me and Dragon Rider are making this run." Carlos looked at Tobias and Habiba, and then at Dragon Rider. "You read the stones, and then I'm jettisoning you back here while I go in and then try to get back in one piece."

"Whoa, whoa, whoa," Damali said. "Since when was that the plan? Who's watching your back out there?"

"Next question I was gonna ask," Yonnie said, stepping forward. "C, didn't you feel that power boost while you was out there fighting . . . like they made another Chairman or something?"

Carlos gave Yonnie a look, pissed off that he'd let the cat out of the bag in front of Damali.

"Yeah," Carlos said flatly. "Got a dark supercharge that I'm not real happy about." He looked at Damali. "At first I thought it was from all the Light harmonics you all were generating . . . but—"

"Your eyes went black just like mine did, bro," Yonnie said, ignoring Carlos's vibe to chill. "Then we got stupid strong and ripped out everything's heart within a reach radius, so I ain't particularly mad about it." Yonnie pulled the toothpick out of his mouth. "Just for the sake of speculation, who you think it is?"

"We can worry about all that later," Carlos said in a low rumble, his gaze boring into Yonnie.

"Peace," Yonnie said with a sheepish grin. "Just kinda leaves you high, you know. But I'm good, I'm good, I'll come down in a minute—damn, we up against two Chair-level vamps?" Yonnie shook his head. "This gotta be a first. No wonder I feel like I do."

"Is that what happened out there?" Jose asked quickly, rubbing his jaw as he glanced at Rider. "*Dayum.*"

"Later," Carlos warned, feeling fangs near the edge of his gum line.

"Aw'ight," Yonnie said, pushing the toothpick he held between his fingers back into his mouth. "Sho' you right, not in mixed company. But I still got your back, man. Figure, me and you get the word on where whatever you need is to do the hit, blow into the Temple—"

"You must be clean," Tobias said quickly. "It is still a holy site, no matter what is going on all around it—this is inviolate holy ground. Ruin that and you could possibly tip the balance of power in this region to permanent darkness! We don't know what could happen." He looked between Carlos and Yonnie, suddenly frantic. "You cannot go in there like commandos and storm the place. All men must take a *mikvah*."

"A what?" Yonnie said, spitting out the old, worn toothpick he'd been gnawing and materializing a fresh toothpick in his mouth to begin slowly chewing on it.

"A ritual bath," Marlene said flatly. "See, this stuff I try to tell you guys isn't some mess I just made up out of thin air. It goes back thousands of years in every old culture!"

"Aw'ight, so we clean up and do the job," Mike said, looking around. "We got your back going in, C. At least let a couple of us go to watch your six."

"Dragon Rider must not be on her menses, if she enters," Habiba said quietly.

"I'm good." Dragon Rider gave Habiba the thumbs-up.

"But no man that has been with his wife even with the ritual cleansing can enter . . . choose warriors that have abstained from this for twenty-four hours, and with a ritual bath, you then will not disturb the hallowed ground." Tobias looked around. "I will go with you—I know the area, know the language, and know how to handle both conventional and supernatural weapons as a tactical."

"Oh, man . . . well, as to the whole abstinence thing . . ." Yonnie flipped the toothpick in his mouth with his tongue, and then shook his head as he leaned against the wall. "Then count me as a liability, bro."

Val looked off into the distance, seeming embarrassed enough to publicly slap him.

Damali briefly closed her eyes and spoke in a private murmur. "I'm betting that's why Heru said to take the Weinsteins and the baby." She let out a long breath and looked away from Carlos. "The Light always has a reason."

"I'm not taking the Weinsteins and definitely not Ayana." Carlos folded his arms over his chest. "Forget that."

Damali's hands found her hips. "You'd have to stab me first

before I'd let you take my niece or put Dan's parents in harm's way, Carlos—so I'm not arguing with you . . . just trying to help."

Carlos let out a breath of exasperation as strained glances passed around the team.

Cordell stepped forward, joining the group. "Couldn't help, as a seer, to *overstand* the situation. When y'all met me in D.C., you knew I was a black Hebrew—know the language . . . know antiquity, can see around corners, and ain't got no problem getting into the Temple Mount. I ain't been engaged in restricted activities."

"But look, man," Carlos said. "You've given enough already, it's cool."

"No, it ain't *cool,*" Cordell replied. "Stop trying to be diplomatic, noble as that might be. You look and see the facts very carefully, young brother. I know I'm a fat old man. Will slow you down, but I'm of more use to you out there than in here, if this place gets laid to siege. You've gotta have a trinity at your back. Me, Tobias, and Dragon Rider. I'm also knighted as a Templar, and after what the darkside took from me, it'd be my honor to die taking some of them bastards out. Tobias got a wife . . . he's like my Dougie used to be . . . don't need to be getting hisself hurt, but he knows the streets of Jerusalem cold and can send me images. Dragon Rider knows the stones. You can send her right back here before she gets hurt, so she can continya to be a fierce warrior to help guard this stronghold."

"He has a point, Carlos," Damali said quietly.

"I know I do," Cordell said, folding his arms over his rotund belly. "So stop arguing, young brother, and just accept the help as it comes to you. If anybody who steps up gets burnt, it ain't on your head. You've gotta let all that go—we at war. Plain and simple. 'Sides, my wife been dead for I don't know how long, so I ain't got cleansing issues, understand?"

Rider ruffled up the hair at the nape of his neck. "Always a technical difficulty on these missions. All right, I'm out of the race."

"You ain't said a mumblin' word," Mike muttered, folding his thick arms over his cinder block chest. "The fact that she's my wife don't make it cool, though?"

"Mike . . . would you *just* shut up?" Inez said, closing her eyes. "No. You can't go and mess up holy ground, *okay*."

"Oh, shit," Carlos muttered, dragging his fingers through his hair. "I got a little technical difficulty myself, truth be told. So, it's gonna have to be a remote job for me . . . I can't go into the Temple, either."

Damali just closed her eyes and shook her head.

"Now I see why your Neteru team is so fruitful and has multiplied," Tobias said with a straight face but a merry twinkle in his eyes. "Why don't you do the stone sensitivity divination underground, pass word to one of our, uhm . . . unburdened seers, who you can then jettison into the Temple Mount to the location—that man can retrieve the relic and be jettisoned back here."

"I don't know what they're talking about," Delores said to Stella. "I never know what they're talking about." She looked down at her granddaughter sleeping on her lap and stroked Ayana's mussed plaits and curls. "This poor baby has been through so much. Why can't we just stay here until all this is over?"

Stella nodded and then reached out her hand to gently lay it against the toddler's back, watching her small body expand and contract with deep breaths of peaceful sleep.

"Nowhere is safe for long, I'm learning. If they tell us we

have to keep moving, then it's for the best, I suppose? But we are so blessed, Delores," Stella whispered. "I saw so much as we tried to escape New York and made our way into the mountains . . . I won't even go into the horrors. Your daughter is alive, and my son is alive. Your granddaughter is alive, and my grandchild is still holding on inside of my daughter-in-law's body. You have a nice son-in-law . . . I have a nice daughter-in-law. They took everything we own, but not everything inside us yet. If they go," she added quietly, motioning to their respective adult children with a tilt of her head, "then I am dead inside."

Delores nodded as Stella kissed her cheek and then stood when her husband, Frank, approached. She watched Frank hug his wife and guide her to stand with Dan for a while before there was yet another change, another move, another battle. Clear pride and respect for their son's valor shone in the Weinsteins' eyes. As their daughter-in-law, Heather, joined the small circle and was warmly received, tears blurred Delores's vision. Why couldn't there be that kind of warmth among her small circle at a time like this?

Deep hurt and a sense of isolation scored her. Delores swallowed hard, allowing a fresh torrent of tears to roll down her cheeks unashamed. In a crowded tunnel she still felt all alone, as though everyone meant something to someone, that is everyone but her. The only person in the world who really cared if she lived or died was Ayana.

And even with that, when danger came, the child naturally went straight for her mother or her aunt Damali or her daddy, Mike, knowing full well that her nana was a complete failure in protecting her . . . just like she'd failed to protect Inez from the predatory stepfather that molested her—the same predator that had gone after Damali and had caused that child to run away from home.

No wonder all Inez did was to make sure she was physically safe and had food and water, but then had gone back into the huddle with the other soldiers. There was no time for a weak momma. Was no time to just sit and put her arms around her to let her cry and make sense of a totally insane new world. Stella and Frank Weinstein were blessed to have a son like Dan and a daughter-in-law like Heather, who made time to make sure their hearts and minds were all right. However, she couldn't even be mad.

Jesus knew that if she'd been a better mother, then maybe someone would have come over by now to check on her—and she certainly wasn't going over there while the team generals were discussing what to do. She'd already been humiliated enough time and time again with the Neteru team for making mistakes . . . last thing she wanted was to get yelled at in front of all of these people she didn't even know.

Guilt lacerated Delores as she sat on the ground, dirty, terror-stricken, tears streaming down her face, head leaned against the wall with her eyes closed. But she gave a start at the sound of someone sitting beside her.

"I'm sorry," Monty said. "I didn't mean to frighten you—and after all we've seen, I should have announced myself."

"It's all right," Delores said in a flat monotone. "It doesn't matter. If something was that close, I was dead anyway."

"How can you talk like that?" Monty said gently.

His gaze was tender, his voice nonjudgmental and caring. He was the first person since her world had turned upside down that had spoken to her with any patience or understanding. Everyone else just pushed her to the side and acted like she was in the way, but he seemed to be waiting for a real answer from her.

"Because," she said after a moment. "I really don't matter.

I'm probably just here to make sure that, while they fight, nothing happens to the baby . . . but then again, look around. There're so many others that can take good care of my pumpkin. Plus, I just make people mad. Won't be long before one of these times I fall, or slip, or can't keep up and one of those things we saw out there takes me."

She pressed a trembling hand to her chest, for the first time really giving voice to her fears. "I'm not special. I don't have the gifts. I've messed up my life so . . . messed up my daughter's life, and for a while Damali's, because I didn't want to see some things I should have seen. Now, in hindsight, the terrible things I'm seeing are all from the same place—they're all demons, just not in disguise. If it wasn't for this little baby girl, I'd be nothing to anybody in the world, not even my own daughter."

"Oh, no, ma'am," Monty said, closing his eyes against her words and shaking his head slowly. He surprised her by taking up one of her hands and patting it between his. "I was on the yacht when your daughter and your son-in-law thought you and the baby had perished." Monty opened his eyes and stared at Delores hard, his intense brown eyes seemed haunted with the memory. "They had to literally tie your son-in-law down to the deck to keep him from hurting himself. Your daughter nearly flung herself overboard at deep sea, weeping at the rails."

"You are kind, sir, and have a good heart," Delores said, sniffing hard. "But me being gone isn't what upset them like that."

"Monty. I am Monty," he stated firmly, also holding her hand tighter.

"All right, Monty," Delores murmured, gazing down at the sleeping child on her lap. "But all that upset was for this little precious angel, as it should be. If they knew she'd made it, no one would scream and wail for me." Delores looked away from Ayana and Monty, staring off into the distance. "I thought I'd be able to make up in Yaya's life all the things I did wrong in my daughter's life . . . and maybe that would help Inez to forgive me for all the mistakes I'd made with her . . . like not seeing what I should have seen, not being there and listening when I should have been there to listen."

Delores swallowed hard as tears refilled her eyes and her voice broke. "That's all I wanted to do. I thought that would give me a role and a place. Do you know what I mean?" She glanced at Monty briefly and then extracted her hand from his palms to wipe her tear-streaked cheeks. "But this baby girl here needs, like, what do they call 'em . . . Special Ops soldiers with guns for a grandma." Delores laughed self-consciously as her voice hitched and her lip began to quiver. "I don't even make a good grandma in this crazy world."

Monty pulled Delores into a loose hug with Ayana still dozing between them. He petted Delores's frazzled hair and rocked her gently. "You are a good grandmother, just for loving that child the way you do. I heard the stories of how you put your life on the line for her more than once."

He made Delores look at him by pulling back a bit. "You're blessed because your daughter is still alive and you have a courageous and wonderful son-in-law. I know about not having those things . . . and about losing them and wondering what role is left for you in the world. So you go ahead and cry and let it all run out of you. This time, maybe, let someone else take care of you—since you've been trying so long to take care of everyone else while so afraid."

"You don't even know me, but you know me," Delores said in a thick, quiet sob. "Why do you care about some old, broken-down woman who is useless?"

"Because you are not some old, broken-down woman—and you are most certainly not useless, even though I am some old, broken-down man without a family or anybody to care about me . . . and after a lifetime of caring about other people, and feeling needed, suddenly I had no role." He brushed her hair off her face with a weathered, meaty palm and then hugged her again for a while. "I know how terribly lonely that can feel."

They sat that way for a long time, her crying quietly, him blinking back tears as he kept his gaze on the tunnel ceiling, each thinking about the gnarled journey of their lives. Finally she pulled back, wiping her nose on the back of her blouse sleeve.

He held Delores away from him and looked at her, wiping tears from her face. "I was all by myself, Delores. They all died. Didn't even have a pretty grand to hug close to my heart to re-member them by. When angel Damali and the others found me, I was sitting in an empty confessional, where even the priests had fled. And I was asking God to excuse me for getting ready to take my own life . . . and then all these young people flooded into my life, needing this and that: 'Can we borrow your boat, Mr. Sinclair, can we use your linens and your navigational skills?' They overran my life and my ship, the only two things at that moment that I had left in this world."

Monty chuckled and wiped his eyes, hugging Delores again. "At first I thought, Am I going mad? And then I remembered that I really wanted all the chaos. I had prayed for it, and now I'm on the adventure of my life." He watched her studying his face and his eyes. "Giving up that last bit of what I was clinging on to from my past made me feel so alive. The yacht is ruined, and I may never see it again . . . but who cares?"

"You think we'll make it?"

"I honestly don't know, but I promise as long as I'm here in this fine quagmire with you, I won't leave you to die alone. That's a vow," Monty murmured, and then looked down at Ayana.

Delores nodded and sucked in a huge, steadying breath. "Thank you for saying that. Everything is changing, our roles are changing . . . better get used to it—life ain't never going back to the way it was before."

"No, I'm afraid not. But, so what if our roles change?" He glanced at Delores directly again. "So what if this tiny angel has more people than you to help her grow up—look at all these magnificent individuals fighting for good . . . and look at all the cousins about to be born. She'll be surrounded by love and excellent role models."

"Yeah, I guess you're right," Delores said quietly. "Funny how things work out. If she was growing up with me in the old neighborhood, the way I had to raise Inez . . . there was nobody good, I mean, really positive for her to emulate. I don't even have anything she could really model herself on, except I think I know right from wrong . . . but some days I'm not even sure about that."

"We all have special skills, Delores. Okay, so I can navigate a ship. You also have something positive you can do. It will be revealed." He smiled broadly. "Or maybe you've already prayed so hard about wanting to take care of children you'll be saddled with a whole kit and caboodle of crying infants at once? Can you actually see the very serious-minded Marlene Stone playing nursemaid to a houseful of Guardian tots?"

When Delores cracked a smile, Monty pressed on. "I promise you, she will bop those children over the head with her magic fighting stick as quick as look at them—being a grandmother and finger painting with peanut butter and jelly is a very highly specialized skill, madam. Not everyone is up to the task. That's Special Forces."

When Delores laughed softly Monty wagged a finger at her. "So, be careful what you ask for, you just might get it."

"Thank you, Monty," she said, taking up his hand again and squeezing it.

"The pleasure is all mine."

He released a contented sigh and let his back rest against the wall with a soft thud. She slowly relaxed to lean back against the tunnel wall, smiling for the first time in a very, very long time.

CHAPTER THIRTEEN

Jerusalem was in ruins. It looked like the smoldering hail had strafed every window and wall with the force of an Uzi drive-by. Buildings were on fire, shelled by cosmic fury. Car alarms and sirens sounded; the smell of burning gasoline and smoke added to the already dust-laden air.

Fist-sized ice fragments still littered the pocked streets, even though it was close to ninety-five degrees outside. The world's geothermostat was out of order. In fact, there was no such thing left called natural order as Carlos peeped out of the safe house window witnessing what Tobias and Habiba had warned of.

Battered landscape laid bare in yawning, silent screams of fractured earth. The sun wore a deep, charcoal mourning shroud. Dead birds and people paved the ground. Moaning echoed from every doorway and building entrance. The sound of human suffering was like a piteous, droning hum. Small rocks and debris flickered with brimstone fury.

Tobias and Habiba had been so right; he had to see what was going on aboveground and clear the tunnels on a solo check before taking Dragon Rider down there with him. He could have inadvertently jettisoned them into a collapsing section, or right in front of a startled military patrol . . . or a feeding den of hiding walkers. Everything seemed like it was on borrowed time, hanging by a fragile thread of existence. Buildings listed, many going down like dominoes to trap the wounded and bury the dead.

But the Temple Mount, the Dome of the Rock, and the Church of the Holy Sepulcher were still standing.

Carlos narrowed his gaze watching for demon sentries and spies, as well as any walking dead. The walkers probably had enough to gorge on by scavenging the insides of all the buildings. But from what he could tell there were still human authorities and people trying to help injured civilians get to the major religious sites that had now been turned into triage units.

"Okay," Carlos said in a low rumble, pulling back from his lookout spot behind a broken window shutter. He wiped both palms down his face and composed his thoughts. "You sure you're up for this, Cordell?"

"Ready as ever," Cordell said, keeping his head low as the small group crouched on the living-room floor. "My age and weight make me less likely to get shot at if I stumble out toward the street and just start crying . . . which after seeing all this ain't hard to do. They'll think I'm a shell-shocked survivor, which will get me into whichever side of the shrine you think best for the search."

"You must dodge the walkers to get to the entrance, though," Tobias warned quickly. "While Carlos is connected below in the tunnels with Dragon Rider, I will have to cover you from the window. Men my age are considered dangerous . . . looters, especially if armed. I can't go with you into the open, or I'll be detained—or worse."

"No," Carlos said. "You fall back, cover him from a window, but I don't want any casualties on this run. We're in, and then we're out. Ain't trying to leave nobody behind." He turned to Dragon Rider. "Okay, two minutes, then I'll pull you to me down below. We do the Wall, you get a location or sense, and then you flip the impression to me, so I can relay it to Cordell." Carlos looked up at Cordell. "The moment you get something, you give me the word to pull you out—then we're all in a fold-away back to the team."

"Sounds like a plan I can live with," Cordell said with a half-smile.

"I'm banking on that, man," Carlos said, his expression completely sober.

"Then we'd better break for it now," Tobias said. "While it is still and the military might not be so quick to shoot first and ask questions later if a survivor stumbles out of a building asking for help in Hebrew. Then they'll take him to the Temple Mount, most likely . . . because they are taking all who are Muslim or speak Arabic, as well as foreigners, to the Dome of the Rock."

Carlos peered out of the window again, watching for rabid stray dogs, walkers, and anything else that could attack Cordell on his short path to the military checkpoint.

"But how do we know for sure which side within the shrine to look in? Until I work on the stones, I cannot tell you if he should be in the Church of the Holy Sepulcher or the Temple Mount or even the Dome of the Rock. And he'll already be segregated into whichever area." Dragon Rider looked at the small squad for a moment, seeming worried for Cordell's safety as he and Tobias edged toward the door.

"Well, we can rule out the Church of the Sepulcher, because it was held by three primary custodians in the eleventh century—Templar time," Cordell said with a faraway look in his eyes. Then as though walking back into the room, he looked at Carlos and the two guardians that were with him. "I know my history. The Greek Orthodox Church, Armenian Apostolic Church, and the Roman Catholic Church—who got the relic via their Templars—had oversight of the shrine then. But in the nineteenth century, the Coptic Orthodox, Ethiopian Orthodox, and Syrian Orthodox churches had coregency over it. In the last days, they wouldn't hide it where you-know-who would assume it would be."

"The thing that came out of Ethiopia," Carlos said, his gaze going back to the window as he fit the puzzle together. "The manuscript wasn't the only thing, the weapon was secreted away there, but came back . . . they wouldn't have it out of Jerusalem at a time like this."

"Right, my Templar brother," Cordell said in a quiet, excited rush. "And the Dome of the Rock is located on the Temple Mount . . . so all I need is a general vicinity and I can work my way to possible hiding spots—not to mention, I do have a few seer skills of my own, you know."

"Yeah, well, just be careful, man," Carlos said. "No heroics."

Tobias and Carlos shared a look.

Dragon Rider nodded. "And Godspeed."

Both Carlos and Dragon Rider watched Cordell and Tobias slip out of the door. They glanced back to the window, barely breathing as they waited for Cordell to exit the building safely and enter the street. From their individual hiding places, Carlos and Dragon Rider kept their gazes sweeping the streets and the Temple Mount area for any signs of danger.

Even in the eerie, dim half-light where night and day fought for dominance in the unnaturally cojoined sky, the bright copper-hued dome stood out like a beacon above the gleaming white, octagonal-shaped structure.

Tobias gave the low double-knock signal and scrambled back

into the room, and then took a sniper's position to cover Cordell so that Carlos could pull back.

"The building is clear so far of walkers," Tobias said, panting from the quick run, his gun trained on the street below. "You go now. Dragon Rider and I will make sure he gets inside without incident while you inspect the tunnels by the Kotel. Travel well, my friend."

His goal had been to get to the Western Stone. Based on what Damali had said, the numerical implications alone made him decide that might be as good a place as any to start. Pitch-blackness met him. All power was out, which he expected. Sulfur and ash stung his nose as his silver night vision adjusted to the surreal darkness. Demon rats had obviously tried to flee along the hallowed corridor—they wouldn't be his problem.

It was so quiet that it made the hair stand up on the back of his neck. However, as he stumbled over a soldier's half-eaten body, he knew there was another equally vicious threat to contend with. Silver light from his focused gaze caught them crouched low over human entrails. Light hit their eyes, giving them the reflective appearance of animals caught in high beams on the road. There were so many that they seemed to go on for miles, filling the entire underground passageway. One hiss from the leader and they all stood slowly. Carlos backed up, drew a blade, and did the only thing he could—send a hard energy charge upward to blow a section of the tunnel ceiling.

Screeches and screams rent the dense tunnel air as huge stones and cement rained down, smashing the walkers. There were too many to risk fighting and bringing contagion back home to the team. Carlos got down low on one knee, covered his head and a section of the Wall with his shield of Heru, and waited as the debris settled. The moment he sensed stillness all around him, he pulled in Dragon Rider under the shield with him.

"Tight quarters and make it fast, sis," he said as she tumbled onto the ground under his shield. "Walkers got here first, and I had to blow the whole length from here to the north end. That's no longer an escape route."

"Give me a minute," she said as they stood, pressing her hands and cheek to the large section of Western Stone by their shoulders.

After only a few moments, Carlos watched the Guardian frown, and then her face contort in agony as tears began to course down her cheeks. Her breathing became so shallow that he feared for her life—and when her nose started bleeding and she cried out, he pulled her away, dropping his sword and shield to pull her into a healing embrace.

"Give it to me," he said, placing a hand on either side of her skull and sweeping her mind with silver sealant. "Let it go, Dragon! Send it to me before you have a cerebral hemorrhage!"

"Oh, God—so much pain!" she gasped, her knees buckling as she held on to Carlos's arms for support. "Thousands and thousands of years of agony . . ."

"What did you see?" he asked, gently enfolding her. "I'm gonna take it from you and send you back to the team . . . you make sure Medic heals you up, all right? You did real good," he murmured as her breathing calmed and the images began to flood his mind.

"Water. An abyss," she said quickly, sending lightning-fast images from her mind into his. "A cave. *Bi'r al arwah.*"

"Say it in English for me," he said, holding her tighter, unable to scavenge his mind for the translation while also receiving her transmission.

"Well. Cave. Spirits," she said, beginning to hyperventilate. "Crusaders. South. Bedrock."

Out of nowhere, fetid hands began to reach through the fallen rock, moving Carlos's man-made dam. His kissed Dragon Rider on her forehead. "You did real good," he said again. "Thank you." Then he sent her away in a burst of white light, reached out and called his blade into his grip, spun and hacked away a clawing hand, and was gone.

He hit the floor of the safe house without warning, almost causing Tobias to shoot him.

"Sorry, man, it was hectic down there. Did Cordell get through?"

"Yes, he is in," Tobias said, his gaze torn between Carlos and the window for a moment before he ducked down. "And Dragon Rider?"

"She'll have a helluva headache, but she's back with the team. So many wars, so much emotion is charged into those stones . . . she almost had a stroke." Carlos wiped his brow with his forearm. "I only got pieces . . . gotta hope Cordell can put it together. She said a word I don't know . . . *Bi'r al* something. Cave, bedrock, water, spirits, abyss, south, Crusaders, which I know is the Templars, but the rest . . . hey. It was hitting her so hard that all I could get was one-word sound bites."

"*Bi'r al arwah?*" Tobias said slowly, lowering his weapon.

"Yeah," Carlos said, still breathing hard. "I think so."

"*Bi'r al arwah* is the Well of Souls. Crusaders hacked an entrance hole into the bedrock of the Temple Mount from the south. Under that rock is a natural cave where it is believed that the Ark of the Covenant was originally hidden during the destruction of Jerusalem before it was secreted away to Ethiopia . . . also in the Talmud, the cave is said to be the center of the world where the waters of the Flood still rage from the abyss."

Tobias dropped down to sit and allowed his back to lean against crumbling plaster. "Carlos, that rock is where they say the archangel Gabriel held it here on earth when it wanted to ascend to Heaven with the great prophet Muhammad. The crack in the rock is from where he made his visionary journey. Souls of martyrs and saints guard that well."

Carlos just stared at Tobias for a moment. "If Gabriel has his handprint on pure bedrock beneath a temple that people from the three major religions have devoutly prayed in for thousands of years . . . pure rock that sits over the rushing waters that began the world and also wiped it out, with spiritual sentries on 24/7 watch . . . I can tell you that if I was trying to keep something safe from the darkside, I would think that would be like a spiritual Fort Knox, don't you?"

Dragon Rider came out of Carlos's jettison, took two staggered steps forward, and dropped. Damali, Marlene, and Berkfield were on her in seconds. But Marlene quickly held out her stick and used it to bar Damali from going closer.

"Me and Richard got this," Marlene said. "If she came back with contagion or a demon presence, you don't need that in your system."

Berkfield squatted beside the fallen Guardian, instinctively placing his hands on either side of her head as Marlene slowly passed the now-glowing ebony walking stick over Dragon Rider's body.

"Her nose is bleeding, never a good sign with a seer." Berkfield stared up at Marlene as Quick came to squat beside her fallen Guardian sister, and the rest of the team gathered around.

"I don't care what you say, Mar," Damali said, pacing behind Marlene. "If she doesn't come around in the next few minutes, I'm going in."

★ ★ ★

People were beyond touching one another. The guards at the shrine entrance lowered weapons and used gun muzzles from their automatics to run up and down Cordell's body to be sure he was clear of firearms.

"There is limited food and water here," a soldier said, not allowing Cordell to immediately pass. "If you are not injured—"

"I don't need to eat, I just want to pray. Bricks fell on my head and—"

"You are not bleeding."

Cordell nodded, his nervous gaze darting around the fearsome retinue of soldiers. "This is why I want to pray. The way the ceiling fell, I was in a pocket. I got knocked out but not bloodied. My neighbors weren't so lucky," Cordell replied in Hebrew, beginning to weep earnest tears. "But I saw the creatures pulling my neighbors down the hall to the deaths—the screaming, the crying. I cannot get it out of my head. What are these things that eat human flesh . . . that murder?"

"He is an old man," another soldier argued from a high post. "He's able to talk, isn't sick. Let him through—it could be your father or your brother . . . and since we're all probably going to die in this Apocalypse, do you want to have it on your head that you left an old man out here to fend for himself against demons? What will you say to Yahveh?"

The soldier that had stopped Cordell lifted his automatic to allow him to pass. "*Shalom.*"

Dragon Rider sat up slowly, coughing as Berkfield wiped his bloody nose with the back of his hand and the collective teams released quiet exhalations of relief.

"You really took one for the team there, kiddo," Berkfield said, dabbing his nose.

"Thanks for going in and putting my poor head back to-gether." She lifted her dark sandy hair off her neck and closed her eyes with a wince. "Can't remember a thing I saw, but have a nasty headache for the trouble."

"You'll be all right," Marlene said, stooping down to massage her neck. "I can draw the rest of it out, but whatever you saw was for Carlos and Cordell only . . . just as well, because it might have been something that would haunt you for the rest of your days."

Dragon Rider leaned into Marlene's nimble touch. "Like none of the rest of this would?"

Damali smirked. "I hear you. Just glad you're back in one piece. We really appreciate everything you did back there."

"Is it getting hot in here or is it just me?" Marjorie asked.

"Hot flash?" Marlene said, joking to relive the tension. "Comes with the territory, lady . . . but I thought it was me from helping with a healing."

"No," Delores said quietly as she brought Ayana's limp body to Damali and Inez. "The baby is burning up. She won't wake up—she's all fevered."

"I noticed Delores felt warm," Monty said, "and then I went to go get her some water and it wasn't cool like before."

Inez grabbed her child from her mother's arms and held her tightly as Guardians got to their feet and stared at the steaming reservoir.

Damali held out her arms at each side, turning around slowly, sensing, listening. It was quiet above them; the hail, fire, and brimstone rain had stopped. She looked up. There was no breach at the mouth of the tunnel entrance.

"Demons can't get in here because of the prayer barriers, de-mon rats will fry on contact, and the tunnel is barricaded against the walkers . . . they won't fry because they aren't technically demons—just reanimated humans with feral, rabid qualities awakened within their dead nervous systems," Shabazz said as sweat trickled down his temples.

"But they can heat the rocks and earth all around this shaft and turn it into an oven," Damali said, watching steam rise as the water in the reservoir begin to bubble. "I've gotta get you all out of here."

"But where?" Frank Weinstein said, panicked, holding his wife closer. "If the demons have enough power to melt the rocks around us and our weapons are almost spent—where do we take women and children?"

There was only one place she knew of from her team's tour there before that was nearby, hallowed ground that they might not violate so terribly by stumbling across the threshold unwashed, with men and women and children all in one huddled mass.

Damali called her Isis into her palm. "Church of the Holy Sepulcher."

Cordell kept his head down and his hands clasped in prayer as his eyelids fluttered with Carlos's strong mental transmission. The images hit his mind so hard and fast that his eyeballs stung and a piercing, clear voice filled his mind.

I can't go in there without violating the cleansing laws and we don't need any variables right through here, Carlos said. *Once you're in the cave, you've gotta sense for it. Can you make it?*

I don't know, Cordell's mind whispered back. *Can you use my eyes to see? There's chaos all around . . . the entire complex has been turned into a giant army hospital and refugee camp here, but they are monitoring movement very heavily. They're shooting walkers that try to breach the perimeter, and there might even be some in the cave.*

Okay, Carlos said on a hard mental exhalation. *Lend me your eyes; let me see what you see as you try very carefully to make your way to that side of the building. If I see a walker or someone coming for you, I'll pull you out of there. Trust me, if I could see exactly where the relic was without having to send a pair of human hands to go get it, I'd pull it in without putting you in this position . . . but that's just the thing—this weapon has been so hidden and prayer sealed that only a righteous human with a pure soul can actually retrieve it. Maybe that's also why Heru said to send the baby . . . but you can understand why me and Damali weren't even trying to go there, right?*

I want to do this—I told you that before. Cordell got up slowly, and continued his prayers aloud, passing military guards. *Take over my eyes. Use my sight.*

Carlos wrapped his arms around his knees as he sat on the floor. Tobias kept a lookout and covered Carlos as silver filled his irises and his gaze became distant. Soon the two seers joined as knighted Templars, sharing the same vision, with Carlos's vision being slightly bowled and distorted, but accurate nonetheless.

"I'm in," Carlos murmured aloud, and then sent Cordell the same message in a mental barb.

It took Carlos's complete concentration to follow the scenes being sent from Cordell's mind into his. Everything coming to him was in a grainy stream of continuous impressions that was like watching a very badly handheld-camera-filmed silent movie.

Pallets, bodies amid Byzantine architecture loomed like a sea of writhing, wailing misery. The triage camp seemed to go on for forever as Cordell navigated his way to the Dome of the Rock. Then the images stopped. Flashed in and out. An angry Palestinian guard halted Cordell. There was a flurry of words that Carlos couldn't hear. A weapon was raised. There was no image. Carlos stood quickly, ready to do a jettison, but Cordell's words stabbed into his mind. *Not yet.* Images came back. A weapon in his focus slowly lowered. Images vanished again for a moment.

I can't talk to them or you and keep my concentration of letting you use my eyes—takes a lot of energy.

It's cool, Carlos replied, sending Cordell protective vibes. *You take care of you, first and foremost. If you need me to pull you out, drop the visual and holler.*

No, no, I'm okay, Cordell shot back quickly. *They said I was on the wrong side, but I said my wife and children were on their side. I told them we'd gotten separated and I just wanted to bring them back to where they belonged. They have so much going on, guarding anything or anybody is futile and those guys are tired. That's the advantage of being my age; folks always underestimate you and let you pass.*

Carlos's shoulders relaxed. *Okay, man, as long as you're good.*

Tell you what would be a big help, Cordell finally said as he crossed the large courtyard.

Name it.

If you see a walker, rather than jettison me and not get what we need—send that sucker into a tunnel or somewhere . . . you keep them things off of me, I can work on frightened human beings by using diplomacy.

Carlos rubbed his hands down his face. *Done.*

(C) CHAPTER FOURTEEN

She could not afford to have any members of her team accidentally shot by nervous soldiers as they came out of an energy
fold-away. Damali kept her focus keen. Marlene was sent in first
as her remote vision. Once the two seers were on lock and in
sync, Damali tried to bring the members into the sanctuary in
small groups jettisoned behind pillars, doing that all from the
memory of their pilgrimage to the site more than a year ago.
Before she could actually see through Marlene's eyes, she could
only pray that things within the holy location hadn't been decimated and hadn't been overrun by the walking dead. Even
worse was the potential of scaring some trigger-happy MP
who'd unload a clip out of reflex.

If she didn't get the first jettison just right, she might have
been sending her mother-seer into instant death, but they had to
take the risk. Guardians were beginning to pass out, the baby,
civilians, and older folks had to get out first. Guardians began
clutching their necks as air became scarce and too hot to suck
in. She had to get her pregnant sisters out of there as the floor
began to melt shoe rubber and turn soles gooey. Had to get her

Guardian brothers out of there to provide cover for the team. Had to not fall down on the hot ground . . . had to keep conscious . . .

Damali! Marlene's voice cut through the broiling oven around her for a moment just as everything went black.

Carlos's head jerked back. Marlene's scream pierced his consciousness and blotted out Cordell's vision. He opened his arms and his wife filled them, her clothes smoldering, her cheek and palms and arms burned where she'd obviously fallen against a scorching surface.

"Damali, Damali, wake up, D!" Carlos shouted, no longer caring if passing forces or spies heard him.

Tobias was at Carlos's side in seconds as Carlos laid her flat on the floor, turned his cheek to her nose, and felt for a pulse. She had one; it was weak, but instantly he began to place his hands a millimeter over her skin to take the third-degree burns from her into him.

"Freshwater, any you've got in the house," Carlos said, wincing as his skin blistered and took the violent injury from Damali's skin into his. "I've gotta hydrate her."

Not even answering, Tobias immediately ran down the hall to honor the request, but within seconds Carlos heard Tobias's weapon report. It wasn't about waiting to see what had happened. Blind, frantic, Carlos jettisoned Tobias to the cave he'd seen in his mind, having no idea what had gone on in the water tunnel. For all he knew, the team could be dead, the water tunnel nuked by conventional weapons.

Standing quickly with Damali half healed in his arms, Carlos was gone in a flash as walkers broke down the front door, came out of the hall, and rushed the living room, snarling.

★　★　★

"I want your permission to send everything we've got into Jerusalem now," Lilith said, staring at her husband as she burst into his private war room.

"And why would I do that, given how wasteful you all have been? After the heavy losses I have just endured, which could take me *at least* twenty years or more to rebuild Hell to its old capacities, you now want me to go into reserve demons *before* the Rapture?" He sat back and laughed in a low sarcastic chuckle, staring at the globe and making a tent with his graceful fingers before his mouth. "Are you not aware that if my demon reserves get depleted, our heir will be forced to rule during the Tribulation period at a severe military disadvantage? There-fore," he added, standing slowly, his gaze menacing her even though he continued to smile, "I suggest you not give yourself over to rage and frustration, darling . . . and that you continue to be strategic."

"I have located and injured the pregnant female Neteru, and her team is on the run."

He picked up a goblet of blood and casually took a sip from it, giving her a sidelong glance. "Forgive my skepticism, but I have heard this sort of overconfident bullshit before, Lilith." He set his goblet down very carefully on the war-room table and leaned forward. "*Produce a witness.*"

"Gladly," she said, fighting an openly insubordinate snarl. "Will *Ialdabaoth* do?"

Icy hands grasped his arms and legs, sending shivers of pure ter-ror into his skeleton. The dark cavern felt like a tomb and as he squeezed the trigger on his automatic, the tragic sound of an empty click reverberated off the walls. Yahveh help him, he would be eaten alive.

Tobias quickly pulled a bowie knife from his fatigues and just as suddenly, dim light let him see that he was all alone in the Well of Souls. He quickly put away the knife and dropped the spent automatic weapon as he fell to his knees and began to pray. An inexplicable knowing told him that whatever had been trying to tear at him from the great beyond had to have been spirits protecting this sanctuary.

"I am not a perfect man, I have sinned," he said in a quavering voice. "I admit that I fear for my wife, for my own life, but I submit to the will of God."

A sound broke Tobias's prayer and made him look up. Footsteps creeping closer in a steady shuffle put Tobias on his feet in search of any small cove he could find to hide in. Every bit of military training he owned took over his mind as he picked up his gun, prepared to use the gun butt to stun a predator before his knife would instantly slit its throat. But instead of a walker or something equally as formidable, a frightened old man stumbled into the enclosure.

Before Cordell could draw his next breath, a strong hand reached out and yanked him against a wall. For a second he couldn't breathe, couldn't fight the gripping strength, but he still tried to free himself in a futile struggle.

"Stop, before you hurt yourself," Tobias said in a low-timbred warning between his teeth. "It's me, Tobias!"

Cordell stopped struggling and Tobias removed his hand from his mouth.

"You weren't supposed to be here!" Cordell whispered, shaken.

"I know," Tobias said more calmly, wiping at the perspiration that wet his brow. "Walkers finally overran the safe house. I don't know how or why, but they did and Carlos jettisoned me here to finish the mission with you."

"Did that boy make it out all right?" Cordell asked, gripping both of Tobias's arms.

"I cannot say," Tobias murmured, and then looked beyond Cordell's shoulder. "I honestly don't know. All I know is that I owe the man my life—he saved me and sacrificed himself back there . . . I heard him yelling as I disappeared."

"Then that's gotta be why I couldn't connect—the signal between us just went black and then nothing." Cordell rubbed his palms over his bald head and walked away from Tobias. "It just ain't right. It just ain't right the way the young is dying . . . the ones who could stand and fight against the coming evil is being called home way too young." He turned and looked at Tobias. "So, we gotta finish this."

"Am I not a woman of my word?" Lilith asked, surveying the Old City from their vantage point in the hills beyond it. She brought her black nightmare around to face her council. "I present to you perhaps the greatest battle theater of them all— Jerusalem."

When Nuit smiled, she offered him an appreciative nod. "My fellow Chairman, this may have been well before your time, but I assure you that, as a man who appreciates antiquity and the finer points of war, feast your eyes on what can only be described as the true art of war."

She waved her arm out toward the sweeping, panoramic view. "The Temple Mount, the Dome of the Rock . . . the Church of the Holy Sepulcher . . . the Tower of David—and we will siege this city like the days of old, when Babylon was at its zenith and the Roman Empire was an unconquerable force. My machinations led those armies into battle to grind Jerusalem under their heels . . . and we will do so again!"

A thunderous demon cheer went up. Vlad rode down the

rows of his Berserkers, looking into the glowing eyes of his frontline captains.

Misshapen faces in massive skulls leered back at him. Maggot-infested pelts barely concealed barrel chests as gargantuan arms lifted swords and maces, battle-axes, and spears. Huge Viking helmets gleamed with black static charges of pure fury as riders tried to rein in their nightmarish, demon warhorses.

"There will be warrior angels!" Vlad shouted. "They will open up Heaven to rain injustice upon you, but your reward is worth the sacrifice! The dark empire will rise again! Take the Tower of David as our fortress, lay siege to the streets!"

Another rowdy cheer went up in a deafening roar. Nuit pulled away from Lilith to bring his mount down the left flank of the Berserkers.

"Master vampires to the air!" Nuit shouted. "Darken the already dim sky. Blot out the gray clouds in a carpet of pure night! They must be holed up in one of the three main citadels that we cannot breach. But use conventional weaponry from the standing human armies to blast at their edifices until they crumble to dust!"

"You three are on recon," Lilith shouted toward Lucrezia, Elizabeth, and Sebastian. "As our warriors fall, bring them back. As the humans flee the destruction—poison them, hit them with contagion, and take them hostage until the Neteru team is forced out beyond the sanctuary of hallowed ground."

When the threesome nodded, Lilith rode off to the right flank into a dark void of nothingness. She stopped as the slow, putrid breaths of Satan's Thirteenth pelted her ears. She didn't turn to meet the colossal presence that dwarfed her nightmare and made the frightened beast rear, snorting fire.

"Your bidding, per my master, my queen?" it rumbled.

Lilith took a moment to compose herself, narrowing her gaze

against the absolute darkness that had bent to address her. "If the Neteru Councils rush in and if the archangels come . . . you are our nuclear option. I will not cede to defeat."

Damali sat up slowly as the combined teams gathered around. Five soldiers took note and rushed over, weapons drawn.

"Get back, get back!" the captain shouted at the teams, leveling gun barrels at Carlos as he slowly unfolded from Damali's body. "He has the contagion! Look at his eyes and his teeth. Get back so we have a clear shot!"

Red dots covered Carlos's chest and forehead. But Guardian brothers stepped out from behind columns, and the distinctive clicks of hammers being cocked made the confused soldiers ease their arms down.

"You need to chill," Phat G said quietly into a nervous soldier's ear, pressing cold steel against his neck. "Things ain't always what they seem."

"Ain't nobody contagious. This ain't got nothing to do with you," Big Mike said into a captain's ear, making him feel the gun muzzle at his back. "Tell your men to stand down—you and I don't want nothin' unfortunate to kick off up in here, right?"

"We'll take care of our own," Shabazz said calmly as he dug the muzzle of Black Beauty into one of the lead soldiers' temple.

"*Americano, comprende?*" Jose said between his teeth, making sure the soldier in front of him could feel the barrel of his 9mm at the base of his skull.

"Just say the word, Captain," Rider called out, while pressing his weapon into a young soldier's cheek. "This is family business and we've got a cure for the man. You don't want an all-out war inside this of all churches, so my suggestion is you call your squad back. We are *not* the enemy. The enemy is out there, trust me!"

"You don't want a full-scale shooting match in here with all these civilians, right?" Big Mike warned the captain.

The captain shook his head as civilians and clerics huddled against the walls and altar. "Stand down," he said quickly. "This is not of our concern—they are Americans."

Cordell and Tobias got down on their knees. Cordell held his hands over a small fissure in the stone floor. They listened, straining, until Tobias glanced up.

"You can hear water," Tobias whispered, awestruck. "But the crack is so small . . . maybe the child's hand could have reached down within it. Our limbs are too big."

Cordell nodded. "If it's water, then it had to be blessed . . . and it's gotta be holy water that could cover anything hidden within this cave that's covered by holy rock. But if something goes wrong out here, would you or I want to have that little girl's life on our heads? She ain't nuthin' but a baby. If I die, so what? If she ran the wrong way or something snatched her along the way, could you live with yourself? Maybe that's what the angels were testing to see, who knows?"

For a moment, neither man spoke, their silence answering the lingering question.

"But how can we get the dagger if it is down there?" Tobias leaned in, peering into the nothingness. "It is an abyss. We have no ropes or climbing gear. I do not think I am supposed to send a tactical charge into the center of the world to take out something so revered . . . that could be considered sacrilege."

"If we're supposed to have it, it will come to us," Cordell said sitting back on his haunches. "My old grandma wasn't a black Hebrew, but she had wisdom that comes down through the ages. She said if two or more are gathered in His name, then that's where He is also." Cordell's gaze trapped Tobias's for a moment. "Me and you make two, so let's do that."

"Are you all right?" Carlos asked in a rush, bringing bottled water to Damali's lips.

She nodded, taking the water from him, and then pushed herself up to balance on her own. "Yeah," she said after a long drink. "They burned us out—or better stated, boiled us out. They turned it into a steam oven. Had to get the team onto serious hallowed ground, and with the heat, and the multiple sends over that distance, next thing I knew I was passed out."

Carlos rubbed his palm over his jaw and dropped his voice. "Next time you get in a box, if there is a next time, you get out first and then pull everybody to where you are. None of this captain going down with the ship—"

"Don't even say it," she warned, her gaze unflinching and her tone nonnegotiable. "Leave them in an oven and—"

"I didn't say leave them in an oven, I said, like they tell you on a commercial flight, put the damned mask over your face first, Damali. If you go down, you can't save anybody else!" He could feel his heart slamming against his breastbone as his voice went from a private whisper to a sonic boom. He stood and walked away from her. Shabazz landed a hand on his shoulder and walked with him.

"It's cool, man, you gonna be okay, she's gonna be okay. Everything is peace. Hetep," Shabazz said.

"Yeah, yeah," Carlos said, thoroughly shook as Shabazz walked him behind a huge stone pillar. "She don't get it, man. I'd take a bullet, the burn, whatever they've got—but I cannot take losing her or the baby."

"We all know that, so pull in a coupla breaths while Mar

gives Damali the once-over and Medic does a double-check, all right?"

Carlos closed his eyes and leaned his head back, trying to get his breathing to normalize. He felt Shabazz pound his fist and heard him walk away, but his bones felt like jelly. His body was still shaking from the adrenaline rush that had swept through him when he'd seen his wife half dead in his arms. "God, just give me the strength," he murmured, and let out a long, weary sigh.

The only noise in the cave that could be heard was the sound of two men breathing and the distant gurgle of water. Now that they'd finished their joint prayer spoken aloud they were at a loss for what to do next.

"Can you feel the presence of what Carlos is seeking?" Tobias finally asked, breaking the silence.

"I know it's here," Cordell said. "I can't exactly *see* it, but I *know* . . . if you understand what I mean."

Tobias nodded. "I am a tactical, I feel things. All of my senses are on alert, but I cannot pinpoint why or where right now."

"Yep," Cordell said, craning his neck. "You hear that?"

Tobias leaned his face closer to the small fissure in the ground and turned his head to the side to listen, then jumped back. "Water is rising. That is the sound of water rising!"

Both men got to their feet, Tobias helping Cordell up. Within seconds, crystal-clear water gushed out of the crack, making them back away quickly. An object wrapped in soaked red velvet thudded onto the floor as the water rapidly receded.

It took them a moment to move. Cordell edged forward first and stared down. "It has a Templar seal on it. The crest in the embroidery."

"Then you open it," Tobias said. "You are knighted, I am not. I will not offend the order."

Cordell nodded and stooped down with a grunt. "All religions are represented at this site . . . I don't think you, as a man with a good spirit, could offend," he said, carefully untying the leather straps and unfurling the waterlogged fabric. "Don't you think it's odd that this has probably been down here for hundreds of years, if not a couple thousand . . . and the velvet is still good, ain't rotted away or nothing?"

"I think it's Divine," Tobias whispered, watching intently as Cordell's hands worked with reverent caution to then begin unwrapping old, brown linen from around an oblong, hard object.

Cordell pressed his fist to his mouth as he stared down. An eight-inch, broken piece of jagged wood terminated into a sharp, flat, iron spearhead. At the neck of it was a Roman seal and rank etching. The edges and face of the ten-inch blade were corroded with a dark, crimson, tarlike substance that also ran down onto the wood. Cordell's hands shook as he carefully swaddled the weapon in the cloth again, treating it with the care of a newborn infant.

"Hey, I'm sorry. Maybe you were right," Damali said, rounding the pillar and handing Carlos a bottle of water.

He accepted it from her but didn't immediately look into her eyes. "I never meant you were supposed to leave our team to fry . . . or to let Ayana die in an oven."

"I know," she said, touching his face. "Everybody knows what you meant . . . tensions are just running high."

Carlos didn't look at her as he opened his water. "How's Ayana?"

"Fine. Everybody is all right. How are you?"

"I'm all right," he said, guzzling his water. "Gotta get a lock on Cordell and Tobias." He finally looked up at her. "I lost my focus, left my men. Haven't been able to reconnect with them, which tells me there's interference in the airwaves real close by. That ain't a good sign, D. Couldn't even look in Habiba's eyes. If I can't get a lock on two men with extrasensory skills who are less than a mile away, then that means at least one of them isn't still on hallowed ground. I sent Tobias to the only safe place I knew—"

A heavy blast rocked the sanctuary. People began screaming and running with clerics. Mortar fire made huge chandeliers and candelabras crash to the floor amid fleeing civilians. Another shell hit and Damali and Carlos were up at the now-shattered stained-glass windows.

Carlos flung a shield of Heru up to cover the façade of the building as Damali sent four white-light pulses from the tip of her Neteru blade to blast the incoming shells out of the air.

"Tactical nets up!" Carlos shouted, causing every tactical squad member to scramble blue-white charges to dome the building.

Folding away, he joined Damali in her window. His blade touched hers, sending a nova of white light toward the Tower of David to chase the direction of the original mortar fire.

"I gotta get over to the Dome of the Rock," Carlos said. "If they shelled here, they shelled there, trying to figure out which location we're holed up in."

"Go," she said, and then turned back to the window. "We'll hold it down here so you can bring those men back alive."

"We'll settle the score later on what I owe you, Fallon," Lilith said with a wicked chuckle. "You are indeed the best at three-card monte—of the three sites, it appears that you've guessed the right one to shell first."

He returned a half-smile as he looked down at the charred

remains of demons that still clung to human conventional weapons. "But it does seem that our female Neteru is quite recovered. Perhaps it's time for Vlad to send in his troops?"

Carlos came out of a fold-away just outside the hallowed ground, not wanting to violate the sanctity of the site. He swept the area with his senses, frantically calling out to Tobias and Cordell in his mind as the ground began to rumble. He watched in horror as a missile headed right for the coppery gold, gleaming dome where thousands of innocent civilians sought shelter. Several quick energy pulses from the tip of his blade exploded them in midair.

"Everything you send to me, I send back to you tenfold!" Carlos shouted.

Prepared to stave off the next volley, he watched in awe as tracers careened toward the dome and then curved, and went screaming back in the direction they'd come. A massive blast threw him off his feet. In the back of his mind he heard people screaming. Thunder seemed to be coming from the earth beneath him, and dazed, he took a few seconds to realize it was nightmare hooves quaking the ground.

He flipped up, and ducked as an iron-barbed mace swung past his head. Berserkers were on the move! Civilians fearing the collapse of the Dome had fled hallowed ground. Those who had tried to make an escape on foot were trampled under cloven horse hooves, heads severed from their shoulders by huge iron balls with spikes or cleaved clean off their shoulders by massive black blades.

Bodies banged his as he swam in the opposite direction of the zigzagging humanity. Thousands of civilians were moving in panicked herds, rushing first one way and then another as demon horsemen gave horrific chase. Human military ranks were decimated. Tanks and conventional artillery was useless against what came at them. It all happened so fast, he was one blade against an entire demon army—and yet he had to find Cordell and Tobias within a sea of flaming, screaming death.

CHAPTER FIFTEEN

Cordell rushed behind Tobias as quickly as he could. Tobias body blocked for him like an NFL linebacker, pushing panicked citizens out of their path and grabbing Cordell by his arm to occasionally help him along.

Walkers careened into the street, snatching at human flesh and adding to the chaos, while rabid dogs fled buildings followed by demon rats that poured into the streets from the sewers. Chunks of brick and falling debris rained down to add to human fatalities. As Cordell and Tobias rounded a corner, a huge Berserker skidded into their path, wielding a fiery spiked ball that wiped out half a building.

The crowd changed direction on a dime like a terrorized school of fish, trampling one another, darting into crevices and bombed-out buildings, individuals getting picked off by demon slaughter. Tobias had Cordell by the back of his shirt, yanking him toward safety against a wall as he reached out using a blue-static tactical energy line and bound the legs of the charging Berserker's nightmare.

As the demon went down it slid the length of the city block, taking out screaming people in its wake to leave a bloody smear.

But a white-light pulse coming from across the street spurred Tobias and Cordell on. The second they rounded the corner, they saw Carlos—he spotted them, cutting through a horde of walkers. Cordell raised the wrapped weapon to let Carlos know their mission was accomplished. Pure darkness entered the tiny street, melting walkers as Carlos reached out to his men for a fold-away. Cordell looked back; Tobias screamed no; every building that had been around them exploded.

Carlos sprawled onto the stone floor of the Church of the Sepulcher with a hard thud. He looked up and saw that Tobias had crashed into a section of pews, clutching a portion of Cordell's shirt as the sacred weapon he'd been holding clattered to the floor. Carlos was on his feet in milliseconds as he saw Cordell's body face down on the stones, twitching.

Guardians rushed in with Damali. An agonized yell suddenly escaped Carlos as he held his face and blood began to leak from his eyes. Torn, Guardians split ranks, going among Carlos, Cordell, and Tobias.

Damali tried to pry Carlos's hands away from his face, and when she did he collapsed as her shriek shattered church glass. His eyes were missing. Huge holes with skull bone and exposed flesh remained where his silver gaze had just been. Carlos began to convulse as Marlene hastened to Cordell's body, flipped him over, and then jumped back, making the sign of the crucifix over her chest. Carlos stopped breathing.

"His eyes are gone," Marlene said, aghast.

"He's not breathing," Damali yelled, beginning to urgently perform CPR on Carlos.

Berkfield was on his hands and knees beside Carlos but got up and ran to Cordell, and then ran back again. "What should I do, Mar? What should I do!"

"It-it-it-," Tobias stuttered as Habiba rocked him in her arms, "it was the most evil darkness I have ever felt. I didn't look back, but Cordell, Carlos, they stared right at it." Tobias broke down and covered his face, weeping. "There was nothing we could do against it!"

"What do we do!" Berkfield shouted again as Damali's hands covered Carlos's wounds and she frantically gave him mouth-to-mouth resuscitation.

"You work on the living!" Shabazz hollered. "We got a Neteru down—Cordell is gone!"

Carlos coughed before Berkfield could even move, and then he sat up quickly, yelling, and shoved Damali away from him. As Cordell's last gasp exited his body, Carlos covered his eyes and released a long, bloodcurdling wail.

"Don't touch him, D, anymore," Marlene said firmly. "He tried to heal that man in a fold-away with a demon charge tracking him."

"I don't give a damn!" Damali said, trying to get back to Carlos's side. "I'm not leaving him like that!"

But Carlos waved her off, keeping his eyes covered against the dim lights with his forearm. "Oh, God . . ." He arched and clawed the stones with one hand, panting as though giving birth, and then finally slumped over. "The light is too bright," he gasped, sliding down to lie on his side. "The light is too bright."

Damali knelt by him, her wings out and covering his shuddering form, blocking whatever oil lamplight and candlelight still existed. "I'm here, I'm right here," she said, ignoring the shelling outside the walls.

"I tried to save that old man," Carlos said in halting jags. "I knew he was a seer, so they'd take out his eyes, try to use them to see the last thing he saw. I thought if they pulled in a little silver,

I could blind them . . . woulda saved Cordell his sight. But the second I could see from Cordell's eyes, saw the streets, I knew they'd—" Carlos stopped speaking and heaved in a deep breath to steady his voice. "It wasn't a swap, it was a merger—they got both for a minute. It all happened too fast to make a clean separation."

"Oh, baby," she whispered, wrapping her arms around him as she pressed her face against the crown of his head.

"Tell me he made it, D," Carlos murmured thickly. "Even if he might be blind."

She shook her head. He balled his hands into fists.

"Do you know what they are doing to people in the streets?" Carlos said in a low, lethal whisper. "Damali, we've gotta take it to the streets. We can't stay in here."

"I know," she said, brushing back his hair. "But right now your eyes need to heal." She gently peeled his arm away from them, looking at the reddened, fragile lids and deep, bruised blood circles all around the sockets. He looked like he'd been in a prizefight, but at least the organs were slowly coming back.

"All I need right now is that blade Cordell brought me, and some sunglasses."

The darkness screamed; the shelling temporarily stopped. It clutched at its eyes with massive claws, reared back, and ripped them out as silver residue blinded it. Silver drizzled down its invisible black pit of a face, sizzling and popping as the beast ripped at its own flesh. Its feral wail in the distance spiked a tornado. Lilith and her generals stopped slaughtering the masses and for a moment all fighting ceased. A huge claw reached up from the broken earth, and from within the pit, the Dark Lord climbed out to challenge her.

Huge bat wings cast a shadow over Lilith as she stared up into glowing eyes filled with pure rage. Cloven hooves advanced in the unnatural quiet, clattering against stone. Her generals withdrew, fearing for their lives, as a muscular, spaded tail with a weapon tip the size of a boat anchor bullwhipped toward her, crashing into buildings and smashing bricks. Vicious, saliva-dripping yellow fangs opened to release a deadly snarl. Fire chased the smell of sulfur from the gaping maw that demanded recompense.

"My Thirteenth was blinded by a Neteru's silver gaze! How could you allow this travesty to happen, Lilith?"

"Listen," Damali said quickly, helping Carlos to his feet as the other Guardians covered Cordell's body and reverently placed his lifeless form on a pew. "It's too quiet and it's too dark."

"I've felt that before, bro," Yonnie said. "No offense, but so have you. We both know who's topside now, for real."

"Truth," Carlos said, facing the direction of Yonnie's voice with his eyes still closed.

"Lucifer has violated the edict," a hollow murmur echoed through the sanctuary. "He cannot be on the battlefield during the time of the pending Rapture. That he has tipped the scales offers us the opportunity to now also do the same."

Guardians looked around, clerics looked around, as civilians wept and ducked their heads low in terror.

"We should go outside," a priest said. "One hundred and forty-four thousand will leave this wicked world. It is the time of the Rapture!"

"Not yet," Father Patrick said, materializing before the shaken clerics. "And a word was left out of the texts in translation . . . one hundred and forty-four thousand *thousand*. One-hundred-and-forty-four-million good people of all races, religions, and walks of life will be called home. The Most High is love unconditional. You will be called from wherever you are. There is yet to be a battle completed. Wait on the Lord."

Carlos stooped down and blindly picked up the wrapped weapon that Cordell had given his life to bring him. He held it out to Father Patrick. "You *know* I know what to do with this."

Father Patrick nodded. "That is why it was given to you . . . and now you know what the Unnamed One's beast looks like and you have its name—but that foul creature is blind to you. The darkness that has been spilled like black ink will not be a weakness for you; use the temporary disability to your advantage. Your wife and the other Guardian females now have their own inner lights to allow the rest of the team to see. Remove that entity called the Thirteenth from the face of the earth so that your children will not be left to battle that as a part of their legacy."

Rabbi Zeitloff slowly appeared, drawing the attention of the team and the sanctuary's clerics. He stared at Dan, his parents, and then Tobias. "We stand with you, as well as all those who've wailed at the Kotel. Send your parents, Dan, to stay safely here with the child—little Ayana—as well as Delores and Monty, to be under the care of clerics and prayers. Let the people pray while the warriors fight—this always reduces casualties."

Imam Asula stepped out of a fold of light, machete drawn. "The Dome of the Rock shall be valiantly defended, as will this vast land. It is the will of Allah."

Monk Lin quietly stepped from behind a pillar with a retinue of ninja warriors, his blades gleaming. "Justice knows no borders; when one has penetrated deeply into enemy territory, the army will be unified, and the defenders will not be able to conquer you. This is the Tao of warfare; this is from *The Art of War.* You are in deep, make honorable use of your position." He bowed slightly and then disappeared.

"Strike now," Adam's booming voice commanded as he stepped out of a splinter of golden light. "The others are on the Temple Mount and at the Dome of the Rock. We say take back the Tower of David and defend this citadel as though it were Giza."

The healing staff, Aset's Caduceus, filled Damali's left hand as her Isis filled her right.

"Heal him," Aset said in a disembodied voice. "He must see using his mind as well as his eyes. Make haste."

"It's too quiet," Lilith murmured, trying her best to restore the lead demon's sight. She glanced up at her generals.

"Although right now it seems that they are holed up on Golgotha—the hill of Calvary—we must make sure they do not double back and attempt to attack Washington, D.C., while our Dark Lord relocates the heir for his safety. The only reason we are alive following the severe injury to his Thirteenth is because the Dark Lord cannot afford any high-ranking casualties this close to a victory. But do not take his temporary restraint as a sign of weakness."

"They will not escape," Vlad said, looking at the flickering silver in the beast's missing eye sockets that made it wail.

"You bet your life they can't," she said, turning away from him and Nuit. "Be sure you keep the Neteru team so engaged that they keep the battle here for now . . . even if it means we deplete our forces and have to rebuild them for the next twenty years during the Tribulation, I want this *finished*!" she hissed.

"We've got tactical charges covering this sanctuary, as well as the stones it sits on, and are drawing power from Calvary so our men don't fatigue," Damali said, using her blade as a pointer. "But through that high front window that got blown out with the first blast . . . I wanna send them a little welcome card—call it a shot over the bow."

Seven Guardian sisters nodded and got into position, drawing down Light energy into their cores and then clasped hands. Marlene stood between them and Damali, serving as a jumper cable, her stick to Heather's shoulder, her palm toward Damali, who was aloft on the thirty-foot-high stone window ledge. The moment their light fused with hers, Damali sent out a long, pulsing blast of multihued light toward the tower.

Rather than the impact terminating with a destructive charge against the building, glowing colored light shimmered over the ancient stones, washing them in pure energy that caused demons to leap over balustrades and out of windows screaming and burning. Instantly, whirling black tornadoes of rage funneled up from the citadel, releasing demon bats.

"Masters airborne," Yonnie hollered. "Aerial attack, archers up!"

From her phalanx of rooftop warriors with wings, Val released holy water–dipped arrow fire that sent airborne vampires plummeting to the ground. A full Valkyrie squadron took to the air with her as Yonnie took ground forces beyond the walls to hunt down Fallon Nuit.

Guardians poured out into the courtyard and went over the walls in a complete frontal assault. Neteru Council cavalry offered ground support cover, while warrior angels swooped down from the sky, breaking the demon ranks from the rear. Black demon blood ran in the streets, eerily commingling with the red human blood they'd spilled only a short time earlier.

Big Mike commandeered an abandoned Humvee and turned over the wheel to Phat G. With his shell crate newly blessed by sanctuary clerics, he leaned out the window as they careened down the street, playing chicken with a demon cavalry, sending

Hellfire rockets into Vlad's oncoming Berserkers, seeming crazier than they were. The team had gone for broke. Jose, J.L., and Bobby were doing recon with Dan, tracking evil building by building, kicking in doors, blowing away walkers and demons with hallowed-earth packed shells, liberating trapped humans to flee to the nearest holy shrine for angelic protection.

Rider, Berkfield, and Shabazz worked the roofs in a fast relay of hard sniper fire, sweeping streets, then pulling back so the team could advance, constantly jumping roofs and lobbing shots. Heather and Habiba kept the pressure on the stones, rushing amid the buildings, lighting them up, creating instant ovens for anything dark within them, while Jasmine erected living flags that gobbled fleeing rats and Harpies.

In the midst of battle frenzy, Dragon Rider caught the long whiskers of a flying water dragon just as it was about to depart from an altar cloth, leaping upon its back and riding it into a cloud of bats.

The holy water from the Church of the Sepulcher that she tossed into the screeching morass had the effect of detonating C4 midair. A thunderous blast rocked her off her mount. But the dragon was faithful, and doubled back to softly land her on the ground before it delighted in gobbling charred bat bits.

"Whoo-hooo!" Dragon Rider shouted, running for cover. "Wanted to do that all me bloody life!" She grabbed Jasmine by her face, kissed her cheek, and got another bucket of holy water as clerics worked as quickly as they could to renew supplies.

Tara and Juanita slipped behind enemy lines like silent assassins with Marlene, using Tara's ability to track a male vampire's energy pulse. Their goal was the necromancer, the one who could continue to replenish fallen demons.

Marlene gave them the nod as she saw Sebastian working amid the ashes. Healer to healer, their eyes made contact at the same time. Overly confident but clearly exhausted, Sebastian bared his fangs with a roar, his arms outstretching at the same time as Marlene's in a white light–black charge stalemate. A thrown Neteru battle-axe culled both of his outstretched limbs away from his body at the forearms. His scream brought in demon reinforcements that were beheaded before they could assess the threat. Black blood flowed like a geyser from Sebastian's severed limbs as he tried to escape, and then his eyes suddenly widened when Marlene's walking stick ripped through his back and pierced his heart. Two seconds later, his head left his shoulders with a silver slug to his temple.

Juanita looked at the gun in her hand as Tara yanked the stick out of his back. The Neteru Amazon Queen slapped Marlene a high-five and cleaned off her blade.

"The fellas said hi," Marlene muttered over Sebastian's body before she spat on it and then damned it to never rise again with a good prayer.

While the New York and Detroit teams rumbled with evil in the streets below, Inez and Marj set up a seer's trap on a rooftop, using Krissy as bait. Liz Bathory's history of luring young women to their deaths would be her weakness they'd exploit. Joan of Arc waiting in the wings, they sent Elizabeth a fake distress SOS as though it were Damali, jumper cabling the Neteru Queen's young, female warrior energy with Krissy's young, living, pregnant energy to bring the councilwoman to the rooftop.

It was a lure too tempting to resist. Elizabeth touched down within moments, surrounded by a retinue of vampire henchmen. Nzinga's blade whirred through the air, Aset's silver-white prayer lines rolled over the rooftop. Elizabeth's head hit the tarred surface with a sizzling thud as her security forces spontaneously combusted.

"I wanted that venomous bitch, Elizabeth, in the worst way,"

Nzinga said coolly, retrieving her blade and wiping off the gore on the bottom of her boot.

A loud echoing yell scattered the rooftop team. Vlad's long "No!" made the building begin to crumble.

In a quick jettison, Damali pulled the Guardians down to safety but remained on the roof. Carlos came out of the fold-away, blade plunging into Vlad's steed at the heart. The monstrous nightmare kept plowing forward, momentum taking its flaming body over the roof's edge in a violent, ember-exploding display. Vlad landed on his feet, black blade drawn, facing Damali, and ready for war. But Carlos decapitated him with a double-handed swing, kicking his head over the roof as he spat.

"That was for my wife, motherfucker! Don't you *ever* draw on her!"

"Thank you, baby," Damali said with a hard smile, as they both folded away in different directions.

Damali nodded as a Neteru blade glinted off the roof a half mile from her. The signal that another council member was down made her open her arms and swan dive off the edge of a tall apartment building, wings spread, into the fray.

The Detroit, Chicago, and Atlanta teams had remnants of the Berserker army hemmed in. Now without a general or a necromancer, they'd begun to flee. But Yonnie was on the ground with the Guardians, having gone hand-to-hand and acquiring a gigantic spiked mace, he sent Berserkers careening into hallowed earth gunfire, folding away like a ninja and reappearing out of the nothingness to do permanent bodily harm.

Carlos studied the battlefield from afar. Heru joined his side with Adam, Ausar, and Hannibal.

"They made another Chairman," Carlos muttered, still half blind.

"So we heard, my brother," Hannibal said, gripping his forearm in warrior support.

"Me and Fallon go back," Carlos said, tilting his head to the
side, trying to sense where he might be. "That punk ain't leaving Lilith's side right through here. They're down three . . . and
if I know Damali, in a minute they'll be down four when she
goes after his wife."

Damali ran along the city streets in a zigzag pattern, searching
for the water source. Although Lucrezia couldn't breach holy
ground, she was into poison as a formidable weapon. All-out
street combat just wasn't that councilwoman's style. But what
better way to ensure that a weary populace and human armies
couldn't live to attack another day than to taint the one thing
every living thing required . . . water.

As expected, Damali found her target at Jerusalem's water
mains. That source would send freshwater down a long aque-
duct to the fountains on the Temple Mount, as well as the cisterns on the lower platform that had been designed years ago to
collect rainwater. Battle-panicked, Lucrezia was more focused
on doing her evil deed quickly and getting back to a safe position behind the wall than watching her back. Too bad she
wasn't looking when seconds mattered; Nuit should have taught
her better.

Damali smiled as Father Patrick laid a hand on her shoulder
and she whispered the words he gave her, blessing the water before she folded out of the nothingness and gave Lucrezia a hard
shove into one of the open reservoirs.

A blast rocked the area as Lucrezia combusted on impact.
Vampire embers floated down in red glowing dust and gook
floated to the water's surface.

"Eiiiww! Nasty. Hope they've got a good filtration system,"

Damali said, wiping water and gook off her face as she jumped up.

"You bitch!" Lilith screeched, materializing behind Damali, who quickly spun to meet the threat. "At long last, you've come out to play."

"But so have I," Eve said, sheering off Lilith's head with one clean cut.

The body dropped slowly as Lilith's hands grappled at her bleeding throat. Eve dispassionately watched Lilith sink to her knees, staring into Lilith's dead eyes as she kicked the body over using the bottom of her golden boot.

"I have been waiting eons to do that," Eve said in a hard murmur. "I didn't take nearly long enough, however, to make that bitch truly suffer." Then suddenly, crazed, Eve released a Neteru war cry and rammed her sword through Lilith's heart so ruthlessly that her blade stuck into the concrete. "For my sons, you whore of Babylon!"

Eve and Damali instantly jumped back as a black electrical charge shot up and out of Lilith's dead body from the wound in her chest, and her open neck, and then connected to her eyes, nose, and mouth, slowly turning her body inside out as it dragged her into the ground in a sizzling puff of black smoke.

Four Covenant clerics immediately appeared, standing at the four corners of the fissure to send prayers down behind Lilith's body, which caused an underground blast that shot up a black geyser of blood.

Adam flung up a shield to keep the gore away from Eve and Damali as the clerics disappeared with a satisfied nod. Adam immediately turned to Eve, speaking quickly.

"That just turned the tide of the battle . . . killing Lucifer's wife could unleash anything." Adam's gaze went between Eve and Damali. "There is no time to savor that victory. We need to get the human teams back onto hallowed ground. Archangels have wanted her for years, and they will protect us until we reach sanctuary, but they hunt the Devil himself while he is weak. We must go."

Eve just stared at Adam for a moment. "No congratulations?"

He chuckled and bowed, taking up her hand to kiss the back of it. "But of course."

"I also heard what you said." Damali strained to see as far as she could. "I'm out. Gotta tell these folks to fall back."

Fallon Nuit stood at the top of the Tower of David staring out in disbelief. *Lilith* was gone? His Lucrezia had been murdered? He was stunned beyond grief. All the others were gone but him? Nuit turned to the Ultimate Darkness behind him and allowed the power of his new office to fill him, but was wise enough to quietly enjoy his rich inheritance.

"In all these years," the disembodied voice said. "I would have never believed that they would have gotten to my beloved. Lilith was like none other."

Fallon Nuit remained very, very still.

"Release my Thirteenth!"

A sense of urgency made Damali take a running leap off the roof. Her energy was low, a fold-away would have used the last of it, and somehow she sensed that she would definitely soon need it. The worst part of all, Carlos was nowhere to be found as she began giving the Guardians mental signals to fall back to the church or whatever shrine they were closest to.

As many humans as could be saved had been sent in all directions to find shelter in the churches, temples, synagogues, and mosques, and she could see her team fighting backward to get indoors. But where was Carlos?

One more circle around the area, and she'd come in and do roll call. But a daggerlike pain gripped her stomach as she began to spiral to the ground. To avoid fatal injury she used what reserves of energy she could to propel herself to drop face down on the roof. Her Guardian sisters' screams pierced her consciousness. Damali pushed herself up and dragged herself to the edge of a building.

Jasmine was being led away by Habiba, trailing blood.

"No!" Damali tried to stand, but a gripping, hemorrhaging cramp put her down on her knees.

Inez's SOS to her made her feel faint. All Guardian females were bleeding. This could not be happening!

Yonnie met Carlos on a roof. "I'm going, too, man. I have to! I'm the only one living that can."

"Where's the female squad at?" Carlos never turned to speak to Yonnie, but kept his shaded gaze searching rooftops.

"Big Mike, 'Bazz, and Mar, all the Guardians got 'em in the Sepulcher. Mar found Damali on the roof." Yonnie walked back and forth, dragging his fingers through his Afro. "They're all inside, man. Got clerics sending up prayers . . . maybe angels will come, too, who knows?"

Carlos nodded. "They're all bleeding. You be my eyes. History ain't repeating itself on my watch."

A tiny voice whispered inside her head. Damali limped into the church and then stopped. Awareness made her stand up taller and then run in. She grabbed each Guardian female who was pregnant and shook her, causing males to gather around, bewildered.

"It's illusion!" Damali shouted. "Your worst fear amplified by mine. They can't touch these children—they weren't created to be lost like this . . . what happened to me before happened while Carlos was dead."

Damali pointed to the floor of the church. "What do you see?"

Female Neteru Guardians stood slowly and looked around and then down at their clothes.

"Right. The moment you crossed the threshold, the blood disappeared."

Nuit spun away from the tip of a Neteru blade as it burned a graze mark in his black fatigues at his chest, and then sent a black charge toward Carlos, who deflected it with his shield of Heru.

"We go way back, motherfucker—and this time you have gone too far!" Carlos shouted, still partially blind as he listened for Nuit to land.

"You're so right," Fallon hissed, bearing fangs and battle bulking behind Carlos. "We go very far back, *mon ami.*"

"So do me and you," Yonnie said, his hand reaching through Nuit's back to rip out his dead heart. "All the way back to plantation days, bitch."

This time Carlos's blade didn't miss. His only regret when Fallon's head hit the ground was that he couldn't get one last good look into his foul eyes. But he never had time to contemplate the philosophical raisons d'être. Something so strong and so massive swept his body off the ground and full body slammed him against the rocks. Neteru Kings surrounded it, drawing the colossal beast that was sheer moving darkness away from Carlos's limp form while Yonnie tried to get him up.

Damali came out of a fold-away and Yonnie waved her back.

"No, D! This is the Thirteenth! Get back to hallowed ground!"

"Not without my husband!" she shrieked, running forward,

but a huge, clawed hand the size of a semi broke through the earth and snatched her out of the air before she could take flight, crushing her wings.

"Then since you helped to kill my wife—fair exchange is no robbery," the voice belonging to the hand thundered, dragging her into a fissure.

Angels splintered the sky, Neteru Kings and Queens charged into the pit behind her, blowing open the empty caverns as Carlos got to his feet. Massive darkness was closing in on Yonnie, who'd tried to throw everything he had within him at it before a wide black charge began to crush the life from him, cracking his ribs as he yelled.

Humans that still ran through the streets exploded into red stains against the ground and buildings. Carlos threw his head back, released a primal yell, and drew the spear into his grip. Insanity replaced all doubt. A foul stench of absolute demon stung his nose, but pure crazy spiked inside his bones. They'd taken Damali and his kid as a hostage? Was killing his boy—not today!

"Ialdabaoth, die you bastard! I rebuke you in the name of the Most High!"

Hurtling toward the beast as it swung away from Yonnie, Carlos met a black charge with the power of a nuclear blast that billowed out from the entity's core. In a split second, he jettisoned Yonnie to the church. But Carlos was coming at the beast headfirst, a silver-white bullet of determined fury covered by Heru's shield. The moment the spear pierced the entity, it exploded into a mushroom cloud of black ash and soot, throwing Carlos to land a half mile away.

Grace broke his fall. He could feel things touching him, gentle hands probing him, lifting him, as though putting him back together to make him whole. But as reality returned, he sat up, fully sighted on the steps of the Church of the Holy Sepulcher, and spun around, crazed. "Damali!" The Unnamed One had taken his wife.

Carlos stomped the ground as buildings fell and burned all around him. He called his blade of Ausar into his hand, trying to open up a fissure in the earth with white-light pulses, creating such a commotion that Guardians opened the church doors. Yonnie barreled out of the doors first, holding his right arm against his rib cage.

"He took her! Oh, shit, he got her, man," Carlos said, blasting the ground like a madman.

"Carlos, Carlos, what's wrong?" Damali said, running out of the church. "I've been looking all over for you!"

Carlos stood still for a moment, disoriented, and then dropped his blade. He turned and ran, grabbing her up and pressing her to him, not caring if the team saw him lose his mind. He squeezed his eyes shut, and grabbed a fistful of her hair, and buried his face in the crook of her neck. "I thought he took you," he said, his voice raw. "I swore that he finally got you."

"It had to be illusion," she said, holding him close. "The rest of the team wasn't bleeding."

Carlos pulled his gaze up and looked into Damali's eyes as her hand touched the edges of his at her cheek.

"They fixed your eyes. . . ."

"Maybe so you could see this, C," Yonnie said, pointing out to the horizon.

Heaven split with a bolt of white light. Legions of Angels filled the sky, lightening skewered the blackened earth, until the team had to look away. The sound of thunderous wings beat the air as a war horn sounded, making every human present cover their ears. A joint vision convulsed the human Neterus while the Neteru Councils began to cheer. Movement so swift in their minds made Damali and Carlos fall, the vertigo impossible to fight. Archangels with white light blades pierced the ground causing it to belch up its remaining demons. Then they heard the voice—Lucifer's bellows.

Carlos covered his wife's head protectively, pulling her to his chest.

"Michael—damn you!" the savage voice raged from beneath them, creating an earthquake.

"You don't own that power!" a forceful male voice shouted. "Gabriel, Uriel, Raphael, all of my brethren, in the Name of ALL that IS, seal away this treasonist!"

As suddenly as the earth had split a roiling energy of glistening golden light sealed the earth. Pure silence followed. A quiet knowing entered both Damali and Carlos as they slowly looked up and stared at each other.

"They sealed away the Devil?" she asked in awe.

Carlos nodded. "But they've still gotta find his son."

"That's supposed to be a battle for somebody *way* bigger than us then," she said quietly. "The real *ONE*." Damali hugged him and laid her head on his chest.

Thousands and thousands of cylindrical lights began to glow, breaking through the darkness as they shot heavenward like a reverse meteor shower. Guardians hugged one another, turning to see that the church, behind them, which was once filled with civilians, had emptied out. All was silent at the Temple Mount and Dome of the Rock, too. The mass ascension was something they could feel in their souls like a quiet sigh from Heaven released around the world.

They all stood gazing at the majestic beauty, while Inez kissed her baby girl. "Momma's gonna see you soon," she whispered into the toddler's ear. "I love you so much, Yaya."

"I love you, too, Mommy," Ayana said, and then squeezed Inez's neck.

But as the landscape slowly dimmed, confused Guardians looked around. People staggered out of buildings crying, some yelling, as they took to the streets.

"What happened?" one man shouted. "Was it a nuclear blast? Did we get nuked? What about the radiation and fallout—we're all gonna get cancer and die."

The team on the church steps looked at one another, every Guardian staggering to a place where they could sit.

"I knew I wasn't going. No big surprise there," Yonnie said quietly, rubbing Valkyrie's hair. "But I don't understand why they wouldn't take you . . . unless you forfeited a ticket on account of me?"

"They didn't take my baby?" Inez said, weeping, her gaze wild. "I know I done sinned up a storm, but Ayana?"

Delores held her face in her hands and wept bitter tears as a stunned Monty just rubbed her back. Marlene sat with a thud beside her and Monty and simply took up Delores's hand, as the Weinsteins hugged each other, rocking with sobs.

A single tear cascaded down Damali's cheek, but she grabbed Carlos's hand still staring out at the horizon. "As long as they didn't split us up."

He nodded. "I can deal, as long as they didn't split us up . . . but I am so sorry I stood in your way. If they ain't taking angels and little kids, just because they hung with us," he said, turning to look at the disheartened team, "then what can you do? It is what it is; we just got re-upped for a tour of duty in Hell."

"After all this time . . . all those battles, all of the insanity," Rider said, rocking and then jumping up to shout. "This is bullshit! You mean it's not over? We put our lives on the line and there's no cool retirement plan—*we* got left behind? I know I drink, and cuss, and yeah, I smoke, but—"

"Don't be mad, Uncle Jack," Ayana said, making the group look at her. "The angel said you can't go, 'cause of the babies." She lifted her little chin with pride and smiled wider. "She said that's why I have to help, too, 'cause I'm *a big girl*."

She pointed a stubby finger at Tara, her voice bright and cheerful as only a child's could be at a time like this, making it all the more surreal. She had every Guardian's complete attention as they drew near the most innocent member of the team.

"Girl," Ayana said with a big smile, looking at Tara. "Aunt Val, you got a boy. But Aunt Jasmine got a girl . . . and Aunt Krissy and Aunt Juanita gots boys. But Aunt Heather got a girl." She looked at Damali and opened her arms wide and then clapped. "You got bof . . . a girl and a boy. Plus there's all the ones coming from the mountains where we was . . . and some more from them," she said, pointing toward the other Guardian teams. "Like Miss Habiba gonna have one soon, don't know yet if it's a girl or boy, but she will. I'm gonna be the big sister little mommy."

"Out of the mouths of babes," Damali whispered, closing her eyes.

"Every time," Marlene whispered as her old, tattered black tome, *The Temt Tchaas,* filled her hands, smoking. She watched in quiet reverence as the frayed black binding slowly covered over with new silver etched with Neteru symbols.

"Babies' names are in there, Nana Mar," Ayana said. "But you can change 'em if you want—that's what the nice lady said."

Guardians laughed. Guardians cried. Some just looked out into the distance too overwhelmed by all they'd recently been through to process anything more.

"Twin Neterus?" Carlos croaked.

Damali's hand slowly covered her mouth.

The child glanced around as Carlos caught his weight against the church's stone wall and she gave him a little shrug, returning her attention to Rider.

"See, Uncle Jack, that's why the angels said stay. You wasn't bad. You not on punishment. But who's gonna be here to teach all the little kids how to fight that big thing that hurts people?"

EPILOGUE

One year later . . .

They clung to life, to survival and hope, dispersed Guardian teams and civilians alike. Tribes of humans determined to live sought refuge in the Carpathian Mountains, and the shelled remnants of the ranges in Afghanistan and Turkey. They flooded into the center of huge landmasses, seeking the Congo, Mount Kilimanjaro, and the highlands of Tibet.

Humanity clawed its way kicking and screaming, some dying along the way, but enough ultimately surviving against all odds to relocate to the Altay Mountains of Mongolia as well as the Ural range of the Siberian plain. People fought their way up Everest, the Andes, across Australia's Great Divide and the Sierra Madre Occidental and Oriental. Guardians led them to clean food and shelter from Templar stashes.

Healers and angels dispatched to hold back disease upon the survivors who still believed, while others used all their human knowledge inspired by Divine insight to set up guerrilla communications systems, interloper lookouts, and security systems. The war for survival against evil was on.

And the Neteru Guardian team went home, calling their

North American squad to safety in the vast Rockies, Sierra Nevada, Grand Canyon, and Appalachians.

The Unnamed held his head in his hands in abject frustration, alone in his fury except for the company of his gestating heir.

"Neterus and Guardians are worse than cockroaches!" he bellowed, and then flung a weak black charge at the listing globe.

He closed his eyes against the devastation of his realms and sat back on his dark throne, spent. He would have to make another wife . . . but who could rival Lilith? Her loss was incomparable. The amount of vengeance he would unleash to redress this offense would smite the world a thousand times over! He would have to make a new Council of Vampires . . . replenish demons, werewolves, phantoms . . . he simply shook his head. *And they'd destroyed his Thirteenth.*

This time his hand would not be forced into play prematurely. There were still humans left behind, many of whom he could compromise. There were still those who'd bought into the illusion even after all the signs were revealed, and those still inhabiting the burned-out cities, those still looking for salvation from a human leader, would be his sheep, his flock; they would bear the mark of the beast. He narrowed his glowing black gaze on the globe and then finally shut his eyes. Defeat was temporary; he had to believe that.

Twenty years to rebuild—so be it.

Quiet peace filled Damali as she gently lowered her son into his bassinet and then placed a light kiss against his soft, cocoa-brown cheek. Unable to resist, she allowed her fingertips to brush against his profusion of silky black curls and stared in awe of his long, onyx lashes that dusted his cherub cheeks. She was still amazed that something so incredible had pushed its way out of her body. Of the two, this one was so calm that Marlene actually had to give him a little whack to get him to take his first breaths of life. So different from his sister. Damali smiled and looked up as Carlos entered the nursery.

"Finally," Damali whispered. "How long did she have you walking the compound halls being nosy until she gave up and closed her eyes?"

Carlos squinted for her to be quiet and Damali covered her mouth not to laugh.

She wanted to be where the action was while me and the fellas were playing cards, Carlos told her, sounding pleased. *Rider had his boo on his lap—Mike had Ayana, and you know Jose and Yonnie had their bruisers on their laps talking smack. She loves that, D. So, our girl here wouldn't go down until every other kid in the place gave in and drifted off. When Ayana finally conked out, this one started rubbing her eyes and I started walking back here. You know motion is the only thing that makes her really go to sleep.*

She's got you wrapped around her little finger, Damali said in a teasing, mental barb.

Yeah, she does. When she looks at me with those big brown eyes . . . Carlos's gaze was tender as he looked down at his daughter. He nestled his nose in her wild shock of walnut-brown curls against her smooth cinnamon-brown forehead, breathing in the child's baby scent with his eyes closed. *This is my angel.*

Damali gave him a look. *Angel, nothing. She's a pure terror. Him, I can still breast-feed—she's been on a bottle from day one, and still bites. And that one came out hollering, fists balled up, with teeny little fangs cutting through her gums—and she won't sleep at night to save her life. Her brother's the angel.*

Carlos chuckled softly and kept his voice to a gentle whisper. "Yeah, that's Daddy's girl. My take-no-prisoners fighter," he said, lowering the sleeping infant into a bassinet next to her brother. He bent and kissed the top of his son's head, admiring the dozing infant with a proud nod. "But that's my boy. Got a grip like Bam Bam. Look at him, 'Mali, the kid is already diesel. Check out the size of his fists and his feet compared to his sister's. He's twice her size already."

"He has your eyes," Damali murmured with a wide smile, sliding her arm around Carlos's waist. "But he's so even tempered, doesn't get angry unless his food is late, and that's when you'll see the silver." She stared up at Carlos. "Earlier today, his bowl fell off the counter while I was trying to get some apple juice bottled. I think he was trying to bring it to his tray—but I'm not sure."

"Uh-huh . . . I can't wait till he takes that first flight, 'Mali. Wings should be able to hold him in a few years, you think?"

"Oh, man . . . please don't rush it," Damali said in a quiet voice, laughing softly. "As it is, we've gotta figure out how to childproof this compound. When they all hit two, I don't know what we're gonna do. They'll be able to outsmart us, using Ayana to see around corners for them like a guided parent-tracking system. Think about it, Carlos," she added, beginning to sound distressed. "We've got our two, plus Yonnie and Val's male Valkyrie, who will be trying to fly off a cliff with our son. . . Jasmine's dragon-painter who also owns wizard skills from Bobby—who knows what she'll create if she spills her cereal on her tray and starts painting with her hands—what, a freaking dragon will break out of the high chair plastic?"

"Baby, just . . ." Carlos let out a long breath. "I know it's gonna be crazy, but we've faced worse."

"Yeah, ya think?" Damali said, her voice soft and teasing. "Oh, it's cool now, but wait a few years and try to pit your skills up against a couple seers with vamp stealth capability, coming from the combos of Rider and Tara and Jose and Juanita, to go with a stoneworker who can kick a tactical charge, courtesy Heather and Dan—who will no doubt be busting things up with J.L. and Krissy's boy."

"Baby, we don't stand a chance," Carlos said, laughing softly. "All I can say is, we'll just have to worry about that later. It's hard enough to figure it out one day at a time."

Carlos chuckled and pulled Damali into a loose embrace, and then kissed the crown of her head as they both stared down at their sleeping miracles. For the first time in his life, he didn't want to rush time, and if he could have, he would have made it stand still . . . but that was the province of a higher power way beyond his comparatively meager Neteru abilities.

As though locked into the same thought, he and Damali looked up in unison, staring out at the barren mountainside that was blanketed by snow. Multihued lights sent dazzling prisms of pastel shades against the stark white backdrop that covered charred trees and foliage. The women had built a sanctuary, a place invisible to the unholy, a place of hallowed earth left to them unspoiled and prayed over by angels, Atlantis resurrected. Everything they'd endured, every lesson learned, had come together in an unfathomable tapestry, a grand design that had been impossible to see episode by episode in their lives. It took an elevated view. The universe was efficient, nothing went to waste.

The women's lighthouses that had been ignited by ancient energy on Monty's yacht now served to set up twelve-hundred-acre, interdimensional havens that were off the human grid, and functioned like a demon blind. All he and the brothers had to do was build within the safety zones. Every Guardian compound worked that way, hid that way, would survive that way.

Stone and wood, everything natural was called into service. Solar panels hijacked from lost warehouses and abandoned buildings, rainwater cisterns, technology stripped from lost military outposts, supplies brought in from hidden Templar silos—blending into the environment without a trace was the goal. It had been a mission of survival that went far beyond just that. It had been a mission of love, a promise to protect the future by shielding the present so that it could live and grow.

Lighthouses of sanity, places of peace . . . all the Guardian squads that had fought with them during the final battle had made it, and word was that so had many more around the world.

Yeah, life was good. Carlos briefly closed his eyes, feeling blessed. They had lived to fight another day and when the time came they'd fight the darkside like guerrillas, always a rebel army that would never cede to corruption. Light-encoded Internet, light-encapsulated telepathy, light tower to light tower communications, they all had to kick it up a notch and function on a new frequency to keep the children safe.

He and all the brothers had watched their wives go through perhaps the most significant ordeal of human existence . . . creating life, bearing its weight, fighting to protect it, and then pushing it forth on their own, bloody and screaming, into the world. And every woman immediately recovered . . . her first objective to hold that which had given her a level of pain that he couldn't even begin to comprehend . . . then brought new life to her breast to nourish it. *Respect* was too shallow a word to describe what he had for what he'd witnessed.

Carlos sent his gaze to the horizon, still awed. The women had been right; it was all about using the Light as the most effective weapon. Everything else brought death, hell, and destruction. Never again. Not on his watch. Uriel had come to them with an archangel's promise of twenty-one years. Carlos tore his gaze away from the huge bay window and pristine Appalachian mountainside to settle it on his sleeping children and then his wife.

Twenty-one years . . . he couldn't even think that far into the future. Damali seemed to know that as her hand went to his face to gently pet soft caresses against it. The one thing he had learned was to savor every precious moment of life to the fullest. She was his living, breathing joy. This woman whom he'd been blessed by was still alive, had given him life, created life, and given him the ultimate gift. Every dream he'd ever owned she'd made come true—not just his, but had orchestrated the deliverance of the entire team's dreams, too, under seemingly impossible odds. She would always be his first angel. *Always.*

Te amo, he mentally murmured, pulling her closer to him. She smelled so good, felt so good, he'd never get enough of touching her soft skin or feeling the extra swell of her now-swollen breasts against him . . . the kids would have to wait a bit and allow their father to indulge his senses in something truly divine—their mother.

"I love you, too, for letting me get some rest," Damali said in a quiet rush as he began to spill slow kisses down her neck. "Why don't you go eat, baby? I think Delores and Monty made breakfast for everybody with Frank and Stella . . . Mar and 'Bazz have this watch with Richard and Marj; wanna get some grub and then a few hours of sleep before these two are up again?"

"I'm not really hungry," Carlos said, tracing Damali's cheek with a finger.

"More tired than hungry," she murmured, leaning up to take his mouth with a quick kiss. "I understand that one . . . c'mon, why don't you go to our room and lie down then. I've got this watch."

"I'm not tired, either," he said, staying her leave for a moment, allowing the pad of his thumb to smooth over her eyebrow and then over the swell of her cheek. "I love you, and I miss my wife."

She smiled as she turned her mouth into his palm and left a gentle kiss there. "And I love you," she whispered as she stared up at him. "But you're gonna have to be real quiet or you'll wake these two up."

"I think I can work that out."

A slow smile spread across Carlos's face as he glanced at their adjoining bedroom door, the babies, and then Damali again. She covered her mouth quickly to stop a belly laugh from tumbling out as he put a shield of Heru over both bassinets and motioned with his head toward their bedroom.

1. How do you feel about the resolution of the battle with the Neterus and Guardians left behind?

2. What do you think about all the major religions coming together as one force of good against evil in the end?

3. Do you see any parallels to real life in the strange weather patterns, incidents in the news, and the new and resurgent viruses?

4. What do you think of the roles of the angel corps and Neteru Councils in assisting humankind?

5. Does the end of the story leave you feeling hopeful or depressed?

6. What special powers do you think the children will have?

7. Can you envision what the children will be like as toddlers, then as young tweens, then adolescents, and finally as adults?

8. What challenges will they face both environmentally and politically during the Tribulation?

9. The young couples and their children, too, will have a solid core of older couples/surrogate grandparents to learn from and interact with (namely Marlene and Shabazz, Marjorie and Richard Berkfield, Monty and Delores, and Frank and Stella Weinstein). Discuss how the influence of these mentors will affect the future of the younger generation.

10. At the end of this 12-book saga, did you feel all your questions were wrapped up and all loose ends tied up? Where would you like to see the story go in the future, if there was an extension?

A
Reading
Group
Guide

For more reading group suggestions, visit
www.readinggroupgold.com.

St. Martin's
Griffin

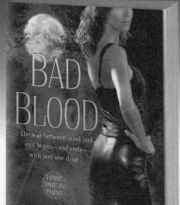
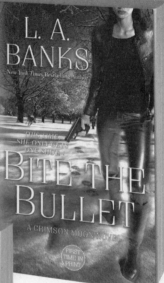
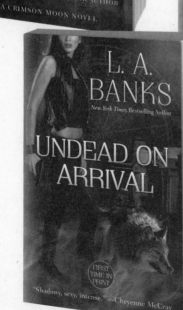